One Sick Puppy

"It's a hard one to figure, Father," the cop said. "This guy didn't have nothing worth stealing. And from the way he's cut up—"

"Mind if I have a look?"

"—he was either killed by a pack of dogs, or one sick puppy, if you know what I mean. Go ahead. Have a look."

The priest pulled back the plastic.

It wasn't what he saw that bothered him, though that was bad enough.

It was the familiar smell, mixed with the faint sweet scent of death.

The familiar smell of Garou.

Wyrm Wolf

Based on
THE APOCALYPSE

Edo van Belkom

HarperPrism
An Imprint of HarperPaperbacks

This is a work of fiction. The characters, incidents, and dialogues are products of the author's imagination and are not to be construed as real. Any resemblance to actual events or persons, living or dead, is entirely coincidental.

HarperPaperbacks   *A Division of* HarperCollins*Publishers*
10 East 53rd Street, New York, N.Y. 10022

Cover illustration by Steve Gardner

First printing: February 1995

Printed in the United States of America

HarperPrism is an imprint of HarperPaperbacks. HarperPaperbacks, HarperPrism, and colophon are trademarks of HarperCollins*Publishers.*

❖ 10 9 8 7 6 5 4 3 2 1

For my wife Roberta,
without whose love, understanding, and support
the writing of this novel would never have been possible,
or have meant very much.

A lot of people helped bring this novel into being. My thanks go to Stewart Wieck and Bill Bridges at White Wolf Games; editor Edward E. Kramer (who first invited me into the world of *Werewolf: The Apocalypse*); and fellow writers James A. Moore, Don Bassingthwaite, Matthew J. Costello, Martha Soukup, David Nickle, and Robert J. Sawyer.

Wyrm Wolf

PART I

Our greatest fight, our most bloody battle, is to survive alone in the world. Though Gaia and Luna turn their backs on us, we will survive. There will come a time when we are the only ones left, and then we will have won.

—*Shakespeare, Bone Gnawer Galliard Grandfather*

1

It was a night like any other in the Tenderloin, a fifty-block hellhole of a neighborhood in the northeastern part of San Francisco.

As usual, the moon hung above it like a naked bulb, bathing its dirty streets and back alleys in moonlight.

Steam rose from sewer grates.

Rats skittered from shadow to shadow, toppling garbage cans and gnawing on the remains of the day.

And while the citizens in most parts of San Francisco slept in the warmth and comfort of their homes, others less fortunate lay in the gutters and alleyways of the Tenderloin cloaked in darkness, waiting for the sun to shed light on their misery.

Or for the night to end it.

In the midst of it all, a werewolf padded silently down the street, sniffing the shadows, looking for prey.

Easy prey.

Human prey.

In a dark alley between a department store and a bank, Randall E. "Sully" Sullivan III rolled over inside the cardboard refrigerator box that had served as his home for the past three weeks. He reached out with beefy, blackened fingers and peeled the soggy brown paper away from the neck of the bottle. Then with a shaky hand he raised the bottle to his lips and upended it. The cheap red wine ran down his throat as cool as ice water, then burned in his stomach hotter than fire.

He was about to take another swig when . . .

He noticed something creep into his field of vision.

He adjusted himself in his box, turned to take a look . . .

And the bottle fell from his hand.

There was something coming toward him.

Something big and hairy.

Monstrous.

He rubbed his knuckles into his eyes, then took another look.

It was a creature of some sort.

More wolf than man.

The thing looked familiar.

Sully thought about it and remembered seeing something like this a few months back. A big wolflike creature running through the alley carrying a man in its arms. At the time Sully had been able to discount the episode as something he'd uncorked from a bad bottle of gut-rot.

It had been as good an explanation as any at the time.

But this time Sully was stone-cold sober.

He squeezed his eyes shut and curled up tight in his box, hoping that the creature's two hind legs would just pad on by. But as he listened to the thing approach, he couldn't resist opening his eyes and taking a peek.

It had to be nearly seven feet tall, maybe even eight, covered from head to toe in a thick ragged coat of dirty brown fur.

Sully inhaled a gasp as the thing stopped less than a foot from his box. Then he held his breath, raised his head . . .

And looked straight into the eyes of the beast.

The alley was full of scents—perspiration and urine, rotting food and vomit.

There was another scent, too. That of a human.

A live one.

The werewolf slowed, sniffing at the air.

Closer . . . closer . . .

And then it stopped, savoring it.

The delicious smell of fear.

The werewolf looked down and saw him lying there. Helpless. A miserable little man, curled up inside a cardboard box like a dog hiding from the rain.

His face was a dirty mask of fear. His wet eyes were opened wide in terror, and his mouth was shaped into the O of a silent scream.

The werewolf pulled its lips back, showing the man its jagged set of razor-sharp fangs.

The human looked afraid.

And rightly so.

Sully wanted to get up and run, but his body wouldn't move. Even if he could have moved he wasn't sure he'd have gotten very far. The beast looked strong, powerful, fast. All Sully could do was gaze up at it and stare helplessly into those angry steel gray eyes, and hope . . .

Hope it would move along, out of the alley and on down the street. Away . . . far away.

But the beast remained. It looked down at him for what seemed like forever, then raised its head and opened its mouth in something like a laugh. Its fangs were long and wet, the points sharp and deadly. A drop of saliva fell from one of them, glistening like crystal in the moonlight.

Sully had the sinking feeling that the creature wasn't going anywhere soon.

The beast's maw opened wider as it let out a twisted, mad howl.

Shivers ran down Sully's spine while something warm trickled down his thigh.

The beast raised its right arm over its head. Fingers spread like points of a star. Claws as sharp as talons glinted like daggers. The clawed-hand remained in the air for a second, wavering slightly—as if just to intensify the terror—before coming down hard and fast.

With a single swipe of its hand the creature sliced the box open, its claws cutting through the cardboard like a knife through cellophane.

In an instant the box was gone. It lay flat and shredded around Sully, leaving him totally exposed—naked to this hulking wolflike creature. Sully looked up one last time, saw the rage in the beast's eyes, and began to feel giddy, delirious.

He closed his eyes until the feeling went away.

The beast did nothing for several moments, content to let him cower in fear.

But then there was movement.

Sully heard the claws slice through the air, felt them pierce his skin and grate against his bones. He let out a scream, then felt the blood bubble out of a hole in his shoulder and run hot down his back and chest. He felt his bowels empty, then smelled the sickening mix of his bodily fluids as they coagulated on the pavement of the alley beneath him.

His eyes still closed, Sully swung his big fists blindly at the beast, striking it in the head, neck, and chest. He kicked at it too, his shoes landing solidly against its haunches, but his ever-weakening blows had little effect against the roiling mass of muscle and fur.

He kept his arms raised in an attempt to fight back, but his efforts steadily grew more feeble until he couldn't even make a fist, let alone raise his hand to strike a blow. He ended up slumped against the wall, a mass of torn and bleeding flesh.

The beast was killing him slowly, letting him bleed to death instead of mercifully going for his throat and breaking his neck with a single bite of its powerful jaws.

There was no purpose to this killing other than making it as slow and painful as possible.

For what seemed like hours, the creature opened fresh wounds along Sully's arms, legs, chest, back, and belly. Anywhere it could find a spot of unbroken skin.

Sully drifted in and out of consciousness a half-dozen times as his will to live ebbed from his body like the blood oozing from his wounds.

At last he felt the fangs sink deep into the meaty part of his neck.

Ripping. Tearing.

But by now he felt no pain.

Because his body had turned cold.

And all he could hear was the sound of dead silence.

"Hello," said Father Oldman, stepping into Jackson's Fruit and Vegetables, a midsized grocery store on Eddy Street near Mason.

"What you want?" chirped Mr. Kim from his familiar perch atop his stool behind the counter.

"You never stop kidding, do you?"

"What you mean?"

"I've been coming to see you every Monday morning for the past three years, and every time I come into your store you act like you don't know what I'm here for."

"What *are* you here for?"

Father Oldman looked at Mrs. Kim, who was standing behind the counter several feet to her husband's right. She was holding her hand in front of her mouth to hide her smile, but Oldman knew she was giggling behind it. She always giggled at her husband's peculiar brand of humor. And, like Oldman, she always grew tired of it after a few minutes, ending her laughter with a sigh and telling Oldman what he needed to know.

"Only one bag today," she said as her husband tended to a customer. "People buy lot of potatoes now. People have no jobs, no money, so they buy lot of potatoes. Potatoes and cabbage."

7

Oldman smiled at the woman. She was probably right. If the government ever wanted a *real* indication of how the economy was doing, all they'd have to do is ask Mr. and Mrs. Kim how potatoes were selling. Not all that scientific, but probably as accurate an indicator as anything Wall Street or Washington used to monitor the rest of the nation's fortunes.

"Then I hope potato sales are bad next week," Oldman said. "And canned salmon sales are good."

Mr. Kim smiled and nodded in dramatic fashion.

Satisfied he'd sufficiently entertained the shopkeeper, Oldman headed for the back of the store and looked for the food that had been put aside for him, food that was a couple hours away from being thrown into a dumpster.

Father Wendel Oldman ran The Scott Mission, a homeless shelter on Eddy Street between Leavenworth and Hyde Streets in the heart of the Tenderloin.

It was a rough little part of the city where too many people lived in too few rundown rooms. There were plenty of homeless here, not to mention drunks, junkies, and prostitutes, all working to keep people like Father Oldman busy.

In recent years the area had been settled by immigrants from Vietnam, Laos, and Cambodia who had opened a variety of small businesses. When people write about the Tenderloin these days, they say that the immigrants have given the neighborhood a stability and respectability that it hasn't enjoyed in years. That might be true, but no one who lives in the Tenderloin knows it. To them it's just an ugly little place where nobody lives unless they *have* to.

While one of the most important goals of Oldman's work was to get homeless people off the streets and back into society as productive human beings, most of his time was spent scrounging for food and supplies. Every few days he made the rounds, going to stores like Jackson's Fruit and Vegetables with cap in hand, hoping to take enough back to the mission to get his flock through another week. It was a hand-to-mouth existence to be sure, but no worse a life than a lot of other people in the Tenderloin were living.

Oldman stepped into the back room. In the far corner resting against the wall was a large plastic bag filled with potatoes. He opened the bag, saw that several of the potatoes were already dry and shriveled, and quickly closed the bag, thankful that it was full.

He walked back toward the front of the store, the plastic bag hanging heavily from his right arm.

"What you got in the bag?" asked Mr. Kim as Oldman approached the counter.

"Nothing," said Oldman.

"You stealing from me?"

"You'll never miss it."

Mr. Kim turned to his wife, his eyebrows raised in alarm. "We're being robbed! Hurry, call the police!"

"Funny man," said Oldman. "I'll see you next week." .

"Not if I see you first," said Mr. Kim.

Mrs. Kim's hand shot up in front of her mouth, and her eyes squinted as she smiled.

Oldman gave a final wave and stepped out the door. It was a lot to go through just for a free bag of potatoes, but in these hard times he had to take whatever he could get. Besides, there were fifteen people who'd be grateful to him for the full bellies they'd be sleeping with that night.

Knowing that helped to make it all worthwhile.

Oldman headed back toward the mission. As he walked west along Ellis Street he saw Bernadine Daly peering into garbage cans. Oldman had long ago dubbed Bernadine "San Francisco's Master Gatherer." Every day for who-knew-how-many years she'd been picking old newspapers out of the garbage as she walked the streets of the Tenderloin. No one was quite sure why she did it, or what she did with all those newspapers, but she was out there every day, rain or shine, walking the streets with doubled-up shopping bags full of newspapers weighing down her arms.

"Hi, Bernadine," said Oldman. "What do the papers say today?"

"It looks like rain."

Oldman looked up into the sky. There wasn't a cloud in sight. He wondered which day's paper she'd been reading, and which year.

"I'll be sure to pick up an umbrella," Oldman said cheerfully.

"Good thing to do. Boots too. There's a frost coming, don't you know." Bernadine closed her eyes and nodded like this was some sort of secret.

"Well," Oldman said, suddenly feeling chilly in his black short-sleeved shirt and white collar. "Thanks for the warning." He turned away and continued on down the street.

He said hello to various people along the way. He didn't really know them all, or at least he couldn't put names to all of their faces, but they all seemed to know him.

One man whose name he had no trouble remembering was "the General." The General was an older man, probably in his mid to late sixties, who spent his days standing in front of vacant storefronts barking gibberish at people and cars as they passed.

"One time only!" shouted the General. "Often imitated never duplicated! Hut! Hut! Hut!"

Oldman had tried to talk to the man on several occasions, had even sat with him for dinner at the mission once or twice, but he'd never gotten through to him. Now he just stopped and said hello, admiring the man's steadfast single-mindedness.

"Company halt! Ready, set, go! All aboard! Hut! Hut! Hut!"

"Morning, General," Oldman said as he passed.

The General saluted, then continued barking out his mantra.

"Toronto goal scored by number ninety-three! Well blow me down! Hut! Hut! Hut! Look out! Look out! Twist and shout! Hut! Hut! Hut!"

Oldman walked several more blocks west along Ellis Street. As he did he noticed that things were growing more quiet, almost solemn. He turned south onto Jones Street and saw a pair of police cars parked by the curb with their red lights flashing. There was an ambulance between the two cars, sitting idle with its doors closed. A crowd of people had gathered on the sidewalk, those at the back trying to see over the ones in front. Obviously something had happened in the alley between the department store and bank.

Oldman crossed the street.

The crowd was getting bigger by the minute as people filtered down from their tenements hoping for a closer look. The only thing that would arouse such curiosity, thought Oldman, was the blood of a dead man. He hoped that wasn't the case, but he had a sinking feeling that it was.

When he arrived at the edge of the crowd, he eased himself into it, then patiently made his way to the front. When he reached the taped-off mouth of the alley, he saw that his guess had been correct.

"Excuse me, Officer," Oldman said to the nearest policeman. "I'm a priest, perhaps I can help."

The policeman turned around, saw Oldman's black shirt and white collar, and stepped closer to him. "Believe me, Father," the cop said under his breath. "I've seen this guy up close. There's nothing you can do for him now."

"Perhaps I can—"

"He's okay," came a voice from inside the alley. "Let him through."

It was Sergeant Metzger, a man who had patrolled the Tenderloin as part of the Tenderloin Task Force for years. He knew all about Oldman and the work he did with the homeless.

"Good morning, Sergeant."

The policeman tipped his cap. "Maybe for you and me, Father. But not for this unlucky sonuvabitch . . . Excuse my language."

"That's quite all right," said Oldman. "I've heard a lot worse in my time."

Metzger smiled, perhaps a little relieved. They stepped into the alley and walked toward the heavy black plastic wrap covering the body.

"Do you know what happened?"

"It's a hard one to figure, Father. This guy didn't have anything worth stealing, so it's unlikely that it was a robbery. And from the way he's cut up it wasn't any ordinary street fight that did him in."

"What do you mean?"

"Well, I can't really explain it to you. It's one of those things you'd have to see for yourself. All I can say is that it looks like he was either killed by a pack of wild dogs, or one sick puppy."

Oldman looked at the policeman.

"You know, Father . . . a psycho."

Oldman nodded.

When they reached the body Oldman set aside his bag and knelt down at the edge of the dark pool of blood that had seeped out from under the wrap. Then he placed a hand on the outside edge of the plastic and looked up at Sergeant Metzger. "Would it be all right if I had a look?"

"Yeah, sure, go ahead. Maybe you can even give us an idea about who the hell he is."

Oldman slowly pulled back the plastic . . .

And gasped.

It was hard to know which part of the body he was looking at because every inch of it was bruised in a mottled pattern of black and blue. There were also dark red slashes intersecting each other from different directions, making the body look as if it were covered in thick dark netting. When he finally recognized the man's feet, Oldman knew he was looking at a leg, or what had once been a leg. Now it was just a mass of bruises, open wounds, and exposed bones.

He turned his head away and fought off the urge to retch.

"It's a mess, ain't it," said Sergeant Metzger, taking a step back to give Oldman some room.

The body was more than a mess, it was utterly decimated.

But that wasn't what had Oldman spooked. The thing about the body that made his hair stand on end was the *way* it had been mutilated. Those wounds had not been made by a pack of wild dogs, or by any psychopath. Those kinds of wounds could only have been made by a werewolf.

He sniffed at the air.

It was faint, but he recognized it mixed in with the stink of decomposition—the familiar scent of a Garou.

He sniffed again.

There was something else hanging in the air. He couldn't put his finger on it, but it was evil, corrupt. . . .

He looked back down at the body. The thought of one of his flock being tortured to death made Oldman sick to his stomach.

He took another minute to compose himself.

Finally, Oldman stood up and looked closely at the dead man's face. There were few recognizable features to it, the nose had been broken, the eyes were empty black sockets, and the mouth had been torn apart. Still, there was something that seemed familiar.

It took a few more seconds for him to realize what it was, but then it came to him all at once. It was the ears. The dead man's ears were two rough-edged cauliflower blossoms sticking almost straight out from the sides of his head. This man was Randall E. "Sully" Sullivan III, former middleweight boxing champ of the state of California and a frequent visitor to The Scott Mission.

Oldman bent over and covered the dead man's head with the black plastic wrap and made the sign of the cross over the body.

He was beginning to feel sick all over again.

"You know who he is, Father?" asked Sergeant Metzger.

"Yeah," said Oldman. "He is a . . . He *was* a friend of mine."

Although it was only a few blocks from the murder scene to the mission, the walk seemed to take forever.

Sully had been a good man. Even though he'd been a professional fighter, he'd never been a brawler. In fact, in all the years Oldman had known the man he'd never seen him raise a fist—or say an unkind word, for that matter—to anybody.

News of Sully's death, or rather, his murder—for that's what it had been—would hit the people at the mission hard. Sully had been well liked by everyone, a person others sometimes turned to for protection from street punks. If such a strong man had been cut down so easily, what would happen to some of the weaker ones in the flock?

Something had to be done.

And soon.

By the time Oldman had reached the mission, he'd recovered enough to put on a brave face. No sense having everyone guess there was something wrong. He'd tell them all when the time was right. Right now there was lunch to prepare.

He stepped lightly down the stairs into the basement where the mission's mess hall was located. It was a makeshift cafeteria at best with an open kitchen at one end and four eight-foot tables sitting side by side in the main room surrounded by two dozen chairs, no two of which were alike.

It looked like hell, but Oldman had had some of the best meals of his life down here, all thanks to Alcina Williams, the mission's cook.

Everyone called her L.C.

Some even called her the Miracle Worker.

While L.C. had never turned water into wine, she had once been able to feed two dozen people for a week with nothing more than a bushel of potatoes and four loaves of bread.

"Hi, L.C.," Oldman said. "I'm back."

L.C. stepped out of the kitchen, leaned against a table, and smoked her cigarette while she waited for Oldman to bring her the goods.

She was a thin woman who never wore anything other

than faded blue jeans and a white T-shirt. Her face was far more wrinkled than was just for her fifty years, and her hair had been prematurely gray for decades. She was constantly surrounded by cigarette smoke, and the index and middle fingers of her right hand were a dirty shade of yellow. Funny thing about that was that for all her years at the mission, Oldman had never found a cigarette butt or fleck of ash in his food. That she was able to accomplish that was nothing short of miraculous.

"Well," she said. "What sorry excuse for food did you bring me back this time?"

Oldman pursed his lips, almost embarrassed to give her the bag of potatoes. "Spuds," he said at last. "Idaho's finest." Oldman held the bag out to her so she could take a look.

She glanced into the bag, inhaled on the tiny nub of her cigarette, and shook her head.

"You want me to feed these people that?"

"The people who come to the mission are grateful for whatever nourishment we can provide them," said Oldman, realizing those kinds of words didn't quite sound right coming from him.

"Cut the crap, Father," L.C. said. "I can't polish a turd."

"No, perhaps you can't." He paused. "But you *can* make some of the finest hash browns and mashed potatoes this side of Chicago."

L.C. looked up at Oldman, gazed into his eyes, and smiled. "You're lucky you're a priest," she said. "If you weren't, I'd *know* you were lying."

Oldman stood there, smiling.

"All right," she said, taking the bag out of his hands. "I'll see what I can do."

"I still can't believe it," said Preston Parker, Oldman's assistant and right-hand man. "Sully was as strong as an ox and twice as tough. What the hell could have done that to him?"

Father Oldman had informed the people of the mission of Sully's death after lunch—a filling meal of soup, mashed potatoes, and home fries. He'd spared them most of the gory details, but Parker had wanted to know more about what had happened.

So Oldman had told him.

And now Oldman sat silently behind the desk in his office watching the younger man anxiously pace about the room. Parker was deeply troubled by Sully's death. Although Parker was now working with Father Oldman, it wasn't so long ago that he had been struggling to survive out on the streets himself. When Oldman first met Parker he'd been wearing a sign around his neck that read

WILL SING
FOR FOOD!

After leaving the navy, Parker had spent some time as a professional lounge singer. And while he did have an excellent tenor voice, he'd been starving to death out on the street. A thin and wiry man to begin with, Parker had weighed less than a hundred pounds and could hardly walk on his own when he first knocked on the mission's door. But coming to the mission had revitalized him, had given him a sense of purpose. He was soon back on his feet, eager to do work that could help others who found themselves in similar straits. Now, people of the Tenderloin looked up to him, admiring his strength of character and dedication to the mission.

That's why the violent and senseless death of a homeless person affected him like that of a brother. It could have just as easily been him lying there dead in some alley instead of Sully. And if a man like Sully had been killed so horribly by whatever it was that was out there, who was safe from it?

"The police have a couple of theories about the killing," said Father Oldman. "The two most popular ones are that Sully was either attacked by a pack of dogs or that it was the work of some psychopath."

Parker stopped pacing a moment and gave Oldman an incredulous look. "Are you kidding me?"

Oldman shook his head. "No, I'm afraid not."

Parker started pacing again. "What do *you* think killed Sully?"

Oldman answered immediately. "A combination of the two, actually."

Parker stopped again, looked at Oldman with his pale green eyes, and found a chair to sit in. "What do you mean?"

Oldman realized he'd just painted himself into a corner. Parker knew that Oldman was Garou, but he didn't know how brutally violent the Garou could sometimes become. Since his only exposure to Garou culture had been through Oldman, his perception of the Garou was that of a noble, merciful, and compassionate werebeast. To tell him the killings were the work of a Garou would shatter everything Parker knew about them. Still, he couldn't hide the truth from him. Not if he wanted the two of them to continue the relationship they currently enjoyed.

Parker remained silent, patiently waiting for an answer.

Oldman resigned himself to telling Parker the truth. It just wasn't in his nature to tell the man an outright lie.

"Well . . . I fear that it might be the work of a Garou. A renegade, someone who is totally out of his mind with rage." Oldman stood there, thinking about it for a moment, and suddenly realized what it was he had sensed there in the alley. "It might even be a Garou in the Thrall of The Wyrm."

"A Garou?" Parker said slowly, as if trying to fathom it. "It *would* have to be out of its mind to do that kind of damage to a human." Parker shuddered at the thought.

"That's what it means to be in the Thrall of The Wyrm. Absolutely insane, corrupt, a manifestation of pure evil."

Parker took a deep breath. "What about drugs?"

"That's another possibility," said Oldman. "It certainly wouldn't be the first time it's happened."

Several months ago, Oldman had scared off a Garou who'd been killing homeless in the Tenderloin as a form of revenge against the pack of Bone Gnawers who had blackballed him for smoking crack. It was possible that the same thing had happened this time, but somehow Oldman didn't think so.

Sully's murder had been far too malicious, as if the Garou had actually *enjoyed* tearing his body apart.

The room was silent for a long time.

At last Parker spoke. "You know, I'm going to miss Sully."

"We all will," said Oldman. "He was a good man."

Later that afternoon, Father Oldman was busy in his office catching up on correspondence.

Operating the mission required countless hours of work, a lot of which had nothing to do with rehabilitating the homeless. The letters he was writing now were to wealthy citizens of San Francisco and to the heads of various companies, particularly those involved in the food industry. Half the letters were thank-yous for past donations, the other half were gimme-pleases for future ones.

It was a boring job, but it was the sort of thing that had kept the mission operating the past six years. Oldman had tried to give this work to Parker, but people seemed to respond better to handwritten letters from the priest who ran the mission rather than a typewritten letter from an underling.

Oldman finished off a letter to Tony Campione of Campione Party Rentals and Restaurant Supplies asking him for anything he could spare that might be put to use in the kitchen. It was a strange place to ask for supplies, but Oldman had long ago learned that the best stuff usually came from some of the most unlikely sources.

Like the time he'd written a letter to a Nike executive and got back a parcel containing twenty-five pairs of white leather high-tops. The shoes were too dangerous to wear out on the streets—they were the kind of shoes punks wouldn't think twice about killing a homeless person for—so they were raffled off for a quarter a ticket. The mission ended up taking in twice the shoes' retail value in cash.

Oldman slid the letter into the envelope and made a check mark on the list of addresses under his right arm. "Three more to go," he sighed under his breath.

Thankfully, there was a knock at the door.

It was Parker, beaming.

"There's someone here to see you, Father."

"Who?" said Oldman, infected by Parker's smile. "Who is it?"

Parker didn't answer. Instead he left the room, leaving the door ajar.

A moment later a middle-aged man in faded pants and a worn sweater stepped through the door.

"I don't believe it," said Oldman, getting up from behind his desk and looking the man over from head to toe. "Eddie Carver."

After hearing his name, Carver smiled broadly. "I was afraid you wouldn't remember me." He stepped forward with an outstretched hand.

"Nonsense, Eddie. I never forget anyone who comes to me genuinely wanting to be helped." Oldman took the man's hand in his own and shook it. "How long has it been?"

"Six months, I think."

"That long." Oldman shook his head. "Time sure flies."

There was an awkward moment of silence between them as they both seemed uncomfortable and at a loss for what to say. Finally, Oldman spoke. "C'mon Eddie, sit down here"—he gestured at the chair across from his desk—"and tell me what you've been up to."

Carver eased himself into the chair. "Well, about a week after I left here I got a job at a Laundromat on Church Street. After working there for three months they made me manager."

"Hey, that's great!" cheered Oldman.

"Yeah. A lot of things have been going good since I met you, Father."

"I'm glad to hear it."

Carver nodded, his head bobbing up and down on his neck as if it were tied to the end of a string.

"Eddie," Oldman said flatly. "You didn't come back here just to tell me that you're working in a Laundromat, did you? From the way you're looking at me I'd say you've got some bigger news to tell."

Carver looked as if he could hardly contain himself, as if he were about to burst open at the seams. "I never could keep anything secret from you, Father."

"C'mon Eddie, what is it?" Oldman was finding Carver's excitement contagious.

"Just a minute," Carver said. He got up from his chair and quickly stepped out of the room.

Oldman listened to the sound of the man's steps fade as he walked down the hall. Suddenly his steps stopped, their sound replaced by a series of faint whispers. There was a moment of silence, and then he heard two sets of footsteps coming back toward the office.

Carver appeared at the door, stepped to the side, and was joined by a woman.

"Father Oldman, meet Marjorie Watts. Marjorie, this is Father Oldman."

She was a short, squat woman, standing no more than five feet tall and weighing in at something close to two hundred pounds. Her smile was bright and cheerful and she looked to be happy. In fact, standing side by side, Carver and Marjorie Watts looked like the happiest couple in the world.

"I'm pleased to meet you, Marjorie," said Oldman, standing up to shake her hand. Her grip was firm, strong. "Please, sit down."

Carver was the perfect gentleman, holding the chair for the woman before taking a seat himself.

"Eddie has told me so much about you, Father. I feel like I already know you."

"I'd like to say I've heard all about you too, but I haven't seen Eddie in months." Oldman paused for a moment. "So . . . Tell me all about her, Eddie."

Carver fidgeted in his chair like an excited schoolboy. "Well, like I said, I manage a Laundromat and I'm there just about every day. One day I saw Marge come in to do her laundry and we started talking—"

Marjorie leaned forward. "We talked so much that day I didn't even get my clothes washed."

Carver laughed. "Which was great, because it meant that she had to come back the next day. We spent time talking again the next day, and the day after that . . . until we were seeing each other just about every day."

"Even when I didn't have any laundry to do," Marjorie said, leaning to her left to rub up against Carver.

"After a while her visits to the Laundromat weren't enough for me, so I started visiting her where she works at the Sunrise Restaurant over on Olive Street. It was four blocks from the Laundromat, a bit of a long way to go for a cup of coffee, but the service was great."

"So, you two have been seeing a lot of each other lately," Oldman said, beginning to suspect the reason why they'd come.

"Yeah," said Marjorie. "And somewhere along the way we realized we were in love."

Carver nodded. There was a glint in his eye.

"That's wonderful!" cried Father Oldman. "I'm glad to hear it."

"Which brings me to the reason we're here." Carver fidgeted nervously in his chair. "I want . . . "

Marjorie gave him a bit of a stern look.

"Sorry. *We* want . . . "

Marjorie nodded approval.

"We want to get married . . . and we'd like for you to marry us."

The couple sat there smiling.

Oldman's face was grim. "I'm sorry," he said. "I can't."

Carver looked stunned. "What?"

There'd always been a danger of this kind of thing happening. Father Oldman wore the trappings of the priesthood, called himself a priest, and let others do so as well, but he had never attended a seminary. There was a record somewhere of him having been ordained, but he knew little about the Church and the Catholic faith. When he'd first set up the mission, he'd needed an identity that would arouse little or no suspicion and that people would automatically look to for guidance and spiritual support. Despite the ass-kicking priests had been getting in the press of late, it had been a perfect cover at the time.

Over the years Oldman had become comfortable with being thought of as a priest. He even began talking and thinking like a holy man. And while he was doing more of "God's work" than a lot of other priests and pastors in San Francisco, he was not a Man of God. He was Garou, a werewolf. A member of the Children of Gaia.

Gaia, the Mother Goddess.

So, obviously he could not marry the couple no matter how much he would have liked to. Even if he knew enough about the ceremony to fake it, they'd never be married in the eyes of God.

Their God.

"But, Father . . . " Carver stammered in disbelief.

"I'm sorry, I'd like to, I really would, but I can't."

"Why not?" asked Marjorie.

Oldman thought about it a moment. He'd answered this type of question before, but it had never been so important. "I'm not a member of any order, and I don't have access to a church."

"You could marry us here in the mission," said Carver.

"It would mean a lot to Eddie," Marjorie said.

I bet it would, thought Oldman. He looked at the couple. It was obvious from the looks on their faces that his refusal of their request had come as a bit of a shock. Probably a big disappointment too. It hurt Oldman to say no to them, especially under the circumstances, but he had no other choice.

"Let me be honest with you. I've been running this mission, and others before it, for so long that I've forgotten most of the sacraments. After all, there hasn't been a lot of call around here for baptisms, confirmations, or weddings."

"I'd thought you'd jump at the chance," said Carver. "I've even arranged to have—"

"Believe me," Oldman said, cutting Carver off. "I'm happy for you, I really am. I mean, this is the kind of thing I work to accomplish. You're a lovely couple and I'd love to marry you off, but I can't. The best I can do is possibly assist your parish priest during the ceremony." Oldman's face suddenly brightened. "How would that be?"

The couple was silent a moment.

Finally Carver spoke. "Well, as long as you're there, Father. The only reason I'm able to get married is because you helped me turn my life around, so I want you to be a part of this."

"Absolutely. You tell me when and where, and I'll be there for you."

"Promise?" said Marjorie.

"You've got my word," Oldman said. "And I'll tell you what. I'll even let you have the downstairs mess for your reception if you'd like. Nothing too fancy, mind you."

"That would be great, Father," said Carver.

"Yes, that would be wonderful," echoed Marjorie.

The couple rose up from their chairs, seemingly satisfied.

"I'm just glad I could be of some help," said Oldman, breathing easier.

The couple exited the mission, stood outside of the front door for several minutes looking up and down the street, then stepped down the stairs onto the sidewalk.

"What time is it?" Carver said.

Marjorie looked at her watch. "Just after three. She said she'd be here at two."

"Well, maybe it's just as well she didn't show up. I'd have hated for her to come all this way for nothing."

They stood on the sidewalk in front of the mission for a few more minutes just in case the woman they were waiting for decided to show. Finally, Carver took hold of Marjorie's hand. "Let's go down to the church and talk to a priest there."

They began walking.

Just then, a cab came down the street in the opposite direction. It pulled up tight against the curb. Then the back door popped open and out stepped a tall, leggy blonde in a full-length tan coat.

The cab remained by the curb as she closed the door behind her. She was so clean, dressed-up, and refined, she stood out on the sidewalk like a fish on the dry side of a dock.

"That must be her," said Marjorie.

"What was your first clue?" asked Carver.

The couple turned back around and approached the woman.

"You must be Miss Caroline Keegan," Carver said, extending his hand.

After he'd asked Marjorie to marry him, Carver had written a letter to the tabloid television show *Inside Affair*. He thought his rehabilitation and subsequent marriage to Marjorie in a ceremony conducted by Father Oldman was the kind of human-interest story the show would be interested in. He also thought some publicity for the mission would be his way of saying thank-you to Father Oldman for all that he'd done for him.

That had been the plan, but Father Oldman's refusal to perform the ceremony had thrown a monkey wrench into the works. Maybe he should have okayed it with Father Oldman first, but he'd wanted it to be a surprise.

Well, thought Carver. *Sur-prise*!

"That's right, I'm Ms. Caroline Keegan," Caroline answered. "Are you Eddie Carver?"

Carver nodded. "And this is my fiancée, Marjorie Watts."

"Pleased to meet you," said the reporter. She took a moment to sigh. "I'm sorry I'm so late, but the traffic was terrible and I couldn't get out of the office until one. So"—she clasped her hands together in dramatic fashion—"when's the big day?"

"Uh," said Eddie. "We don't know yet."

Caroline stared at them with a confused look on her face. "What do you mean?"

"Well . . . we're still getting married," said Carver. "It's just that Father Oldman doesn't want to do the ceremony."

"What? Did he say why not?"

"He's not too up on his sacraments."

"You mean he flat-out refused you?"

"No. Not really. He did offer to assist our parish priest, and he's letting us use the mission's mess hall for our reception."

"But he didn't want to marry you?"

Carver and Marjorie both shook their heads.

"Isn't that strange? You'd think this would be the kind of success story he lived for." Obviously, Caroline Keegan's curiosity had been piqued. Something wasn't right here. "Did you tell him about me, that we were planning on doing a story about you and the mission?"

"I never had a chance to tell him," said Carver.

"Hmm? Can you think of any reason other than the ones he gave why he wouldn't want to marry you?"

Carver was silent, thinking.

"Maybe he won't marry you because you didn't go up to that ranch in the hills like they wanted you to," said Marjorie.

"Nah," said Carver. "That wouldn't be it. Lots of people don't go up there. It's no big deal."

"What's this about a ranch?" asked Caroline, her eyes opening wide at the hint of an even bigger story.

"There's a place called The Scott Ranch just north of Mount Tamalpais State Park where people from the mission go to continue their rehabilitation."

"How come I've never heard of it?" said Caroline.

"From what I gathered when I was living inside the mission, the ranch is a sort of special place. They don't like too many visitors up there."

"I see," said the reporter. There was suddenly a strained quality to her voice, as if she was in a hurry to get away. "I'm sorry Father Oldman didn't want to marry you. It would have made a great story. But if he does end up assisting the wedding ceremony, give me a call." She handed Carver her card and slipped back into the cab. As it pulled into traffic, the cab's rear window rolled down and the reporter's long blond hair began to flutter in the breeze.

"Call me," she said.

Carver looked at Marjorie.

Marjorie looked at Carver.

"What the hell got into her all of a sudden?" asked Marjorie.

"You know how television types are."

"What? Pushy?"

"No, busy. Our wedding didn't pan out so she's got to start working on another story."

"So soon?"

"It's the nature of the beast."

"I wonder what she's going to do a story on next?"

"Well, we'll just have to watch *Inside Affair* and find out."

———

Father Oldman finished writing his last letter, a note thanking Regina DiMaio of the Regina Quilting Company for the dozen comforters she had recently donated. They were all well made and warm and would probably last for years. He stuffed the letter in an envelope and placed it on top of the pile of letters in his "out" box.

That done, he got up from his desk and walked over to the calendar hanging on the wall by the window. According to the calendar, there would be a full moon tonight.

"Good," he whispered under his breath.

Garou weren't affected by the changes in the moon like the werewolves of legend and popular movies. Garou could change their form at will, day or night, full moon or empty black sky. Still, he was glad the moon would be full, it would help him in his search for the murderer.

Oldman looked out the window at Eddy Street for a long time. Somewhere out there was a killer, a Garou killer who appeared to be killing the homeless solely for the pleasure of it.

For the fun of it.

For kicks.

Anger rose in the back of Oldman's throat, and he resisted the urge to howl.

Tonight, he would howl.

Tonight, he would rage.

Tonight . . .

Caroline Keegan sat across the desk from *Inside Affair* assignment editor Sam Barlow. When she was sure Sam was looking at her, she crossed her legs, making sure her skirt slid up well past her knees.

"Don't give me that forget-about-the-story-I-didn't-get-and-look-at-my-legs routine. I asked you to get a simple human-interest story for the weekend edition, and before it's even happened you're telling me to forget about it."

"It's a nonstory, Sam. The priest doesn't want to marry

them. Besides, if he is involved with the ceremony, you can always send a camera."

"Send a camera. Send a camera. That's your answer for everything." Barlow paused a moment, his anger simmering. "Let me ask you something. Why do you think we pay you a shitload of money each week?"

Caroline was silent.

"Because people like to see your beautiful smiling face and long blond hair on their television screens. But for that to happen, you've got to do some stories that we can put on the air. Preferably the ones that I assign you."

"What if I told you I've got a better story. A hard-news story. A story about a cult situated up in the hills on the Marin Peninsula."

The assignment editor's eyes narrowed. He slid easily into the seat behind his desk. "I'd say, let's hear what you've got."

"I thought you might."

4

There was a knock at the door.

"Father Oldman." It was the voice of Preston Parker. "It's beginning to get dark out."

"Thank you, Parker," Oldman said, stirring from a light sleep. He listened to the sound of Parker's steps fade down the hall, then rose from his bed and went to the window. He pulled aside the curtain and looked outside. The moon was bright and full, hanging over the city like a watchful eye.

Oldman moved into the center of the room and removed all his clothing in preparation for the change. It had been many weeks since he'd last changed his form, and he was looking forward to it. Besides that, the rage he felt over Sully's death made it necessary.

Because most of the mission's day-to-day business was best conducted with a gentle touch and patience, Oldman remained in the Homid, or human, form most of the time.

But there were times when he felt the need to run free. At those times he would change into the Lupus form of the wolf and run wild through the city headed for the greenery of Golden Gate Park.

Still at other times, when the mission ran critically

low on things like food or medicine, things that couldn't be obtained through the usual means, Oldman would change into the half-man, half-wolf Crinos form and rely on the power of The Delirium—the madness that overcomes humans whenever they look upon a Garou in the Crinos form—to take whatever he needed from nearby stores and warehouses.

But those times were rare. Cases of extreme emergency. Like tonight.

Tonight, he would use his rage to change into the Crinos form, that of the wolfman, and use his increased strength, speed, stamina, and heightened senses to help him find the killer.

Oldman began the change.

To attain the Crinos form, he would first have to "cross over" the Glabro form of the near-man. Moving through the Glabro form would usually take but a second, while the final transformation into Crinos would take longer, approximately six seconds. However, Oldman was in no hurry and went through the process slowly, taking the time to enjoy it.

First it was his hands, slowly curling into claws, the nails turning hard and black. Then his bones began to grow, doubling and redoubling in thickness while his body became massively muscled, more so than a champion bodybuilder. While this internal growth was going on, his skin crawled with a pleasant sort of itch as hair sprouted thick and gray all over his body.

His entire body surged with power.

And as he continued to change form, he grew bigger and taller, stopping only when he was almost nine feet tall and weighing well over four hundred pounds. His arms were longer, apelike, suitable for running on all fours. His teeth had lengthened, sharpening into fangs, while his claws had become deadly, knife-edged talons. His tail was short and furry and would do well to help him maintain his balance.

His face had become wolflike, his lips easily pulling back in a snarl. While he was the embodiment of the beast, those who knew him in his Homid form might still recognize the thick shock of white hair upon his head and the salt-and-pepper beard that was now a thick mat of white and gray fur around his muzzle.

He stood for a moment in the center of the room feeling currents of strength course through his body. Then, after making sure the hallway was clear, he stepped out of his office and walked casually toward the back door of the mission. He stood at the door a moment, listening to the sounds of people having dinner downstairs.

And he sniffed at the air.

Potatoes. What else?

Then he opened the door and was outside, hidden by the hazy black shadows that shrouded the alley behind the mission. As he began to move, he stepped into the light, and for a brief moment the hair atop his head gleamed as white as a halo before another step returned him to the shadows.

He padded down the alley, his feet sounding as if they were barely touching the pavement.

At the end of it he leaped over a five-foot fence in a single bound and suddenly vanished into the darkness.

He'd been surprised at how much fun it had been to kill, surprised that causing so much pain to a human could bring a Garou so much pleasure.

Killing had become sweet for him.

And he wanted to taste that sweetness again.

The Garou pulled the trench coat tight around his body and headed north along Larkin Street, hunting for humans. He looked into each alley and doorway that he passed, searching patiently for the right one.

He stopped in a laneway behind a row of tenements. There were four men standing around a fire burning inside a steel drum. They were passing a large brown bottle between them. The Garou thought about slipping up behind them and taking one of them out, but with three others there it was just too risky.

He moved on.

A block later he came upon a woman slumped over in the doorway of a vacant store. She was curled up tight under a dirty blue blanket with little more than her head exposed to the cool night air.

He stepped closer for a better look, but before he could take a second step, her blanket opened up and a switchblade *snicked* open in her hand.

"Another step and I'll cut you down at the knees," the woman said, barely looking up at him.

He was enraged by her threat and wanted nothing more than to change form, pounce on her with all his Crinos weight, and tear her body to shreds. But as he contemplated this, her knife blade glinted in the light from the streetlamps. He considered the pain that blade might inflict, even with the faintest glancing blow, and thought it would be easier just to move on.

He walked away, trying to look indifferent, as if he hadn't even heard what she'd said.

He continued walking for several more blocks until he found just what he was looking for.

The man was half a block ahead, stumbling from lamp-post to garbage can either piss drunk or in need of a fix.

He followed the man closely, being careful to main-tain the half-block buffer while patiently waiting for him to find a secluded place to crash.

Together, the Garou and human walked the streets of the Tenderloin for another half hour, the hunter and his prey.

And then the man made a mistake, took a wrong turn.

He turned into the alley behind the Hotel Jefferson.

The Garou made up the distance between them in seconds, then peeked around the corner into the alley.

The alley was dark, less than four feet wide and closed off at the other end, leaving the human no means of escape. There was no way out other than back past the Garou.

Perfect.

The man reached the end of the alley, squatted down onto the ground, and curled himself up tight with his back up against a garbage can. Judging by the way he'd been walking, the man would probably be asleep in seconds.

The Garou slid out of his trench coat and readied himself for the change into Crinos form.

Readied himself . . .

For the kill.

Oldman felt free and alive.

The streets of San Francisco were a poor substitute for Gaia's green grass and thick, deep woods, but it still felt good to run.

He bolted down the quiet back streets, alternating between all fours and his hind legs to let every part of his body warm up to its long-neglected form.

When all the kinks were gone from his body and it flowed with a powerful rhythm all its own, he turned north and headed for one of his favorite places in the city.

The house was a three-story Victorian home at the east end of Cedar Street at Larkin. Unlike most of the tightly spaced homes in Nob Hill, the extremely affluent neighborhood ridiculously juxtaposed to the Tenderloin, this one was set apart from its neighbors by a wide band of thickly grassed lawn on either side of it. Oldman bounded across the grass, reveling in the feeling of the earth giving slightly to accept his weight as he ran.

He ran around to the back of the house and stopped at the fence.

The garden was huge, rich, and lush. As spectacular as ever. All the flowers, bushes, and plants were coming into full spring bloom.

Oldman knew little about the man who lived there, only that his first name was Michele, and that he must be a wealthy retiree because he spent his days outside in his garden—all day, every day.

Oldman hopped the fence with ease and slowly walked along the garden path. Here was Gaia, the Mother Goddess in all her glory. It was refreshing to see a human's love for Gaia rivaling his own. Oldman knew he was trespassing on the man's property but knew the man wouldn't mind, especially if he knew how much joy his garden was giving him.

He spent a few more minutes taking it all in before admitting to himself that he had no more time to waste on self-indulgence. It was a magnificent garden, a wonderful place to spend an evening.

Perhaps some other evening.

He bounded over the fence and headed south into the Tenderloin.

But instead of running back through the streets he scrambled up the fire escape of a tenement building and climbed onto the roof. Up here, from four stories above street level, he had an excellent view of the city. He also liked the feeling of being surrounded by wide-open spaces. It gave him a truer sense of freedom than he could ever get on the ground.

As he stood on the rooftop scanning the streets below, his other senses were also hard at work. His nose was busy sniffing at the air in search of the familiar scent of a Garou in the midst of the city stink. His ears were also active, swiveling around on his head searching for any unnatural or primal sound.

He stood there, deathly still for several minutes—watching, smelling, listening.

Nothing.

He moved a half block east, bounding over the rooftops, his leaps sometimes spanning alleys ten feet or more across. Then he'd stop on the roof of another building, using his keen senses to scan the streets below.

Again nothing.

He moved to four different rooftops, covering an area of five city blocks . . . but came up with nothing.

He was considering calling it a night and heading back to the mission when he heard something.

A scream.

A woman's scream. High-pitched and terror-filled.

He tracked the sound until he was fairly certain of where it had come from, then headed for it, covering yards of ground with each mighty hurtle.

He scrambled down another fire escape, covering the final fifteen feet in freefall and landing silently on his powerful hind legs.

The sound was louder here, clearer.

It was coming from a vacant lot, across the street and half a block away.

He fell down onto all fours and ran down the street as fast as he could.

He was at the edge of the vacant lot in seconds.

At the far end of the lot, partially hidden by a pile of old tires lay the woman who'd been screaming. She was still screaming, but her cries had now been made mute by a strong hand placed over her mouth.

The hand belonged to one of the two men hovering over her.

Clearly, she was being raped.

Oldman's mind and body filled with a new kind of rage.

His lips curled back in a snarl as he bounded across the lot, headed for the two men.

He targeted the larger man first, the one kneeling between the woman's legs with his pants pulled down around his ankles.

He took one last leap, flying several yards through the air before knocking the man over with the full weight of his Crinos form.

Oldman was instantly back on his feet while the man was lying on the ground in a daze, gasping for the wind that had just been knocked out of him.

The second man released his hold on the woman and looked up. His eyes grew wide with terror, then glazed over in fear as he was overcome by The Delirium.

Oldman looked down, away from the second man and at the woman. She was also being overcome by The Delirium, passing out from its compounded effect on the physical and emotional trauma she had just suffered.

Just like that, the crime had been stopped.

But it wasn't enough.

Not for Oldman.

It wouldn't be just to let these men get away without being punished for their crime.

Oldman raised his arm above his head and stretched his claw-tipped fingers to their full length. Then with one swift motion he raked his hand across the second man's chest, easily tearing open his clothing and the soft, warm flesh beneath it.

Bright red bands bloomed across his chest.

Oldman raised his hand again, this time slashing horizontally across the man's groin. The waistband and crotch of his pants tore away like tissue, exposing another set of deep wounds arcing over the top of his genitals.

That will give him something to think about the next time he gets the *urge*, thought Oldman. If he ever gets it again.

The man looked down and saw the blood running down his legs, staining his pants. His eyes turned up as he swayed back and forth on his feet. He dropped to his knees, then fell forward onto his face.

Oldman then turned his attention to the first man, who was slowly coming around. He grabbed the man by the collar of his shirt and used his free hand to administer a fresh set of wounds down the length of the man's back.

For a moment the man's eyes popped open.

And he gazed at Oldman.

Oldman's own eyes narrowed, boring into the man like parallel drill bits. He opened his maw and spoke. "Me, you'll forget," he said, his speech a mixture of words and guttural snarls—the most that was possible in his Crinos form. "But this . . ." He drew his claws across the man's belly and down along his crotch, leaving four long blood lines in their wake. The wounds looked like a red rainbow ringing the outer and inner edges of his pubic hair. "You'll remember forever."

Oldman put the man down and watched him stumble off the lot.

Then he grabbed the second man, slapped his face until he was semiconscious, and gave him a push in the direction of the street.

That left the woman.

She was a young black woman, probably still not out of her teens. She looked as if she might have had a sweet young face at one time in her life, but now she looked streetwise and world-weary, old beyond her years. Oldman felt sorry for her. She was at an age in which she should be discovering things and enjoying life, not coming face-to-face with all its brutal realities.

Oldman gathered her up in his arms, carried her to the edge of the lot, and set her down with her back up against the wall of the building next door.

He stayed with her a few minutes more, stroking her face gently with the thick fur on the back of his hand.

When her eyes began to flutter open and he was sure she'd be all right, he turned his back and ran, vanishing into the night as quickly as he had appeared.

The Garou shifted through Glabro and took several seconds to fine-tune his Crinos form. His face stretched into a long, sharp muzzle, looking more canine than lupine. Fur covered his body in a series of ragged thatches, growing in thick unruly tufts that would never untangle. His body grew taller, his frame roiling with large, well-defined muscles. His fangs were short and stubby, and his claws were razor-sharp and finely pointed.

He entered the alley a werewolf, able to see as clearly in the shadowed darkness as he could in the middle of the day. He moved in on the sitting man slowly, careful not to make any sudden movements.

He was seconds away from the kill.

His body was enthralled by the godlike power he had over the human.

He stood there a moment, letting the excitement and anticipation of it wash over his body.

Shadows flickered over his closed eyelids.

There was someone there.

Someone, or something, had followed him into the alley. A couple of punks probably looking for a drunk to roll or some bum to cut up for kicks.

He sighed in disappointment.

This was the kind of thing he was trying to get away from.

He moved his fingers deeper inside his jacket pocket, fingering something hard and sharp there . . .

And slowly opened his eyes.

The man's eyes opened just as the werewolf was about to strike.

There was surprise in them, but no fear.

The werewolf swung his arm, aiming for the meaty part of the man's trunk, but the man quickly jumped aside and the blow caught him high up on the right arm.

The werewolf's claws came back covered with tattered strips of clothing. Dry.

The man backed away from the werewolf, but there was nowhere to run. After a few steps his back came up against the wall and he was cornered. He assumed a fighting stance, slightly bent forward, feet spread, and hands out in front.

The werewolf's laugh sounded like a vicious snarl. He hadn't been in the mood for a fight, but now that he was in the middle of one, he was going to enjoy it for all it was worth.

He began by taunting the man, bobbing lightly on his hind legs and feinting jabs like a boxer, first with his left, then with his right.

Each time the man quickly moved aside, almost in anticipation of the blows.

This one moves well for a human, the werewolf thought. Almost as well as a Garou. A worthy opponent. Too bad it won't be enough to save his life.

The werewolf continued the cat-and-mouse game

with the man, expecting him to go insane with The Delirium at any moment.

But the man stayed on his feet, and the werewolf quickly grew tired of playing games. It was time to get down to business.

He moved closer to the man, within striking distance, moving both his arms at once. First, he motioned to strike a blow with his right hand. As the man moved to one side to escape the blow, the Garou caught hold of his shoulder with his left hand, then clawed at him again with his right. The blow was a glancing one, but raked the man down the left side of his face.

The man let out a weak cry and tried to wrench himself free of the viselike grip on his shoulder.

The werewolf held on to the man, pinning him high enough against the wall so that his feet were no longer touching the ground.

"You fight good . . ." snarled the werewolf. "For a *man*." Then he reached over with his free right hand and dug his claws into the soft flesh under the man's chin. He pushed his claws about an inch deep into the flesh before pulling them out again. They came back red and wet. Then, with his claws set deep enough to cut open the skin but not the muscles and tendons underneath, he drew them down the man's neck and across his chest and belly.

Blood spurt out of the wounds in a fine mist, then ran down his skin in thick red lines.

The man screamed, a loud yelp of pain that came from somewhere deep inside his chest.

When his scream faded, he looked at the werewolf, his eyes narrowing in defiance. "And *you* fight like a girl." He reached into his jacket for his knife. When he had it firmly in his hand, he pulled it out of his pocket and jabbed it into the werewolf's left arm, burying the long wide blade all the way to the hilt.

The werewolf instantly dropped the man and looked down at his arm in shock. The knife stuck out horizontally from his forearm like a nail from a piece of wood.

Blood spurted out from the entrance point in ever-quickening pulses.

The werewolf grabbed at the knife, pulled on it, and felt the blade scrape against his bones.

He arched his head back and howled, long and loud.

Windows along the alley vibrated and shook from the sound. One of them even cracked.

With one mighty pull, the werewolf yanked the knife from his arm and threw it onto the alley floor like just another piece of garbage.

He stood there, hand over his wound, his breath coming in great blasts of air, like a horse after a hard run.

His eyes clouded over in rage.

He was going to tear the man apart.

He scanned the length of the alley . . .

But the man was gone.

Oldman went from rooftop to rooftop, searching the streets.

He saw prostitutes picking up johns and turning tricks in the backseats of cars. He saw drugs and money flowing through hands like water on fifteen different street corners. He saw homeless people sleeping on park benches, picking through garbage for something to eat, or walking the streets waiting for the donut shops to open so they'd have someplace warm to sit.

He saw all of this, but he saw no Garou.

Tired and disappointed by his fruitless search, he turned his back on the city for the night and headed for the mission.

He was a block and a half from Eddy Street when he heard the first scream. If he wasn't mistaken, it sounded like the yelping howl of a Garou.

But then he heard a second scream, this one louder, more powerful and wolflike than the first. Definitely the howl of a Garou. A Garou in Crinos form.

Surprisingly, it communicated great pain.

This is it, he thought.

He headed in the direction of the howl, first over the

rooftops, then sliding three stories down a drainpipe to the street below. He scrambled across the street on all fours, then headed north, covering great stretches of ground with each mighty leap.

He judged the sound's distance and volume one last time and guesstimated that he was nearing its source. He turned headlong into the alley, expecting to come upon a gory murder scene, but the alley was empty.

He stopped dead in his tracks, realizing he was vulnerable with his back exposed to the street. He turned around quickly, expecting the Garou to be standing there.

Nothing.

But although the Garou was nowhere to be seen, he could feel its presence nearby. Instinctively, he knew he was in the right place. Something had happened here.

He stepped deeper into the alley, sniffing at the air.

He came upon two distinct pools of blood on the pavement.

Oldman fell to his knees and sniffed at the stain closest to the alley's back wall.

Human.

He moved over to the second bloodstain, this one just as large as the first, and sniffed at it.

Garou.

While still on all fours, his eyes caught the glint of something metal. He reached out and picked up the knife, still wet with the blood of—he sniffed it—Garou. . . .

He took a moment to formulate a scenario that would account for what he had found here. Apparently the human had fought back successfully enough to wound the Garou. Not much of a wound by Garou standards, but a wound that had been severe enough to give the human time to escape.

The thought of one of his flock being strong enough to fight off a Garou caused Oldman's lips to pull back in a smile.

But even though the human had escaped, he'd probably not managed to get very far considering the amount of blood he'd lost. And the Garou would heal quickly, especially when the wound had been inflicted by a human.

The fight might not be over yet.

Perhaps it was still going on somewhere else along the street.

The fur along the back of Oldman's neck bristled as he spun around on his hind legs and darted out of the alley.

On the street he looked left and right, but could see nothing that would tell him which way to go. He sniffed at the air; the scents of both the human and the Garou went off in the same direction. He turned right and ran down the street, glancing through storefronts and into alleyways along the way.

The human's scent was getting stronger, the Garou's more faint, until it finally disappeared—as if he had jumped on the back of a passing truck or car.

Oldman turned down another alley, this one large enough to drive a truck through. The human's scent was unmistakable.

He was in here.

Somewhere.

Oldman moved slowly through the alley. Although he could smell the human's presence, the man was nowhere to be seen.

There were piles of old boxes and pallets on one side of the alley, and it was from here that the scent seemed to originate.

Oldman pulled aside several pallets, then moved the boxes and other cardboard that looked as if they had been hurriedly brought together in a makeshift pile. He knocked aside one last box and, as he suspected, found the man lying down in a slight depression, surrounded on all four sides by boxes.

He'd been in a fight with a Garou all right. There were long bleeding scratches on one side of his face and another even longer set across the front of his neck and chest.

The man had been jostled by Oldman's efforts to

clear away the boxes. When moonlight finally shone down on him, he opened his eyes. After taking a few moments to focus, the man's eyes widened in fear. He was likely confusing Oldman with the first Garou that had attacked him.

Indeed, his hand balled into a fist as he took a swing at Oldman, but the blow bounced harmlessly off his shoulder.

This one certainly is a fighter, thought Oldman.

The man tried to strike again, but his arm fell limp before he could gather enough strength to throw another punch.

Oldman knelt closer to the man, carefully gathered him up in his arms, and carried him out of the alley.

Once he was on the sidewalk, Oldman firmed his grip on the unconscious man and ran swiftly down the middle of the street, depending on the power of The Veil to explain the sight of a werewolf carrying an unconscious man to any of the night owls or insomniacs who might just happen to be peeking out their windows.

He was at the mission in minutes.

With three . . . four . . . five . . . strides he bounded up the steps to the mission's front door.

There, shrouded in the darkness of the unlit portico, Oldman eased his burden onto the ground. When the man's head bumped against the concrete, his eyes opened. He looked up at Oldman, and another brief pulse of terror flashed in his eyes. He tried to remain awake, but his eyelids had become too heavy to keep open any longer.

Slowly, they fell.

And before his eyes were fully closed, Oldman was gone.

5

The sun peeked over the horizon, a blazing orange ball chasing the darkness and shadows from the day.

A light came on inside the portico in front of The Scott Mission. A moment later the front door opened and Father Oldman stepped onto the porch. Though the casual observer might have missed it, there was a slight trace of blood on his hands and a buildup of dirt beneath his fingernails. He looked down, ran a hand through his shock of ragged white hair, but didn't look too surprised to find a battered and bloody body lying on his front doorstep.

"Parker!"

Parker was an early riser. But even if he weren't, Oldman had made sure he'd made plenty of noise when he'd returned just to make sure Parker would be there when he needed him. With any luck, Parker could probably hear Oldman's call echoing down the hall to his room.

"Parker!" Oldman called again.

Oldman's assistant appeared in the doorway a few seconds later. When he saw the body he gasped. It was a mass of open wounds, dried blood, and bruises. "Is he alive?"

Oldman knelt down, moved his head closer, and made a token examination of the body, more for Parker's benefit than for his own. Finally, he said, "Yes, he's alive. Hopefully it's not as bad as it looks. Come round here and take his feet."

Parker moved around to the far end of the man and grabbed hold of his ankles just above his naked feet. Parker, a slightly built man not particularly strong in a physical sense, adjusted his grip several times to make sure he had a firm hold before lifting.

Oldman placed his hands under the man's arms and lifted. He stood up easily then waited patiently as Parker struggled to get the man's legs off the ground.

"Into my office."

Parker nodded appreciatively. Oldman's office was the second-closest door to the entrance of the mission.

They carried him down the hall, and then into the fair-sized room on the right. Inside, there was a floor-to-ceiling bookshelf standing against the outside wall and a great wooden desk in front of it. Pictures of presidents and clerics, and one oil painting of a timber wolf howling at the moon, adorned two of the walls, while a couch was set up against the fourth next to the door that led into Oldman's bedroom.

They laid the man down on the couch, raising his feet and placing a few pillows under his head.

"Do you want me to call the police?" asked Parker, his tone slightly solemn.

"No!"

Parker gave Oldman an incredulous look. "But Father," he said, looking away from the priest and at the man on the couch, "he survived the attack. When he regains consciousness, he might be able to give the police a description of his attacker."

Parker had a point.

If circumstances were different and the murderer was a psychopathic human, then it would be a problem for the police to handle. But this man had been attacked by a Garou, and Garou took care of their own problems.

Therefore, in Oldman's mind, the less involvement by the police on this matter the better.

Oldman turned to face Parker. "This is no different than the last time," he said. "This is a Garou matter. I don't want the police to be involved in it any more than they have to be."

Judging by the look in Parker's eyes, Oldman knew he'd been too harsh with him. The young man knew little about the litany of the Garou and had only meant well. "The police will never catch this killer." His voice had become friendlier now, like that of a father talking to his son. "I will have to stop him myself. There is no other way."

Parker opened his mouth to speak but remained silent as if he'd thought better of it. He had far too much respect for Oldman to go against his wishes. And although he didn't fully understand what was going on, he trusted Oldman's judgment in the matter enough to go along with him.

"All right, Father." He nodded. "If you say so, there will be no police."

"Good," Oldman said. He released his hands from Parker's shoulders and gave him a gentle slap on the arm. "Thank you."

"But what about medical attention?" Parker said. "Perhaps I should call for a doctor." From the tone of his voice it was clear that Parker expected the same response to this suggestion as he'd received to his first one.

But Oldman simply shook his head. "I can heal this man faster and better than any doctor ever could."

This seemed easier for Parker to accept. How many times over the years had he seen Oldman suffer a deep gash or cut that would have sent a normal man to the hospital, only to see that same cut virtually gone by the next day with hardly a scar left in its place?

"All right," said Parker, smiling. "I give up." He threw his hands in the air in mock surrender. "You do what you think is best. I'm going back to bed."

Oldman escorted Parker to the door. "Pleasant dreams," he said, then locked the door behind him.

The man on the couch let out a moan.

The sound reminded Oldman of the task ahead.

He went to the locked cabinet in the lower right-hand corner of the bookshelf and opened it. From inside the cabinet he took out several white plastic jars, a roll of gauze, and a bottle of alcohol. Then he gathered everything up and brought it over to the table next to the couch.

With ease, Oldman tore away the man's clothing, then quickly began cleaning the dark red streaks on his chest with a gauze pad soaked in alcohol.

The fiery sting of the alcohol made the man cry out in pain, but his eyes remained closed.

"You'll be all right . . ." Oldman's voice was soft, reassuring, but still quite powerful. "What I am doing will help you heal."

The man nodded, swallowed once, and did his best to tolerate the pain in silence.

"That's good," said Oldman, impressed by the man's strength. "Very, very good." He picked up one of the large white jars from the table and opened it. Inside was a thick, oily white paste that filled the room with the smell of pine needles and moss, rich black earth, and freshly cut grass.

He scooped up a good amount of the paste with his fingers and began applying it to the wounds on the man's face, taking care to completely cover every jagged inch of ruptured flesh.

As he continued to work the paste into the cuts, down the man's neck and across his chest, his patient's breath—which up until now had been short and ragged—slowed into a nice regular rhythm.

When Oldman was done and all of the man's wounds had been given a thick protective coating of the salve, he wiped the excess off—as he always did—onto the back of his neck. It gave him a tingling sensation, and felt pleasantly cool against his skin.

The man soon fell into a deep sleep.

Oldman took the opportunity to get some rest himself.

After sealing his jars and locking them up in the bookshelf, he went over to the seat behind his desk and sat down.

It had been a long night, and he wasn't getting any younger.

He put his feet up on the desk.

And immediately dozed off.

Hours later the man stirred in his sleep, twisting on the couch as if he were in the throes of some horrible nightmare.

Oldman opened his eyes, took a moment to blink the sleep from them, then looked over at the man.

He was asleep, but looked as if he were still fighting for his life. His arms were crossed over his chest as he turned ever so slightly from side to side. His legs kicked at the couch's far armrest as if something was there. Of course there wasn't, but Oldman knew that in the man's mind the werewolf *was* there, bearing down on him, clawing at him with talon-tipped hands, snapping at him with long, dripping fangs.

The man cried out.

Oldman rose from his chair and hurried across the room. When he reached the man's side, he placed an arm firmly against his shoulder and knelt down so that his mouth was close to the man's ear. Then he opened his mouth and began to sing. The song was imperceptible at first, but steadily grew louder, until its soft melodic howls filled the man's head with peace and tranquillity.

Slowly the man calmed down, eventually falling back into a light but peaceful sleep.

Oldman ended the song, took his chair out from behind his desk, and placed it in the center of the room so he could watch the man come around.

A few minutes later the man's eyes fluttered open, and he turned his head from side to side with a where-the-hell-am-I sort of look.

"Good morning," said Oldman, cheerfully. "If you're wondering, you're in The Scott Mission."

At the mention of The Scott Mission the man relaxed slightly. "Good morning," he said. He rose up onto his elbows for a look around, but the painful pull on his fresh wounds created by his movements forced him back down onto the couch.

He let out a sigh.

"You've got to take it easy," said Oldman.

"You mean I have a choice?"

Oldman paused long enough to smile. "Well, I suppose it is obvious enough."

"What the hell happened?" asked the man.

Oldman wasn't about to answer that question. It was better for the human to formulate his own conclusions. That way Oldman would be able to pick an explanation that would produce the strongest Veil.

"Why don't you tell me?" said Oldman.

"Geez, it's pretty hard to remember it all, since I started out a little drunk." The man's eyes were directed at the ceiling. He raised an arm over his head as he tried to remember.

"I was walking around, stumbling is probably a better word for it. After a couple bottles of malt liquor I'm not much good to anybody . . ."

Oldman remained silent, waiting for the man to continue.

"Anyway . . ." He paused to regain his train of thought. "I turned into my favorite alley, the one behind the Hotel Jefferson. There's a vent at the end of it that sometimes blows out warm air. It wasn't blowing last night, but I wasn't feeling up to going to any of my other spots so I decided to crash down right then and there.

"Well, I couldn't've been asleep for more than a few seconds when this thing . . ."

Oldman leaned forward in his chair. "Yes."

"This thing . . ."

"What was it?"

"I don't know. It was like a werewolf or something."

Oldman shook his head, dismissing the man's words with a wave of his hand. "That's impossible."

"No, no. I remember, it's coming back to me clearer now. It was like a half-man, half-wolf kind of thing, seven feet tall, covered in dirty brown fur and smelling like a sewer."

Oldman couldn't believe what he was hearing. It was as if the man had been totally unaffected by The Delirium.

He shook his head again. "A werewolf indeed. You were most likely delirious at the time."

It was the man's turn to shake his head. "No, I might have been drunk, but I certainly wasn't delirious. It was a werewolf kind of creature, but not in the way they look in the movies . . . you know, with a man's head covered in fur. This thing was big and strong like a wolf, but it had a body shaped like a man . . . a really big man. And his head . . . it was long and pointed like a dog's. . . . No, maybe it was more like a wolf's too. The thing even sounded like a wolf. Especially when I stuck him."

"You mean, when you wounded him with this?" Oldman reached over and picked the man's knife up off his desk.

"Hey, yeah, that's my knife. Where'd you find it?"

"In the alley."

The man reached out for his knife, but the stretch on his skin proved too painful, and he had to pull his arms back in and place them over his chest.

"Why don't I just hold on to this for you until later?"

"Yeah, sure," the man grunted, still in pain. "Okay."

The room was silent for several moments.

"You know," Oldman said. "I'm fascinated by that story of yours. Surely it didn't end when you, uh . . . stuck him?"

"No," the man said. "He dropped me when that happened and started howling in pain . . . *like a wolf*!" The last three words were delivered as if they were a solid declarative statement.

"Really?" Oldman was doing his best to sound skeptical.

"Yeah, really. So I hightailed it out of there, found a quiet alley, and curled up under a pile of garbage. I thought I was going to die there, that's how banged up I was."

Oldman was eager to hear the man's version of what happened next, but played it cool.

"But you didn't die there."

"No. There was this other *werewolf* that came along . . . and he wanted to help me."

"You're kidding?"

"No, there were two of them," the man said, his voice strong with conviction. "At first I thought it was the same one coming back to finish me off, but this one was different."

"How so?"

"It was bigger than the first. And there was a patch of solid white hair on his head—and I mean white, like a china plate. And around his face—or what do you call that part on dogs—his muzzle, he had this white and gray hair that looked like . . . "

The man turned on his side and looked at Oldman.

"That looked just like your beard."

Oldman laughed nervously. "That's very funny."

"No, it's not." The man was adamant. "He looked a lot like you."

"Of course he did," Oldman said, trying hard to hide his utter astonishment at the man's recollection of the previous night's events.

By rights, The Delirium should have prevented him from remembering anything. The only way he could have remembered all of what happened was if . . . he were . . .

Kinfolk?

Oldman shook his head, dismissing the thought from his mind as being too hopeful. He'd brought others back to the mission that seemed to remember him in his Crinos form, but they'd all turned out to be simply highly imaginative. There had to be another explanation for this man's recollections, an explanation that wasn't making itself apparent at this time. He would figure it out later. Just then it was important that the man— Oldman realized he didn't even know the man's name— continued to heal.

"I'm sorry, but through all this I've neglected to introduce myself," said Oldman. "My name is Father Wendel Oldman. I run the mission here."

"Father Wendel Oldman," he said curiously. "I think I've heard of you." He paused a moment, thinking. "And this place is a homeless shelter, isn't it?"

"You could call it that."

"Good, I'm in the right place then because I ain't got no home."

"And you are?" Oldman said.

"Oh, sorry." The man tried to roll over and extend his arm. "My name's Ken . . . " He cleared his throat. "Kenneth Holt. But everyone just calls me Ken."

"I'd prefer calling you Holt."

Holt looked at him strangely. "How come?"

"First of all, I call all the men at the mission by their last names. It keeps a bit of formality between them and myself. Second of all, I prefer it to Ken."

"Really?"

"Yes," said Oldman. "Do you know what the name Holt means?"

"Nope. Never really thought about it much."

"Well, it's an Old English word that means, 'from the forest.'"

"Okay, uh . . ." Holt hesitated, unsure what to call the priest.

"People around here call me Father."

"Okay . . . Father, call me Holt. Just don't call me late for supper." Holt let out a laugh, but it hurt too much and he had to stop. "Which reminds me. I'm starved. You got anything to eat?"

"We have a mess hall downstairs. I'll see that you get some breakfast."

"Thanks," said Holt, lying back on the couch and starting to fall back to sleep.

Oldman went over to the door, opened it, and stuck his head out into the hall. "Parker!"

"Yes, Father?"

"Bring this man downstairs. When he's finished eating,

take him into the dorm and let him sleep for as long as he needs to."

"Sure thing, Father." Parker stepped into the room and walked over to the couch. He stopped for a moment when he saw the man's wounds covered over with the white salve, then reached out to help the man off the couch.

Holt grunted in pain as he got up, holding his breath until he was fully upright.

"Put your arm around my shoulder," said Parker.

Holt left the room leaning heavily on Parker. He grunted in pain with every step, but the salve seemed to be working better than Oldman had hoped. At this rate he'd be free to move around on his own by the next morning.

As the two men trudged down the hall toward the stairs, Oldman stuck his head back out of the door.

"I'm going to try and get some sleep, Parker. See that I'm not disturbed until after lunch."

"Okay, Father," Parker said. "Will do."

Oldman began to retreat into his room when he noticed the two men slowly turning back around. He waited in the doorway of his office until they were facing him.

"Thanks," Holt said.

Oldman laughed under his breath. "For what?"

"For . . . " He paused, clearing his throat. "You know . . . for fixing me up and all. I don't know how to repay you."

"Don't worry, Holt," Oldman said. "I'm sure I'll think of something."

"Okay, be careful," said Parker, helping Holt down the stairs. "Just a few more steps."

Holt's body ached. Even the spots where he hadn't been cut open were soft and tender. He hadn't taken a close look at the bruises on his body, but he didn't even want to think about what color they were.

He looked down the steps and counted them off. Four more to go, then an easy walk over to a chair where he'd have to make himself comfortable enough to eat something. It was a lot of painful work for a bit of food, but he was hungry and would have walked a mile for a bowl of soup.

He took a deep breath, feeling the expansion of his chest pulling at the wounds that were already starting to heal, and held it. He did the final steps in one last push and was standing in the basement, smelling the delicious scent of something good coming from the kitchen.

"Hungry?" asked Parker.

"Don't you know it," said Holt. "I haven't had a decent meal in days."

"Yeah, I know what that's like." Parker pulled a chair out from the table. "Have a seat, I'll go and find you something to eat."

Parker headed for the kitchen, leaving Holt to fend for himself. He took two lurching steps closer to the chair, then grabbed a firm hold of the chair's backrest and the top of the table. Slowly, being careful not to move his neck, chest, or stomach, he lowered himself into the chair. Just as his rear was about to make contact with the seat, he lost his grip and fell the final two inches into the chair. He closed his eyes and winced as fiery streaks of pain burned across his body. When he opened his eyes, he realized that the dozen or so people in the room were all looking at him.

They were an odd-looking mix of people, dirty and disheveled. All homeless people like himself. All of them there because they got the short end of the stick at some point in their lives.

Holt always felt that way when he saw a gathering of the homeless. If just one thing had been different in their lives, then maybe they would have turned out for the better, been doctors or lawyers, or just people lucky enough to have jobs, families, and places to go home to at the end of the day. Instead they got shafted, this one with an abusive father, that one with an alcoholic mother, this one introduced to drugs or alcohol at the wrong time in his life, that one bounced back and forth from orphanage to foster home until the street looked like a better place to live.

How did that public service commercial go?

Because a mind is a terrible thing to waste.

Yeah, well, here was a terrible waste of minds and bodies, hearts and souls. Old people, retards, bums, junkies, addicts, runaways, ex-cons, and vets. The homeless.

The bottom rung of the ladder.

And here he was smack-dab in the middle of them, belonging here. One of them.

He took another look around. They looked happy.

At least there's hope in these people's eyes, he thought. Hope for the future.

That's what Holt wanted.

A future.

A second chance at life.

Maybe this was the place that might help him get it. It was worth a try. Anyway, one thing was for sure. Things were already looking up. Being inside here with a meal on the way, he was a lot better off than he was the day before.

A hell of a lot better.

He decided to keep an open mind and give this place a try.

Parker returned to the table with a tray full of food, and a woman—an older woman, but not necessarily unattractive.

Things were looking better all the time.

"Kenneth Holt," said Parker. "Meet Alcina Williams. She's the woman you have to thank for the meals we get around here. If it wasn't for her we'd all go hungry."

The woman's face didn't change its expression as Parker spoke, leading Holt to believe that what he'd said was true.

"Hi!" she said, shaking Holt's hand. "People here just call me L.C."

"Hello, L.C. So far, people round here call me Holt."

"Well, Holt . . . welcome to the mission. Eat up and

don't complain about the food, even when it's bad, if you know what I mean."

She had a drop-dead-serious look in her eye. Holt figured she wasn't kidding.

"Smells great from where I'm sitting."

"I think I'm beginning to like this guy already."

Parker slid the tray in front of Holt. L.C. lingered a little longer to see the man's reaction.

There was a steaming bowl of potato soup in the top-right corner of the tray and a package of crackers to the side of the bowl. In the tray's opposite corner was a plate with a pile of crisp home fries and a small meat patty on it. The gravy sliding off the patty formed a thick, greasy puddle around the fries.

Holt reached out and ate one of the fries. It was a little stale and could have used some salt, but it was hot and eased the empty pangs in his stomach. "Tastes great," he said.

L.C. nodded in satisfaction and headed back to the kitchen.

"Very good," Parker said, sitting down next to him. "You've passed your first test here at the mission with flying colors."

"What? Her?"

"Yeah, don't cross L.C. if you're fond of eating regularly."

"Understood," said Holt.

"Good," said Parker. "Dig in."

Holt began to eat, hungry as a wolf and eating like one too.

Parker sat quietly by his side, giving the man the opportunity to sate his hunger.

"Would you like some more?" Parker asked when Holt had reached the bottom of the bowl.

"Mmm-hmm," said Holt, his mouth full of potatoes and his chin streaked with gravy.

Parker got up from the table and took Holt's bowl back to the kitchen. He came back a minute later with a fresh bowl of soup and a bun.

"The bun's a day old," he said. "But the way you're going I don't think it matters. Anyway, you might want to use it to sop up your gravy."

Holt nodded his thanks.

Parker was silent again for several minutes.

When Holt began to feel stuffed, he turned to Parker and said, "What's the story with this place anyway? And who are all these people?"

Parker took a breath, as if the answer would require a lengthy explanation. "This is The Scott Mission. It's a place where street people, the homeless, and anyone else without any place to go can come for a warm meal and a place to sleep, and hopefully get a hand in turning their lives back around."

"You make it sound easy," said Holt, immediately wishing he hadn't been so sarcastic.

Parker looked at him a moment, then continued. "It's not that easy, but it's what we *try* to do. Some people respond well to what we do and manage to get themselves jobs, get off the street, and feel good about themselves again. Some others don't want or aren't ready to be helped, but still like to drop in from time to time for a meal or a bed to sleep in, or a hot shower. That doesn't help get them off the street, but at least they know we're here for them when the time comes."

Holt looked around the room, nodding. It sounded like nobody had any delusions here. They were just trying to help people one person at a time, not trying to fix the whole homeless problem all by themselves.

"For instance," said Parker. "See her." He pointed to an old woman sitting two tables over, wearing a dirty beige coat and an imitation fur hat on her head. "That's Bernadine Daly. She's been coming here about once a week since the mission opened six years ago. She's beyond rehabilitation really, spending all of her time collecting old newspapers—"

Holt glanced at Parker.

"I don't know why she does it, nobody does. And

nobody knows what she does with them either. But . . . we're here for her, making her life a little more bearable."

Holt heard something and looked behind him. There was a man sitting at the next table, huddled over a bowl of soup, continuously mumbling to himself. He listened more closely.

"And the Oscar goes to . . . Hut! Hut! Hut! *Three Men and a Baby*. Hut! Hut! Hut!"

"Oh, him," Parker said, smiling as he looked over his shoulder. "He's harmless. Everyone calls him the General."

"Gentlemen, start your engines. Hut! Hut! Hut! I can't believe it's a girdle. Hut . . . Hut . . . Hu-tahhh!"

"He talks to himself like that all the time," Parker continued. "In here he's kind of quiet, but outside he barks out the stuff like he's giving orders."

"You're kidding?"

"Nope. He's actually something of a local celebrity. Sometimes kids drive over from Sunset or down from the hills just to listen to his chants."

"You gotta love this town," said Holt, cleaning the last of his gravy off his plate with a hunk of bread.

"What about Oldman?"

"What about Father Oldman?"

"Something's different about him. He seems too tough to be a priest, even for one that works with homeless people."

"What do you mean?"

"I don't know. He looks strong, like he works out, and he seems tough, like he wouldn't hesitate to crack somebody's head if they ever got out of line."

Parker's eyebrows arched as if he'd never heard anyone sum up Oldman so informally, or so accurately, before.

"I sure wouldn't want to cross his path in some dark alley."

Parker took a breath. "I'll admit that Father Oldman is a hard man, but he has to be." Parker's voice rose slightly in volume. "He's a good man, and he's done a lot of good things for the people around here."

"All right, Parker. Take it easy," said Holt. "I was just making an observation, not a condemnation. I know he's a good man. He helped me out, didn't he?"

Parker was silent for a long time.

Finally, it was Holt who spoke again. "What about you?"

"Huh?"

"What's your story, Parker?" Holt said, looking him over. Sizing him up. "You come across like a smart guy, maybe you've even been to school. What are you doing here?"

"I work here."

"I know that," said Holt. "But why would you work here if you could do better someplace else?"

Parker hesitated, as if he had to think about it. "Father Oldman has been good to me. I like working here. And I get a lot of satisfaction out of my work." He crossed his arms over his chest. "Anything else you'd like to know in your first few waking hours inside the mission?"

Holt squinted his eyes shut and laughed. "I've been asking too many questions, huh?"

Parker was silent.

"Sorry, but I can't help it. I like it here, and I want to know as much about the place as I can before I decide to get comfortable."

Parker remained silent.

"Look, my body's aching. Any chance of me lying down in that dormitory Father Oldman was talking about?"

Parker inhaled a long breath. "C'mon, the dorm's this way."

Holt struggled to his feet. He was still in considerable pain, but he could handle it better now that he'd eaten.

Parker waited for Holt to stand up straight, then scooped his shoulder under the man's arm.

Holt firmed his hold on Parker, then turned to him and said, "Thanks."

Parker gave him a friendly smile. "Don't mention it."

Caroline Keegan nestled the phone firmly between her cheek and shoulder and sipped coffee out of a Styrofoam cup. The coffee was four hours cold. She pulled the cup away from her lips and resisted the urge to spew it over the pile of papers haphazardly collected on top of her desk. Reluctantly she swallowed, then poured the rest of the cup into the wastepaper basket, where it suddenly became somebody else's problem.

"Come on, come on," she said under her breath, waiting for someone to pick up the phone.

The priest in Augusta, Maine, who'd given her the number said there was someone in the rectory only between two and three in the afternoon each day. "So you might want to let it ring for a while just in case you catch somebody coming or going."

She wasn't sure where Harlock, Maine, was. Someone had told her it was an old logging town situated near the borders with Quebec and New Brunswick, which would put it just about as far away from San Francisco as you could get without leaving the continental United States. And knowing her luck, this Father—she glanced at the name she'd jotted onto the slip of paper in front of her—Jean-Louis Trudel, was probably a French Canadian whose English was as bad as her French.

Her fingers drummed across the top of her desk. She decided to let it ring five more times.

One . . .

Bonjour, she thought, trying to remember the bit of French she'd learned in school.

Two . . .

Comment ça va?

Three . . .

Ça va tres bien, merci. Et vous?

Four . . .

This isn't going to work.

Five . . .

She was about to put down the receiver when someone picked up on the other end. "Hello?"

Caroline was so surprised that she'd actually reached someone that she almost didn't respond. "Oh, hi, hello there."

"Hello," the voice said again.

"I'm looking for a Father Trudel . . . Jean-Louis Trudel."

"This is he."

English, Caroline marveled. Perfect English with a charming French accent.

"Father Trudel, my name is Caroline Keegan. I'm a reporter with the television show *Inside Affair.*" She paused a moment. This was when people usually said, "Hey, I've seen that show," or "Are you the blond one?"

But Father Trudel was silent. Obviously they didn't watch much television up in Harlock, Maine.

"Yes," he said, expectantly.

"Um, Father, I'm doing a story on a local priest here in San Francisco, a Father Wendel Oldman."

"Oh yes," said the priest, his voice suddenly sounding very interested.

"I was looking into his background when another priest in town, a Father Rizzuto, said I should contact you."

"Very good. What has happened to Father Oldman?" The man's voice was excited now, hungry for details.

"Well, Father. He hasn't done anything wrong. It's just that a couple he knew had asked him to marry them and he refused. It was kind of strange, since the man was one of the homeless people Father Oldman had helped to rehabilitate."

"I see . . . That is curious."

"I'm also trying to find out all I can about The Scott Ranch that's run in conjunction with the mission. And that's where you come in, Father. I was told you know a lot about Father Oldman."

"Well, I don't know much about this ranch you're talking about, but I do know a bit about the man himself."

"Like what?"

"Well, where should I begin?" The words were drawn out, as if Father Trudel was making himself comfortable at the other end of the line. "I first became curious about Father Oldman when . . ."

She turned the switch on her answering machine to *record*, then sat back and listened.

6

Oldman hadn't seen the Garou who had attacked Holt, but he had smelled its scent. It was a dirty animal scent mixed with the smell of garbage and motor oil. A distinct smell, one he'd come across before.

There were actually few possibilities about what tribe the Garou belonged to. Assuming he wasn't a Lone Wolf without a pack, the Bone Gnawers were the only tribe that had a Caern inside the city, so the chances that it had been one of them were good.

Bone Gnawers lived among the homeless as well, most of them in the tent city in Golden Gate Park. But while that put them in close proximity to each other, it didn't explain why a Gnawer would want to kill off the homeless in the Tenderloin.

It just didn't make any sense.

Still, all the signs pointed to the Garou being a Gnawer, and Golden Gate Park seemed to be a logical place for him to begin his search.

Oldman walked south down Hyde Street and turned right on Turk heading west. When he reached that part of the city known as the Richmond, he turned south on Stanyan Street and entered the park from its northeast corner.

He loved the park and visited it as often as he could. It was a marvel of human ingenuity and resourcefulness—over one thousand acres of greenery, museums, and recreational facilities stretching from the Haight-Ashbury district all the way to the ocean. Work on the park first began in 1866, but it really didn't start to flourish until thirty years later when a Scotsman named John McLaren took on the task of transforming the barren, sandy soil into a lush greenbelt. Today, as a result of McLaren's more than half a century of hard work, the park was a literal countryside of flower beds, meadows, lakes, gardens, waterfalls, rolling hills, and forests.

Oldman and other Children of Gaia in the Bay Area revered McLaren, often joking that he was probably a Kinfolk, since it was unlikely a human could have so much love for Gaia as to make her reclamation his life's work.

Oldman strolled down John F. Kennedy Drive past the Music Concourse and Pioneer Log Cabin. As he continued to walk, heading toward the shores of Spreckels Lake, he began to feel a presence following him, eyes watching him. Although a human out for a walk and admiring the sights wouldn't have noticed anything out of the ordinary, it was obvious to Oldman he was being trailed by several Bone Gnawers.

He glanced around, trying to remain inconspicuous. One of the Gnawers was a couple dozen yards behind him, walking along nonchalantly with his hands dug deep in his pockets. There were two others, one each in the Marx and Lindley meadows on either side of the road. Finally, there was a fourth Gnawer standing on the corner of 30th Avenue where it connected with John F. Kennedy Drive. Oldman was surprised he was able to spot them so easily, but then again they probably weren't trying to be inconspicuous.

As he neared Spreckels Lake, it was obvious that he wasn't going to find Bongos there. The place was practically deserted, and Bongos would have had plenty of time to get away if he didn't feel like talking. Still he needed to talk to Bongos, and one of the Gnawers tailing him would be able to tell him where he could find their leader.

Oldman walked up to the shore, sat down on a bench, and waited.

Five minutes later he found himself circled by a ring of Bone Gnawers.

"Gentlemen," said Oldman. "I assure you greetings from just one of you would have been a more than adequate reception."

"Wendel Oldman," said one of the Gnawers, a scrawny dark-skinned Garou named—if Oldman remembered correctly—Kurry. "What brings you into our neck of the woods?"

"I was hoping to speak to Bongos," said Oldman calmly. "Do you know where I might find him?"

"Yeah," said the Gnawer standing to the right of Kurry, a dirty-blond beach bum named Wave-Rider. "We know where you can find him."

The air was filled with silence and the smell of garbage.

The Gnawers laughed at Wave-Rider's joke.

"I admire a Garou with a sense of humor. It's a rare thing to be able to laugh as well as *rage*." Oldman said the final few words in a slightly threatening tone. Even though he was outnumbered four to one, he was still a powerful Garou, especially in the Crinos form. The laughter subsided, and the mood of the gathering suddenly turned serious.

"What do you want to talk to him about?" asked Kurry.

Oldman didn't want to talk about the killings with any of Bongos's underlings, but after a moment's thought he realized that the killings affected these Garou as much as anyone.

"I want to ask him about the homeless murders. I think . . ."

The ring of Garou moved in close.

"I think it may be the work of a Garou."

The Gnawers all looked surprised, turning from one to the other as if saying, "I didn't do it, did you?"

"It isn't any of us," said Kurry.

Oldman's eyes narrowed skeptically.

"Honest."

Oldman nodded. "I need to talk to Bongos."

Kurry's answer came quickly, without hesitation. "He's at the bookstore."

"The City Lights Bookshop?"

"Yeah, that's the one."

"When is he coming back?"

Kurry shrugged his shoulders. "Who knows? It's open until eleven-thirty."

Oldman got up off the bench and towered over the Gnawers, almost a head taller than the tallest of the four. "Thanks," he said.

He began to walk away, but before he'd taken a half-dozen steps, he stopped and turned around. "Do me a favor, will you?"

"Sure," said Kurry.

"If you happen to see the killer Garou," he said, baring his teeth, making his words more of a threat than a request, "tell him I'm looking for him."

From the expression on each of the Gnawers' faces, his message had been understood.

Perfectly.

It was a long walk to the bookshop from Golden Gate Park, but Oldman preferred constant movement, however slow, to standing around waiting for a bus.

So, Oldman headed east. His path would be taking him back past the mission, but he decided not to stop in. His business with Bongos was important, and he wanted to get it done as quickly as possible. Besides, the sooner he got this over with the sooner he could get back to the mission and back into bed. In his younger days he'd been able to rage all night and still function normally during the day, but that was a long time ago. These days he needed his sleep, as much of it as he could get.

He walked along Fulton Street through the Western Addition and headed north on Laguna, passing through Japantown on his way to Pacific Heights. On Broadway he turned right and followed the street until it intersected with Columbus Avenue, the corner where the City Lights Bookshop was located.

Oldman didn't visit City Lights very often. It was an old bookstore, opened in 1953 by a poet named Lawrence Ferlinghetti. After it opened it quickly became a place where writers like Jack Kerouac and Allen Ginsberg would meet and read poetry, and where the idea of the Beat Generation first got off the ground.

But that was almost forty years ago. Although it has remained in the literary stream of things by publishing a number of little-known West Coast poets—including one dismal little chapbook by Bongos called *The Rage Pages*—it was a place that had clearly seen better times. Now it was a place where wanna-bes and others stuck in the Beat Generation time warp hung out trying to recapture something that belonged—and perhaps rightly so—to an earlier generation.

Bongos was one of those literary wanna-bes, writing bad poetry ever since he'd read Kerouac's *On the Road* in the late 1950s. He was a regular visitor to the store, browsing through its extensive poetry section, checking almost daily on how many copies of his book were still left on the shelf.

Oldman neared the store, stopped in front of a small sign in the window that read:

CITY • LIGHTS
• POCKET •
BOOK • SHOP

He peered in through the window. A blond-haired woman sat in a chair near the window reading a paperback, another older woman sat at a table behind her reading through some newspapers. Deeper inside the store a young man with a braided ponytail and several earrings stood perusing one of the white bookshelves that kept the books displayed face-out.

Oldman peered further into the store and saw Bongos

at the back, in the poetry section where his one book was on the shelf.

Oldman entered the store. It smelled a little musty, like some of the books had gotten wet over the years.

When he came up behind Bongos, the Garou hardly moved, his eyes too fixed on the copies of *The Rage Pages* on the shelf in front of him to see anything else.

"Three copies," said Bongos without turning around.

"What?" said Oldman.

"Three copies . . . of my book."

"Oh."

"Do you know how long there have been three copies there?"

Oldman shook his head, then realizing the gesture was lost on Bongos, he said, "No. I don't."

"Since July 1989."

Bongos turned around, his face sad and forlorn.

Oldman did his best not to laugh, but couldn't help a hint of a grin from creeping into the corners of his mouth.

"It's not funny, Oldman," said Bongos. "That was some of my best work and nobody seems to care."

"Perhaps you should take some consolation in the fact that many great writers and poets never really received the accolades they deserved during their own lifetimes."

"Is it too much to ask that people buy a few copies of my book?"

Oldman remained silent even though he'd bought a copy of it when it first came out.

At last Bongos turned his attention away from the bookshelf. "What brings you here?"

"I need to talk to you about a very serious matter," Oldman said, glancing left and right to let Bongos know it was best that their conversation not be overheard.

"All right. Let's get out of here." Bongos headed for the door. Oldman followed.

Outside, Bongos turned to Oldman. "Let's go next door." A few doors away from City Lights was the Vesuvio

Bar, a watering hole that was wet with bohemian atmosphere and frequented by burned-out artists and poets from the Beat era as well as a few Johnny-come-latelies to the scene.

Oldman followed Bongos inside, noticing the strange-looking objects on the wall some considered to be art—or *objet d'art*—then followed the Garou upstairs where it was much quieter and they'd be able to talk in private.

Bongos sat down at a table off in a dark corner, and Oldman joined him. The waitress came by a few minutes later.

"What'll it be?"

"A glass of white wine for me," said Bongos.

Oldman didn't really want anything alcoholic, he was tired enough as it was. "Just a mineral water, please."

The waitress jotted their order down on a pad, then turned away.

When she was out of earshot, Bongos turned to Oldman. "So, what is it?"

"It's about the homeless murders in the Tenderloin."

"Yeah, what about them? That's a human problem. Why are you concerned about it?"

"Because I don't think it's a *human* problem." Oldman hesitated a moment. From the look on Bongos's face the Garou seemed to have a good idea where the conversation was heading. Still, Oldman felt it was best that he spell it out for him. "I think it's a Garou problem. I think it's a Garou that's doing all the killing. In fact I'm almost certain of it . . . ."

Bongos looked at him, unconvinced.

"What's more, I think the Garou is a Bone Gnawer."

Oldman suddenly felt the tension thicken in the air between them. Bongos's easygoing demeanor was suddenly gone, replaced by clenched teeth and narrow, brooding eyes.

"Here you go, gentlemen," the waitress said, placing the glass of wine and bottle of water on the table. She also handed them the bill, then stood there waiting to be paid.

Bongos did not move.

Reluctantly, Oldman dug into his pocket for a few bills and gave the woman a five. "Keep the change," he said.

"Thanks," said the waitress, spinning away from the table.

"Care to repeat that," Bongos said, this time not waiting for the waitress to leave before speaking.

"I said, I think the killer is a Bone Gnawer."

"And what makes you think that?"

"I saw one of the dead bodies before they bagged it. There were marks on it that could only have been made by a Garou. The wounds ran parallel to each other in lines of four, too precise to be done by anything other than the claws of a Garou."

"The claws of *a Garou*," repeated Bongos. "You say the wounds looked like they could only have been made by *a Garou*." Bongos took a sip of his wine. "Tell me, Sherlock. What makes you so sure that these Garou marks were made by a Bone Gnawer and not by *a Garou* from any of the other twelve tribes?"

Oldman sipped his water, fresh, clean, natural—it felt refreshing as it washed down his throat.

"Because . . ." he said, pausing. He hadn't wanted to reveal this part of it, but now it looked as if he didn't have any choice. "I managed to save one of the victims and brought him back to the mission. He was able to give me a pretty good description of his attacker. From what he said, it had to have been a Bone Gnawer."

Bongos was silent for a long time, twirling his glass between his fingers before drinking half of it in a single gulp. "It can't be," he said at last, shaking his head. "I keep a close tab on all the members of my pack, and when I'm not around I have others who do it for me. If the killings were being done by a Bone Gnawer, I'd know about it."

Oldman looked at him skeptically. In his mind he had decided that Bongos was probably telling the truth, but he still felt that something was a bit off. Somehow Oldman didn't feel he was getting *the whole* truth.

"You have my word as the leader of the Bone Gnawers that nobody from my pack has killed any homeless in the last week. And you can rest assured that we'll be looking out for this Garou . . . as I'm sure you will be too."

The more Bongos talked, the more Oldman felt that something was amiss. Then it occurred to him to ask another question.

"Have you blackballed anyone lately?"

"What are you talking about?"

Bingo, thought Oldman.

Being blackballed from the pack was the equivalent of banishment. A blackballed Bone Gnawer didn't exist as far as the pack was concerned, and that's why Bongos could speak truthfully about how no one from his pack had done any killing.

"You know exactly what I'm talking about, Bongos. The last time you blackballed someone, that Garou came into the Tenderloin killing homeless as a form of revenge."

"That's not the case this time." Bongos's voice was grave.

"No, so tell me, what is the case this time?"

Bongos sipped his wine, then began to speak. "His name is Wingnut. He drifted into town about a month ago and asked if he could join us. There aren't too many of us in the park, so we were glad to accept him into the pack."

Bongos paused . . . as if he felt he'd said enough.

Oldman leaned forward and spoke through clenched teeth. "Go on."

Reluctantly, Bongos continued. "He seemed to fit in all right for a week or two, but one night we found him eating the rats that came out at night to rummage through the garbage bins."

Oldman drew in a breath, knowing how sacred rats were to the Bone Gnawers.

"It didn't take us long after that to figure out he was in the Thrall of The Wyrm, absolutely corrupted. We even found him gnawing on his own tail one night. . . . When we confronted him about it, he just smiled at us and went right back at it, chewing all the way down to the bone."

Oldman closed his hand firmly around his bottle of water as he realized the killer would be harder to stop than he'd first imagined.

"So we blackballed him and sent him packing." Bongos shrugged his shoulders and sipped his wine.

"Just like that," said Oldman, feeling his anger starting to build. "You just sent him on his way, like a boy off to school."

"Basically." Bongos's tone was smug.

Oldman was incensed by it. "No, you stupid jackal. What you really did is release The Wyrm into the city. And now he's killing members of my flock . . . for sport."

"The Garou has been blackballed, Oldman," Bongos said coyly. "To me, he doesn't exist anymore. So as far as I'm concerned it's not my problem."

Oldman was livid. "And you call yourself Garou?" Oldman's body roiled with rage. If they weren't in such a public place, he would have thrown aside the table and throated the Bone Gnawer right then and there. Instead he controlled his rage, taking a deep breath and narrowing his eyes into two tiny slits. "I assure you Bongos, you will pay for releasing this . . . *Wyrm wolf* on the people of my protectorate." He leaned in closer, baring his teeth. "You will pay."

Bongos seemed outwardly unaffected by Oldman's words, but Oldman knew his threat had shaken the Garou. He raised his wineglass to Oldman and emptied what was left in a single gulp. "Thanks for the drink, Oldman. Come back and see me again sometime."

"I'll be back," said Oldman, getting up to leave. "But you won't see me when I return."

The wineglass trembled slightly in Bongos's hand.

Oldman was full of rage over what he had learned.

While it was true that there wasn't much of a spirit of cooperation between them, Oldman's relationship with the Bone Gnawers could best be described as mildly abrasive, yet ultimately peaceful. He couldn't imagine why Bongos hadn't warned him about this Garou named

Wingnut. Releasing a Garou in the Thrall of The Wyrm into the city was something to warn others about, not something to be ignored.

Obviously, Oldman wouldn't be getting any help from the Bone Gnawers on this one. They'd already punished Wingnut with the harshest, most severe penalty they had. Normally, blackballing would be looked upon by Bone Gnawers as a fate worse than death, but somehow in this instance Oldman didn't think the punishment carried much weight. If Wingnut was truly in the Thrall of The Wyrm, he'd probably look upon the eight-ball fetish they'd hung around his neck as just another pretty bauble.

Well, thought Oldman, the police were partly right. The murders were the work of a psychopath.

A Garou psychopath.

Oldman took control of his rage, putting it aside for the time being, storing it up for later and the confrontation he hoped to have with Wingnut.

Wingnut.

Even the name sounded crazy.

Oldman shook his head and began walking south down Grant Avenue through Chinatown and into the shopping district of Union Square. After a short walk west on Geary Street he turned south again on Hyde.

When he reached the mission, things appeared to be quiet. There were a few men sitting on the benches out front, while others had made themselves comfortable on the sidewalk, resting up against the building to no doubt digest their hearty potato-based lunches.

"Afternoon, Father," the men greeted Oldman as he passed. "Hi, Father."

Normally Oldman might take the time to stop and chat, but he hadn't had more than a few hours' sleep in the last twenty-four and desperately needed to rest.

He hurried up the mission steps and went inside.

Things were as quiet inside as out. The most prominent of the faintly discernible sounds was the *clink-tink* of lunch dishes being washed downstairs. Aftermeal cleanup was a rotating responsibility shared equally among those who ate and stayed at the mission. Right now it sounded as if someone with four thumbs was hard at work. Oldman listened for another moment. Sounds like the General, he thought.

He went down five steps into the basement and listened.

"I didn't know I was soaking in it. Hut! Hut! Hut! Soap leaves a film . . . Ask for Kodak paper. Hut! Hut! Hut!"

Oldman smiled, turned around, and headed back upstairs.

He poked his head into Parker's office. "I'm back," he said.

Parker looked up from some paperwork on his desk and nodded.

"How's everything?" asked Oldman.

"Quiet."

"How's our new guest Mr. Holt doing?"

"He's sleeping, soundly," said Parker. "I was checking in on him every half hour or so after you left this morning, but I gave up on that. He hasn't moved in over two hours, and he's snoring like a seventy-year-old man."

Oldman nodded approvingly. The salve was working.

"He might as well be in a coma," said Parker.

Oldman smiled. The longer and deeper Holt slept, the faster the salve would work to heal his wounds.

"Speaking of comas," Oldman said. "I only got a few hours' sleep this morning, so I think I'll try and get some rest this afternoon."

"Another late night tonight?" asked Parker, his eyebrows arching.

"Yes."

"All right. I'll come wake you around seven."

Oldman was about to head for his office, but he stopped himself, turned back around to face Parker, and said, "Thanks."

"Don't mention it," said Parker. "Just make sure you catch the bastard."

Oldman was taken aback. It wasn't like Parker to use words like *bastard*. He looked at Parker for a moment, then simply said, "I'll do my best."

An elderly woman sat on a park bench in Union Square feeding the flocks of greedy pigeons that gathered round for a bit of feed.

Wingnut walked over and sat down next to her in the center of the bench, not even bothering to keep his distance.

The birds who had been ten or twenty deep slowly began to fly away, leaving behind a thin layer of seed covering the ground.

The woman turned and gave him a prim and proper now-look-what-you've-done sort of look.

Wingnut pulled back his lips to expose two rows of dirty, uneven teeth, then flitted his tongue at the woman like a lizard.

The woman's eyes widened in surprise and she inhaled a gasp. Then she sniffed at the air, crinkled her nose, and got up to leave. As she walked away from the bench, the pigeons followed.

Wingnut made himself more comfortable, slid out of his trench coat, and let it fall around his waist. He was wearing a cotton blue-plaid lumberjack shirt that had seen better days. He rolled the sleeve up on his left arm.

The wound was about two inches across, healed over now with dark red flesh and sensitive to the touch. Deep inside the arm he still felt some pain. He tensed his arm, clenching and unclenching his fist. The pain became more acute, as if the knife were still embedded in his flesh.

Rage began to roil within him.

Humans were supposed to feel pain, not inflict it.

Not against Garou.

And certainly not against Garou in the Crinos form.

Something had gone wrong.

He balled his left hand into a fist one last time. The pain was still there, but slowly diminishing.

He'd be fully healed in a few more hours.

He'd be ready by tonight.

But this time he'd be more careful.

He pulled his arm closer to his face and began licking at the wound, ignoring the gawking stares of passersby.

Finally, he folded his arms across his chest, closed his eyes . . .

And dreamed contentedly of . . .

Rivers flowing red and rich with human blood. . . .

Faces racked with unspeakable terror, contorted by incredible pain . . .

The air filled with the anguished cries of great torment and suffering . . .

And hundreds of Garou standing idly by, watching the carnage, but absolutely powerless to stop it.

7

Oldman dreamed . . .

Of soft grass and the fresh scent of pine.

Of black earth and blue sky.

And of water, flowing free, fresh, and clean, its taste as sweet as wine.

The pack was all around him, bounding through the forest, exhilarated by the run, charged by the power of the Wyld.

He'd been running for miles, surrounded by Gaia in all her glory, the Mother Goddess stretching out in all directions covering the planet with her lush and bountiful bosom.

He continued to run with a supply of what seemed to be unlimited energy, snapping playfully at the heels of the wolves before him, his own heels being nipped by those behind.

But slowly the forest darkened, the branches of the great redwoods intertwining overhead like a canopy, preventing the sun's rays from reaching the forest floor.

And then the air began to smell with a foul odor, man-made and toxic.

The Wyrm.

The wolves up ahead stopped in their tracks and

began to howl, a somber and strange mixture of two howls—The Wail of Foreboding and The Curse of Ignominy.

Oldman bounded over and through the mulling wolves until he came upon what looked like a riverbank.

But it wasn't any normal riverbank.

Water didn't flow here.

The liquid that flowed past was a mix of black oil and blue-green solvents, with rainbows of other neon colors glowing off its shiny waxen surface.

Oldman lowered his muzzle to the ground, sniffing at the grass in search of cleaner air.

The other wolves had retreated, heading back into the heart of the forest from which they'd come.

Oldman, however, lingered, looking up and down the bank. As he did, the level of the liquid rose, wetting his front paws where they stood on the grass.

The liquid burned his fur, ate away at his claws.

He stepped back.

Then he heard it, a low cackling howl coming from across the river. He looked over and saw a mangy jackal-faced Garou in Crinos form digging its muzzle deep into body of a dead human.

"No," Oldman growled. He wanted to hurtle across the flowing black river and stop the Garou, but he dared not set his paws into the muck. Instead he paced up and down the bank, snapping and snarling at the Garou.

Then the Garou dug its front claws into the body, digging deep inside it. Black liquid began to spurt from the body cavity like water from a hose. The Garou grabbed the body with both hands and turned it onto its side, allowing a torrent of black and green liquid to gush out of it and into the river.

The water level on Oldman's side began to rise. "No!" he howled, moving away from the rapidly rising river.

The Garou laughed, a loud mocking cry that came from somewhere deep within his throat.

Oldman ran, fast . . .

Faster . . .

As fast as he could, but always the river was right behind him, gaining on him until . . .

He began to tire.

To feel old.

His hind legs became wet.

Began to melt away . . .

And then . . .

He was awakened by a knock at the door.

Oldman sat bolt upright in bed, his skin damp and pasty, the room filled with a distinct animal scent. "Yes, what is it?"

"It's Parker, Father," he said through the door. "Night's falling." A pause. "Are you all right?"

Oldman ran a hand across his forehead, pulling away the damp white hair stuck to his brow. "Yes, yes, I'm fine." He took a deep breath. "Thank you."

He rolled out of bed, his body tired and sore, and slowly began getting out of his clothes in preparation for the change.

I'm getting too old for this, he thought.

He padded out from the alley behind the mission in his Crinos form, walked out onto Eddy Street, then headed west toward Larkin. He crossed over Larkin and passed 620 Eddy, the place where the detective writer Dashiell Hammett had lived for several years. As he looked at the building, Oldman wondered if Bongos had read any of Hammett's work, or if he even knew who Hammett was. He suspected not, since Hammett had never tried his hand at writing Beat poetry.

He continued on to Van Ness Avenue, climbing up the fire escape of an apartment building and heading north over the rooftops to Ellis Street.

He scanned the alleys below with the keen eyes that saw through the veil of night almost as if it were the middle of day. But despite his superior vantage point and vision, he saw no sign of the Garou.

He went back down to street level and continued heading north to O'Farrell Street. His eyes pierced the alleys and laneways along the way, but it was his sense of hearing that first told him someone was in trouble.

The faint sound of someone crying out for help somewhere to the north and east.

Oldman dropped down onto all fours and ran as fast as he could up Van Ness. At O'Farrell he stopped for a moment, listening. The cry was coming from a block east. Polk Street. He set off in that direction.

At Polk he turned right. The cries became louder. He came upon a laneway halfway down the block and turned into it.

Oldman looked down the lane. Two Asian punks were roughing up a third, most likely over some drug deal that had gone sour.

The Tenderloin was full of Asians, refugees from Cambodia, Laos, and Vietnam, some decent hardworking people like the Kims, and others not so law-abiding, like these punks.

Oldman knew he should help the third punk. After all, he was currently outnumbered two to one and a minute or two from being either hospitalized or dead. But protecting drug dealers and junkies from each other wasn't what Oldman did. Even if he did try to help him, it wouldn't do a damn bit of good. All it would do is let the punk live long enough to sell drugs tomorrow and the next day and the next.

Still, if he didn't do something, one or more of those kids was going to get hurt.

He stood at the end of the laneway, making sure the streetlights were behind him. Then he opened his maw and growled as loud and as long as he could, ending the roar with a menacing snarl.

The two punks beating on the third were the first to look up. They stared at the silhouette of Oldman's hulking form for a few seconds before their jaws dropped low in awestruck wonder. The knife held by the one on the left fell from his hand, the metal sounding cold and hard as it hit the pavement.

At this distance, and under these lighting conditions,

the effects of The Delirium would be minimal. Even so, as they turned to run away, the two punks still ran a ragged zigzag pattern as they raced out of the laneway.

Then the third punk got up off the ground. He rubbed his sore head with his hand and grabbed his ribs where the other two had been kicking him. No doubt a few of his ribs were cracked, if not broken. When he was on his feet, he turned in Oldman's direction. His reaction to the sight of Oldman was like that of the other two.

He set off down the alley, crying out in pain as he stumbled and fell headlong onto the pavement. But the fall seemed to jolt him awake, because he got up quickly and continued running in the same direction as the other two only in a much straighter line.

Oldman nodded, satisfied he'd done as little as possible, but still just enough to prevent his conscience from bothering him.

He really didn't have the time or energy for these kinds of distractions.

Not tonight.

Tonight, he was on the hunt.

He was out for blood.

And he would have it.

He walked back out onto Polk Street and headed north to Post. Then he headed east to Larkin, where he turned right and headed south back to Eddy Street.

When he reached Eddy, completing a circuitous route covering almost ten city blocks, he realized that with the exception of the one minor crime scene, he had hardly come across *anybody* out on the streets, let alone another Garou.

He leaned against a wall in the shadows of an alley and thought about it. There were two possible reasons that he hadn't come across anyone. First, maybe after being wounded by Holt, the Garou had been scared off, realizing the homeless weren't as easy a prey as he'd first thought. Second, with the number of homeless people that had been murdered in the last week maybe people were beginning to spend more of their nights inside.

The latter made sense, more so than the former.

Although Holt was a fighter, he had hardly done enough to scare off a Garou, especially one in the Thrall of The Wyrm. Besides, Garou healed fast, and the wound made by Holt's knife was probably little more than a scar by now. If anything, Wingnut was probably back out on the streets tonight, more enraged—maybe even a little embarrassed—by the incident with Holt than scared.

Oldman pushed himself away from the wall and headed east back toward the mission.

He was almost at the corner of Eddy and Hyde Streets when he heard it.

The terrible bloodcurdling scream of someone looking straight into the jaws of death.

This was it.

Had to be.

He turned his ears into the direction the sound had come from, and then he was off and running down Hyde Street. At Turk he turned right.

He could still hear the screaming, but now he was close enough to be directed by the smell of blood.

And fear.

He found the alley, a large wide space between a Vietnamese café and a flower shop, and ran into it, stopping after a few steps to assess the situation.

At the end of the alley, a smallish Garou in Crinos form was standing in front of a human.

It was Wingnut.

Had to be.

He had the man pinned up against the wall, claws set deep into the man's shoulders, his maw digging hungrily into the meaty part of the man's neck.

The man struggled in vain against the werewolf, his futile efforts weakening with each passing moment.

Oldman sprang into action, bounding down the alley in great long strides, jaws wide, teeth bared.

Wingnut turned, his wolflike face a mask of shock and surprise. He let go of the human, but could not move fast enough to get out of the way of the charging Oldman.

Oldman made a final leap through the air, attacking the Garou with the full battery of his tensed claws and sharpened fangs.

The two Garou came together in a heavy thud of muscle and bone, then rolled around on the asphalt in a dirty mass of claws, fur, blood, and fangs. Their growls were wild and angry, only slightly muffled by the gathered flesh between their teeth.

Garbage bags were ripped open by flailing claws.

Rats skittered, ran for cover.

Neither Garou wanted to let go of the other.

Finally, Oldman managed to get his maw free and bit down on the other's haunches as hard as he could.

Wingnut yelped in pain, releasing his hold on Oldman.

Oldman let go too, preferring to confront the Garou face-to-face rather than scrambling around in circles waiting for one of them to end up on top.

Oldman crouched down on all fours, watching his foe with a malicious stare. Wingnut was no more than seven feet tall, with scrawny arms and legs—compared to other Garou in Crinos form—and his ears were short and rounded, his muzzle long and pointed.

He looked more like a jackal than a wolf.

Slowly, Oldman rose up onto his hind legs, making sure Wingnut had ample opportunity to see his larger, more powerful body.

"You've killed your last," said Oldman, his snarling words coming out as a series of low, choppy growls.

"No, *ape*-shepherd," replied Wingnut, his words similarly disjointed. "That honor will be yours."

The insult was obvious. This Garou had no respect for anybody, or anything.

Oldman stared at Wingnut for a moment, shaking his head. He couldn't help feeling sorry for the mangy, jackal-faced Garou. Not only was he in the Thrall of The Wyrm, but he'd been blackballed by the Bone Gnawers as well. There wasn't much lower a Garou could fall.

Oldman thought about bringing this pathetic mutt back to the mission to try and rehabilitate him, just as he'd rehabilitated humans with similar problems, but the thought was quickly forgotten. It would never work, he was far too corrupted by The Wyrm.

There was only one thing to do.

Kill him.

Eradicate The Wyrm.

The only mercy he would be shown would be a quick and painless death.

Oldman tensed to attack, but before he could spring forward, Wingnut was upon him. Claws tore into Oldman's shoulders and arms, while toeclaws ripped up his thighs. Oldman held Wingnut's snapping maw at bay with his hands, then managed to tear the Garou away from his body. He threw him up against a Dumpster, his body slamming into the great metal box with the sound of a huge Chinese gong.

Oldman moved in, but before he'd taken two steps, Wingnut was gone from in front of the Dumpster.

"Looking for someone?"

Oldman stopped. The words had come from behind him and had sounded low and menacing, and perhaps even a bit playful.

Oldman turned around just in time to see the heavy metal drainpipe arcing down upon him. He put up his arms to protect himself, but only managed to deflect the blow. The pipe glanced off Oldman's skull, staggering him. He fell down onto one knee, shaking his head to clear away the fog from the inner folds of his brain.

Wingnut raised the pipe over his head in preparation for a second blow.

Oldman looked up, saw the bend his head had put in the heavy pipe, and vowed not to bend it any further. He shot out his hand, claws first, embedding his fingers deep into Wingnut's midsection.

Wingnut still held the pipe in the air.

Oldman brought his fingers together and tore out as much flesh and entrails from Wingnut's belly as he could.

Wingnut howled in pain, releasing the pipe and dropping it onto the alley floor behind him. As it clanged against the ground, Wingnut reached down and placed his hands over the wound in his gut as if to prevent any more of his internal organs from sliding out of the hole.

Oldman got to his feet and grabbed hold of Wingnut by his right arm and leg. Then he lifted him up over his head and threw him headlong into the brick wall on one side of the alley.

Wingnut hit the wall with a hard *whump!* then fell to the ground, limp and lifeless.

Oldman walked over to the prone Garou, grabbed him by the scruff of his neck, pulled him off the ground, and lifted him into the air.

Just as he was about to throw him against the wall a second time, Wingnut's body sprang to life, squirming wildly to break free of Oldman's hold.

The movement put Oldman off balance. He released Wingnut halfway through his throw, and the Garou tumbled awkwardly through the air, landing inside the nearby Dumpster.

For a moment Oldman wasn't sure where Wingnut had gone. It was as if he had suddenly disappeared from the alley.

But then he heard a soft bang of metal and knew the Garou was crouched down in the Dumpster on his left.

Slowly he stepped over to the open Dumpster . . .

And looked inside.

Claws shot out of the Dumpster heading straight for his eyes. Oldman moved his head left, and the claws wound up raking his face and neck. He tried to peer into the Dumpster again, but the claws were there, swinging wildly for his eyes. Finally, Oldman had to step back to avoid being blinded.

And that was the chance Wingnut had been hoping for.

He scrambled out of the Dumpster on the far side, trying to make his escape.

Oldman realized what Wingnut was doing, ran over to the Dumpster, and pulled down the heavy metal lid.

It closed with a tremendous BANG!

The sound was loud enough to wake the dead. . . .

And then all was dead silent.

Oldman looked up and down the alley.

It was empty.

Wingnut was probably inside the Dumpster.

He walked over to it and, making sure to keep his distance, flipped back the lid.

The great metal hinges creaked in protest, and then the alley was once again silent.

Oldman listened closely, trying to hear the sound of Wingnut whining in pain, or at least breathing hard after the long drawn-out battle.

But he heard nothing but silence.

He moved closer to the Dumpster, looked inside.

Wingnut wasn't in there . . .

But his arm was.

Still twitching as if plugged into a wall socket.

Then Oldman looked down at the alley pavement.

And saw the thick line of blood leading out of the alley.

Oldman followed the trail, but the blood line ended at the mouth of the alley, as did his scent.

Wingnut was gone.

Oldman hoped it was for good.

Then Oldman remembered the human and went back into the alley. He was still lying there sprawled out across the garbage, bleeding.

He was an elderly man, probably in his mid-sixties. Oldman didn't recognize him, especially now, since most of his face and body was covered with bright red wounds. His breath was weak, and he was already in shock from loss of blood.

He was too far gone, even for Oldman to revive.

"Help me," the man cried.

Oldman looked upon the man with pity.

He hated to do this to a human, but there was only one thing that could be done for him now.

And that was put an end to his suffering.

Oldman got down on all fours and leaned forward, bringing his mouth in close to the man's ears.

"I will put an end to your pain," he whispered, being sure to make his words coherent.

And then for a brief moment, the alley was once again filled with the sound of ripping, tearing flesh.

The mission was only a few blocks away.

Oldman took his time getting there, reaching it just before dawn.

PART II

Do not belittle that which you do not understand. Our ways are rooted in millennia of life among the Pure, but when the Apocalypse is hard upon us, we shall not fall to ignorance or inflexibility. We travel far to gather what aid there may be, and our ranks swell with every refugee who flees from the camp of the Enemy.

—Kara Two-Nails,
She-Who-Saw-The-Sky,
Uktena Philodox

8

The morning sun rose bright in the clear blue sky over San Francisco.

The start of a new day.

Oldman saw the sun peek over the horizon, then tucked himself under the covers for a few more hours of sleep.

He got less than three before Parker knocked on the door.

"Father!" he said. "Father Oldman!"

Oldman rolled over, and said, "Yes, Parker. What is it?" through the open door leading into his office.

The outside door opened a crack, and Parker stuck his head into the room. "I'm sorry if I woke you, it's just that . . . " Parker hesitated, as if trying to break it to Oldman gently. "The people coming in for breakfast just told us . . . there's been another murder."

Oldman hesitated a moment, thinking how he should handle the situation. Although Parker was a good man, and Oldman's best friend, he might not understand if he told him the truth about last night. When he'd killed the man, he was already as good as dead, but that would be a hard thing to explain this early in the morning. Besides, it might be better if Parker didn't know.

"Oh no," Oldman said at last, trying to sound distraught. "That's terrible."

Parker stepped into the office and walked over to Oldman's bedroom door. "And this one happened not more than a couple of blocks from here."

Oldman lay back down on the bed and pulled the covers up tight against his neck to cover his freshly healed wounds. His head still pounded but would likely feel better by the end of the day.

"Did it have the same wounds as the others?" Oldman asked.

"Everything was the same, except . . . "

"Yes?"

"Well, you know how the other bodies had been splayed all over the place, even with a few scattered body parts?"

Oldman nodded.

"People say that this body was neatly set up against the wall looking almost comfortable. He was covered up to the waist by a blanket, his arms were crossed over his chest, and his eyes were closed. People who saw the dead man said he looked almost at peace."

"Isn't that curious?"

"Yes," said Parker, his eyebrows arching. "I wonder how that might have happened?"

Oldman looked at Parker and realized that he probably understood more about the Garou than Oldman had previously given him credit for. "Sit down," he said at last. "There's something I have to tell you."

Parker stepped into Oldman's bedroom and eased himself down onto the edge of the bed.

"I came across the renegade Garou last night," Oldman began. "His name is Wingnut."

"Did you kill him?"

"Unfortunately not," Oldman said with a sigh of disappointment. "But he might be gone for good."

"What happened?"

Oldman began talking.

Parker made himself comfortable and listened.

Kenneth Holt walked down the steps toward the mess by himself, leaving Parker behind to watch him from the top of the stairs.

Holt still needed a firm grip on the handrail, and he held his breath every step he took, but at least he was walking around unaided. Considering the wounds he had suffered, his recovery seemed almost miraculous.

When he reached the bottom of the stairs, he turned around and looked back up at Parker. "How about that?"

Parker seemed impressed. "Very good. Now let's see how well you fare with the second part of your recovery."

"Huh?" said Holt. "What second part?"

Holt felt he had already made a full recovery. When he got off his cot this morning after sleeping for almost twenty-one straight hours, he'd felt like a recharged battery and hurried to the bathroom to take a look at his wounds. The pasty white salve was gone, leaving bright red slashes of scar tissue across his face, chest, and neck.

His cuts had healed.

Overnight.

Holt had always been a good healer, but never this good. There must be something in that paste of Father Oldman's, he thought. But when he pressed a finger against the tender red skin of one of his wounds, he had to pull it back with a sharp cry. He had healed on the surface, but the pain of his wounds still ran deep below the skin.

Parker stepped lightly down the steps. "The second part," he said, "is the one administered by L.C."

Holt remembered the woman from yesterday morning and how good her food had tasted. If part of his recovery included food prepared by her, he was sure it was going to be both nutritious and delicious.

As Holt followed Parker to a table at the far end of the room, he looked at the plates of food in front of the others stacked high with what looked to be potato pancakes. There was also plenty of syrup and jam on the table. Looks good, thought Holt, suddenly looking forward to the second part of the recovery process.

As he sat down, Parker walked over to the kitchen.

A few moments later he returned with the woman, L.C.

"It's about time you showed up," she said.

"What do you mean?"

"I've had this stuff on the stove for two hours waiting for you to roll out of bed." She slid a bowl of foul-smelling oatmeal in front of him.

"What the hell is this?" asked Holt, his nose crinkling from the acrid stench wafting up from the bowl. It smelled a lot like the salve Father Oldman had put on his chest.

"This," Parker said, sitting down to a plate full of pancakes, "is part two of your recovery. You've healed on the outside, now it's time to work on the inside."

"But it smells so"—he lowered his head and sniffed at the bowl—"bad."

L.C. glared at him. "Just so you know, this wasn't made from any recipe of mine. This is Father Oldman's recipe, and it's only the second time I've made it. So don't blame me for the way it tastes. I did my best."

Parker looked at Holt and smiled. "Consider it medicine."

"You mean like Listerine and Buckley's?"

"That's right," said Parker. "It tastes awful because it works."

Holt picked up a spoon, dipped it into the bowl, and lifted it toward his lips.

He held his breath as he opened his mouth, then slid the spoon inside.

It tasted even worse than it smelled.

He swallowed as quickly as he could, then gulped down a full glass of water.

"You see," said Parker. "Nothing to it."

"I can't eat any more of this."

"I don't think you have a choice in the matter," said Parker, gesturing toward L.C.

She stood over Holt, hands on her hips, head cocked to one side. "Father Oldman told me you had to finish all of it. So don't expect to get up from the table until the bowl is clean."

Holt sighed. The salve had helped him feel better, so he had no reason to think this wouldn't help him as well.

"All right," he said. "If Father Oldman says it's important . . ." He held his breath and swallowed another spoonful.

It went down easier than the first, but he had to fight off a strong urge to retch just to keep it down.

Oldman was just about to settle down behind his desk to write a new batch of letters when Parker knocked on his door.

Oldman was grateful for the distraction.

"Yes, Parker. What is it?"

The young man opened the door slightly, then slid through the tiny opening he'd made as if he didn't want anything else to slip through the door. "Someone to see you, Father."

"Who is it?"

"I'm afraid . . . it's the police."

Oldman's brows arched in surprise as he inhaled a deep breath of foreboding. "Well, let's not keep them waiting, then. Send them in."

Parker nodded, turned around, and opened the door wide. "Gentlemen, Father Oldman will see you now."

Oldman rose up from his chair and walked around his desk. Two plainclothes police officers came into the room, one a tall, muscular black man, the other a shorter but stocky Asian. Oldman shook their hands, making sure his grip was firm.

"Father Oldman," said the black man. "I'm Detective Michael Garrett, this is Detective Ben Chong." The two men showed Oldman their badges.

"Please sit down, gentlemen. Would either of you like a coffee?"

Garrett shook his head, the gesture apparently helping Chong decide that he didn't want one either.

Oldman looked up at Parker standing in the doorway

and said, "Thank you, Parker." He sat down behind his desk. "Now, what can I do for you?"

"You're no doubt aware of the murders of homeless people in the Tenderloin over the last week or so . . ." said Garrett.

"Oh, of course. It's a terrible thing to have happen."

"We're investigating those murders."

"I see," said Oldman. "So what brings you to the mission?"

"We were talking with a Sergeant Metzger, who, as you know, patrols this area regularly," said Chong. "Anyway, he told us that it might be worth our while to stop by and talk to you."

Oldman nodded. "Sergeant Metzger is a good man and a fine police officer."

"Yes, well," the detective continued, "Sergeant Metzger said that if anything strange was happening in the Tenderloin, you'd probably know about it."

"Strange?" said Oldman, feigning confusion. "You mean in connection with the murders?"

Garrett nodded. "Exactly, Father. Have you noticed anything peculiar of late?"

There it was. The question that couldn't be deflected by another question or benign comment. He didn't want to lie to these men, nor did he want to tell them the truth.

Well, there is that nasty little business about an insane werewolf running wild through the city. . . . But you don't have to worry about that anymore, I took care of him myself. Sliced his arm clean off, I did. He won't be coming around this part of the city for a long, long time. . . .

No, he couldn't tell them the truth.

Or at least he couldn't tell them the *whole* truth.

Maybe they'd be satisfied by just a part of it.

He decided to give it a try.

"Well, gentlemen. I don't have to tell you that the people around here are afraid for their lives. There's something out there terrorizing them, and nobody seems to be able to stop it."

He paused a moment to gauge their reaction. It seemed to have worked. They both rolled forward slightly in their seats, eager to hear more.

"To hear people talk around here, you would think we were being overrun by a pack of werewolves or something. . . ."

A light seemed to switch on in the faces of the two police officers, as if they'd heard mention of werewolves before.

"Have people said they've actually seen anything like a werewolf?" asked Chong.

"Or something that might be mistaken for a werewolf?" added Garrett.

Oldman was surprised to see that the police officers were taking him seriously. The people of San Francisco were well known for their remarkable tolerance and open-mindedness, but not looking twice when two men were kissing in the park wasn't the same as believing in the existence of werewolves. The Garou world couldn't survive without the protective shroud of The Veil. Oldman realized he had to wipe the thought from their minds.

"No, of course not," Oldman said, beginning to have fun with the part he was playing. "Everyone knows that there's no such thing as werewolves. Maybe they have them in Hungary, or in—what's it called?—Transylvania, but not in such a modern city like San Francisco."

Garrett leaned back in his chair. "You've lived in this area for a few years, Father. You know the people around here. Who or what do you think is killing them?"

"Well, I did happen to see one of the bodies, Randall E. Sullivan, the man I identified for Sergeant Metzger." Oldman's voice became softer, sadder. "Just by looking at the wounds I'd have to guess that they were caused by a mad dog of some sort, or perhaps a pack of them. I've seen plenty of them sniffing at garbage over the years. If it was a dog, or a pack, that would at least explain why it's the homeless that are being killed off."

Chong turned to Garrett as if to say, "You see! I told you it was dogs."

Garrett's eyes remained on Oldman, ignoring the icy stare coming from his partner. "But somebody would have seen a pack of dogs running through the streets, wouldn't they?"

"Perhaps," said Oldman. "If they were in fact running through the streets. There's a big enough network of sewers, alleys, and laneways in the Tenderloin to enable someone to cover the entire fifty blocks without being seen from the street. . . . Believe me, I know."

"What about during the day? Someone would have seen these dogs during the day?"

Oldman lowered his head and looked at Garrett.

"There are all kinds of empty buildings in the Tenderloin. If a dog wanted to stay out of sight during daylight hours, it wouldn't have any trouble finding some abandoned building to sleep in undisturbed and out of sight."

The two police officers adjusted themselves in their chairs. The prospect of doing a building-by-building search of the Tenderloin for a pack of wild dogs didn't seem to sit well in their stomachs.

Oldman sat back, smiling inwardly with the knowledge that all of this was moot because he'd scared off the offending Garou the night before. Still, it had been fun leading them on and helping draw The Veil over their minds.

"Well," Garrett said at last, rising from his chair. "We'll be beefing up our nightly patrols in the area, and maybe we'll see if we can get a canine unit out here to sniff out any wild dogs. Even if we don't find anything—"

Chong shook his head slightly at his partner's stubbornness against believing the wild dog theory.

"—at least we will have eliminated that as a possibility."

"It sounds as if you have a plan," said Oldman, his voice as congratulatory as he could make it.

"In the meantime, Father," said Chong, "will you keep an eye out for us? You know, for anything suspicious." He handed Oldman his card.

"I'll keep this handy," Oldman said. "Now if you'll excuse me, gentlemen. I have some paperwork that requires my immediate attention."

"Yes, of course," said Garrett.

Oldman escorted the two police officers to the door of his office and opened it . . .

Just in time to witness Parker helping Holt walk by as the two were making their way outside.

"What the hell happened to him?" said Garrett.

Everyone looked at Holt. In the light of the hallway the scars on his face and neck were dark red and stood out dramatically against the white backdrop of his skin.

"He fell down," Parker said quickly.

"Into what? A meat grinder?" asked Garrett.

Oldman stepped into the hall and gestured for Parker and Holt to continue on down the hall.

"He did fall down . . ." Oldman said. "After he'd gotten into a fight with one of the other men downstairs."

The policemen nodded, skeptically.

"Uh-huh . . ." muttered Garrett.

"You see, by the time people come to the mission they're hungry and angry. It's not uncommon for me to have to break up a fight over something as simple as a carrot stick or piece of meat. This one"—he tipped his head toward Holt—"had slipped some home fries off another man's plate while the other wasn't looking. When the man realized what had happened, he pulled out a knife."

Oldman ran a finger around his collar, checking to see that his own faint scars were well hidden.

"Needless to say the one with the knife is long gone from here. I don't allow weapons inside the mission. After all, it is a mission, not an armed camp."

At last the detectives seemed satisfied.

Oldman began walking toward the door, making sure that the two other men got the hint that it was time for them to leave.

At the door, Chong turned to face Oldman. "You will remember to call us, Father, if you see anything suspicious?"

"Of course I'll call," said Oldman. "Believe me, I want these killings stopped as much, or maybe even more, than you do. This is my flock, and what good shepherd would stand idly by while his lambs were being slaughtered one by one?"

"Right, Father," said Garrett.

"Yes," said Chong. "Thanks for your time."

"My pleasure," said Oldman. "And remember, don't get discouraged if you don't find the killer right away. I'm sure he's out there . . . somewhere."

A half hour later, Parker stuck his head into Oldman's office. "Are they gone?"

Oldman looked up from his desk, saw Parker standing there with Holt by his side, and smiled. "Yes, they're gone. Come in, you two, and have a seat. I'd like to talk to you."

Parker helped Holt through the door, then led him to a chair. That done, Parker turned and was about to leave when Oldman called him back.

"No, Parker. Stay here. I want you *both* to be here for this."

Parker spun back around and sat down, smiling.

"The police just wanted to ask me a few questions about the killings," Oldman said to Parker. "Nothing specific." He shrugged and turned his attention to Holt. "Now, you look like you're making an excellent recovery."

"I'm still a little sore," said Holt, placing a hand over his ribs. "And that stuff I had this morning . . ." Holt stopped talking as if the memory of its taste might make him throw up right there in Oldman's office.

"Sorry about that," said Oldman. "It's a very precise recipe, and unfortunately nothing can be added to improve its taste. But, it is making you feel better."

"Well, it did make me nauseous there for a while, but I have to admit I did feel better after eating it."

"Excellent, then you'll have no trouble with the follow-up dishes you'll be having for breakfast over the next three days."

"What?"

"But never mind that now," Oldman said with a wave of his hand. "I have a more important matter to talk to you about. It's about your future."

Holt's face lit up in surprise. Obviously, the future hadn't been one of his more popular discussion topics in the last few months. He tilted his head to one side. "I'm all ears."

"How much do you know about the mission?"

Holt shrugged. "People on the street say a lot of things about this place. Some say you're a saint for the work you do for the street people, while some others say you're a demon running a cult."

"And which one do you believe?"

"What can I say bad about this place? You've only done good by me."

Oldman nodded, smiling at Parker. "Do you like it here?"

"It's okay, I guess. Better than being out on the street, that's for sure."

The room was silent.

The clock behind Oldman *tick, tick, ticked*.

"Say, why are you asking me all this stuff for anyway? I don't owe you any money for staying here, do I? Because I don't have any."

Oldman raised his hands. "Hold on a minute, nobody's asking you for anything. I just want to know if you like it here, because I was wondering if you'd like to stay on with us?"

"What?" Holt looked at Parker and Oldman.

"I want you to stay here and help out at the mission. Then when you feel well enough to travel, we'll take you up to our ranch in the Muir Woods where you can complete your rehabilitation."

"Whoa!" said Holt. "Don't you think you're going a little too fast? I haven't even been here a couple of days and you're already talking about shipping me out—"

"Nobody's going to be shipping you out anywhere," said Oldman. "The ranch is a place where you can get a different set of surroundings and forget about the city for a while. It's important for your recovery. Not just the physical part of it, but the"—Oldman tapped his right index finger against his head—"mental part of it too."

Holt wasn't responding as well as Oldman had hoped, but Oldman didn't blame him. He hadn't yet told the man he might be Kinfolk, that he belonged up in the Muir Woods, helping to protect the Caern. He would tell him eventually, but he wanted to make sure he was Kinfolk first. That would happen in a few days. For now, all he wanted was to get Holt used to the idea of being part of the mission and leaving his street life behind him.

Hopefully forever.

Holt sighed, a thoughtful look on his face.

He looked at Parker.

"Is this how you came to work here?" he asked.

Parker sat up straight in his chair. "Yes. I lived on the street for years, and when I finally ended up coming here, I was probably in worse shape than you were."

"Really?"

Parker nodded. "Of course, I hadn't suffered the injuries you had. I was severely malnourished with sores all over my body. I had a pneumonia, too. But Father Oldman helped me back to health just like he's doing with you. Then when I began to feel better, he asked me if I wanted to stay. Obviously I said yes." A pause. "I would have been stupid not to."

"Oh yeah," said Holt, as if Parker were trying to sell him a vacuum cleaner he really didn't need. "Why is that?"

"Call me crazy, but I've gotten used to the idea of regularly eating my meals indoors. I like sleeping in a bed in a room that's dry and warm all year-round. It makes me feel good to have something *to do* when I get up in the morning, even if that thing is cleaning toilets." Parker was silent a moment, as if considering his next comment. "This might sound a little selfish, but I also like the feeling of being somebody, of having people look up to me with a certain amount of respect for who I am and what I do. Here"—he gestured with his hands at the four walls surrounding him—"I'm Father Oldman's assistant and general manager of The Scott Mission." He leaned closer to Holt and looked him straight in the eye. "When was the last time you did something that you could put on a résumé?"

Oldman had been sitting back in his chair the whole time just listening to Parker speak. Parker had the ability to talk to street people in a way they could understand. He was passionate and persuasive, a rare combination.

Holt sat in his chair, pensive. His eyes moved back and forth between Oldman and Parker while his thumbs twirled around one another like a cat chasing its tail. Finally he looked up at Oldman.

"I don't have to sign anything, do I? And if I don't like it I can leave?"

"Anytime you want," said Oldman.

He took a final look at Parker, then turned back to Oldman.

"Ah, why the hell not."

The next few days were uneventful. Homeless people came and went, meals were made and eaten, dishes were cleaned, laundry was done, but compared to the week before things seemed downright peaceful.

The biggest contributing factor to this new calm was the fact that the murders had stopped. Almost a week had gone by without another mutilated body added to the list of victims.

The whole Tenderloin seemed to breathe a sigh of relief, and slowly, people stepped back out onto the streets. The police had remained quiet about the end to the killings, probably hoping the problem had taken care of itself, or that the killer had just gone away.

The thought of it made Oldman smile.

That kind of outlook on the part of police could usually be discounted as wishful thinking, but in this case it just happened to be true.

Wingnut was probably miles away by now in some big city where he would blend in with ease. He'd probably gone into Los Angeles, or maybe further south into San Diego. One thing was for certain, he wasn't in San Francisco anymore, not if he knew what was good for him.

Oldman scribbled something onto a piece of paper, a reminder to himself to keep up-to-date with the news from LA and San Diego, just in case homeless people started popping up murdered there in the next few weeks. Then he leaned back and took a moment to relax. It felt good.

The quiet time had also been good for Holt. The young man had continued to heal well, and he was now moving around as if the attack had never happened. Every so often he would double over for a moment as a sharp pain shot through his side or neck, but it was nothing serious enough to keep him off his feet.

Nothing seemed to be able to do that.

In fact, Holt turned out to be just what the doctor ordered as far as the mission was concerned, proving himself to be quite the handyman. With the few tools he found lying around in the mission's furnace room, Holt fixed several annoying leaks in the main washroom, got doors to close right and stay closed, and even installed a light switch in L.C.'s pantry so she didn't have to reach for the chain hanging from the fixture in the middle of the ceiling.

Holt seemed to fit in well at the mission.

Better than anyone Oldman had taken in before.

Oldman thought about that a moment.

He had a theory as to why that was, and he found himself coming back to it over and over again.

Kenneth Holt was Kinfolk.

Had to be.

Well, he thought. There's only one way to find out for sure.

Oldman reached out, picked up the receiver of the telephone sitting on the far corner of his desk, and dialed.

The phone rang once before someone answered.

"Celeste," said Oldman. "This is Wendel Oldman. I have a problem I think you can help me with."

Celeste Snowtop was the leader of the Sept of the Western Eye, the group of Garou who lived in and around

San Francisco and tended to the Caern in the redwoods of the Muir Woods National Monument. In addition to being the Sept leader, she was also a Philodox, which meant she was well versed in all the litany of the Garou and knew every rite necessary to the functioning of the Caern. If anyone could determine Holt's status as Kinfolk, Celeste Snowtop could.

Parker and Holt set out for her home on Union Street just after lunch, walking the few blocks north slowly, just in case whatever test she had in store for Holt required some physical strength on his part.

"Tell me again why I have to go see this woman?" said Holt as the two walked east along Ellis toward Powell Street where they would take the Powell-Mason Cable Car north to Union.

"Celeste . . ." Parker began, choosing his words carefully, "is a very special woman. She's going to help Father Oldman determine what role you're best suited for in regards to the mission, and the ranch."

"So, she's like Father Oldman's boss, then?"

"Not really," said Parker. "That person would be God."

"Yeah, right," said Holt.

"Think of her as more of an adviser, a consultant."

"I didn't think Father Oldman needed advice from anybody."

"Well, in this matter, he does. In fact, she'd be pretty upset if he hadn't asked."

Holt gave Parker a confused look, but Parker didn't seem to be interested in discussing the matter further.

When they reached Powell Street they were lucky enough to catch the cable car right away. They got on the car, paid their fare, and hung on to the outside of the car as it moved north on Powell.

Although he had lived in San Francisco for years, Holt had rarely ventured outside of the Tenderloin and had had little cause, not to mention the money, for a ride on the city's landmark cable cars. Now that he was riding one again, he had a renewed appreciation for their well-designed and well-constructed mechanics.

"Amazing, aren't they?" he said.

"What?" answered Parker. "What is?"

"The cable cars."

Parker looked around. "I never thought about them much, other than the view."

The view from the car, Holt had to admit, was spectacular. Each time the car crested a slight hill, he got a sudden dramatic view of the Golden Gate Bridge, the downtown districts, or the waters of the Bay. But as dramatic as the view was, it was the machinations going on under the ground that fascinated him.

Each six-ton cable car attached itself to the heavy cable moving beneath the street at a steady rate of nine and a half miles per hour. The driver, or "gripman," started the car by mechanically gripping the cable and stopped it by letting go. The system was perfectly suited for the steeply hilled streets of San Francisco. Not bad, thought Holt, for something that was designed over 120 years ago.

With Parker admiring the view and Holt awed by the machinery, it wasn't long before they reached Union Street. They got off the cable car and headed east.

Celeste Snowtop lived in a pale green apartment building on Union between Grant Avenue and Kearny Street. Like most of the buildings in the area, it was an old structure that looked its age. The shades strung across the rounded bay windows on each corner of the building were a mix of dirty white and beige, each one looking as if it could use a wash.

When they reached the door to the lobby, they found a big empty hole in the wood where the door handle should have been.

"Father Oldman's adviser lives here?" said Holt, looking at the hole in the wood. "You've got to be kidding me."

"I'm afraid not," said Parker. "Celeste is a woman of simple means. She's more concerned with spiritual riches than financial ones."

"She'd have to be, living in a place like this."

Parker stuck his right index finger in the hole in the door and opened it up as if it was the most natural thing in the world to do.

In the small room that served as the building's lobby, Parker scanned the mailboxes for the right apartment number.

Holt took a look as well—*Joe, Princess, Sam, Loverboy, Gregory, Axeman*—and grew more skeptical by the minute.

"There it is," said Parker. "Snowtop. Four-D." He pushed the small white button for 4-D.

They waited a moment for an answer.

Parker was about to push the button a second time when a tinny-sounding voice answered through a small speaker set into the wall.

"Yes?"

"Celeste, this is Preston . . . Preston Parker. I've brought a gentleman named Kenneth Holt to see you."

"Preston, honey, come on up here. Wendel's got me all excited to meet this new friend of yours."

"Right," said Parker. "We'll be right up."

Holt gave Parker a suspicious look. She doesn't sound much like a spiritual adviser to a priest, he thought.

"Don't worry," said Parker. "You'll like her. She's a lot of fun."

They stepped through the lobby door and headed upstairs.

When they reached the fourth floor, Celeste was standing in her doorway waiting for them.

"Hello, boys," she said.

"Celeste, this is Kenneth Holt. Kenneth Holt, this is Celeste Snowtop."

She was a strong black woman in her late fifties or early sixties, with the kind of weather-beaten look that one gets from spending most of her life outdoors. She had a full head of white hair that she kept cut short, and her face was creased with deep laugh lines. She wore sandals and a multicolored wrap that hung loosely from her body. As he shook her hand, Holt was amazed at how rough her palms were, and how strong her grip was.

"Come on in, boys, have a seat."

Parker stepped into the apartment. Holt followed.

It was a sparsely decorated place with a salad set of old furnishings that, despite their age, still looked fairly new. Obviously, Celeste Snowtop didn't spend much of her time in this apartment. Perhaps it was just her home in the city.

Parker sat down in the love seat by the window, leaving the rocking chair in the middle of the living room for Holt.

When they were both settled in, Celeste began to speak.

"So, tell me, Kenneth Holt, how do you like things at the mission?" Her voice was warm and friendly, and Holt immediately felt relaxed in her company.

"It's all right," he said. "It's certainly a lot better than some of the other places I've lived."

"Oh, I'm sure it is. Father Oldman works very hard to make the mission as comfortable as he can with what little means are available to him." Celeste leaned forward. "Are you going to stay on there?"

"I've said I would. And I have to admit that the longer I'm there the better I like it."

"Wonderful," she said, flashing a wide smile full of bright white teeth. After a moment she turned to Parker. "Preston, honey. Would you mind drawing the curtains for me? When you're done doing that there are a few new books in my den you might be interested in reading."

"Sure thing, Celeste."

"Where is he going?" said Holt.

"Just into the other room," said Celeste, getting up from her chair. "He'll be within earshot, but out of sight."

Holt leaned back reluctantly. She seemed like a nice enough lady and probably meant well, but there were a few things about her that seemed a little strange.

Parker drew the curtains across the corner bay window, and the room was suddenly filled with shadows and dark corners.

Holt sat there for what seemed like forever. He could

hear Parker in the other room flipping through the pages of a book or magazine, but the woman, Celeste Snowtop, was nowhere to be seen.

Then a voice growled softly in his left ear. . . .

"You are in no danger."

And a stone tied to one end of a rough-hewn cord swung around him, its motion forming a sort of cone around his head and body.

"What are you doing? What is that?" he asked.

"Don't worry," said Celeste. "It's just a fetish stone which will immobilize you for the duration of the test."

Fetish stone? What the hell is that? Holt tried to turn around, but his body felt sluggish, leaden.

"You will be unharmed."

Again he tried to turn around, but his body was getting stiff, his muscles weaker. He tried one last time, but his body would not move.

She lifted the stone away, and he felt a chill pass through him, like the cold brush of an icy wind penetrating all the way to his bones. His body fell completely slack, the muscles powerless to keep his right arm from falling off the armrest of the rocker. It wound up hanging limply by his side.

Celeste grabbed the hand and replaced it on the armrest. Then she pulled up a chair so that she could sit down facing him. She looked at him for a long time, gazing deep into his eyes as if she were looking right through them and into his brain.

Holt stared back at her, his eyes open and unblinking.

"Can you see me?" she said.

The muscles in Holt's jaw suddenly came alive. "Yes."

She was silent for several seconds as dark strands of hair sprouted from her face like tendrils.

"Do you see me now?"

Holt didn't know what to make of what he was seeing, but he was seeing it. The woman's face and head, and every other part from her chin to her forehead, were suddenly covered with hair. "Yes."

She moved her chair closer. When she sat back down,

her face was less than a foot away from his. He could see
the individual strands of hair snaking across her face,
joining up with others to form a heavy mat of thick brown
fur.

"And now?"

Her ears had grown long, ending in points, almost like
a dog's. In fact her whole face had lengthened, her lips
pulling back tight against her mouth, then stretching
forward along with her nose until they formed a long,
pointed muzzle.

Holt felt his heart beginning to race. This is too fucking weird, he thought. But at the same time he remained
calm, safe in the knowledge that he would be unharmed.

"Yes," he said. "I see you."

The thing that used to be Celeste Snowtop shook its
head, almost in disbelief. It had grown long, sharp teeth,
and its eyes glowed a yellowish gold. It snarled and
snapped at him, moving in close enough for him to feel
the hot press of its breath against his cheek.

Holt's eyes remained open and unwavering.

The wrap covering the rest of the beast dropped to
the floor, and what was once a human body suddenly
grew large, twisting and changing its shape until it was a
hulking mass of muscle and fur towering over Holt with
its snow white head brushing up against the ceiling.

Then it crouched down, letting Holt see all of its massive body and snarling wolflike head.

"See me . . . now?" it said in a series of low grunts.

"Yes," said Holt.

The werewolf took a stance on all fours, and for the
first time since he stepped into the apartment, Holt felt
threatened. The thing looked at him as if it were going to
attack, as if it were going to tear his body apart.

Suddenly, the memory of the attack in the alley began
to come back to him, and his whole body began to shake.
He tried to stop quivering, but like everything else about
his body, he was powerless to do anything about it.

The animal, the werewolf, before him tensed, crouch-
ing down almost like a big cat ready to pounce. Holt held

his breath as it growled and snapped its jaws . . . then leaped.

Right over him.

He felt the fur of its underbelly brush against his hair, then heard it land with two soft thuds—front legs, then back—on the floor behind him.

He let out his breath.

And the memory of the attack in the alley began to fade.

A moment later the stone and string began to spin around him, this time in the opposite direction.

"You can move now," the voice whispered in his ear a few moments later.

He tried lifting his arm. It moved. He tried to get out of the rocker, but his legs were still too weak and wobbly. He eased himself back and waited to regain his strength.

Celeste Snowtop walked around in front of him wearing the multicolored wrap. "Do you feel light-headed at all? Giddy, nervous, frightened . . . afraid?"

Holt still felt pretty groggy. "How do you expect me to feel after I watch you change into some kind of wolf-man . . . wolf-woman-thing?" His words were little more than mumbles, but he was still coherent enough to make himself understood. "Of course I was afraid. . . . Wouldn't you be?"

Parker appeared in the doorway of the living room. He looked over at Celeste. She smiled at him. "He did very well."

"Really?" said Parker, a trace of excitement in his voice.

"Yes," said Celeste, beaming. "Tell Wendel that he'll make an *excellent* addition to the Sept."

"What?" asked Holt, perking up slightly. He turned to Parker. "What the hell is she talking about?" He shook his head as if clearing out the cobwebs. "What the hell just went on here?"

"Don't worry," said Parker, putting his arm under Holt's shoulder and leading him out of the apartment. "I'll tell you all about it when we get back to the mission."

———

With Parker and Holt gone to see Celeste Snowtop, Oldman lent a hand in the basement, helping L.C. clear the tables after breakfast.

He was on his way to pick up a mop to clean up a dollop of butter someone had dropped on the floor when he heard a woman's voice calling him.

"Hello, there."

Oldman turned around and saw the woman, an attractive long-haired blonde, coming down the stairs into the basement. Something about her looked familiar.

"I'm looking for a Father Wendel Oldman."

"Look no further," Oldman said.

"Are you Father Oldman?"

"The one and only."

"I'm Caroline Keegan, Father. I'm a reporter with the television show *Inside Affair*."

She paused a moment, and Oldman got the feeling he was supposed to be impressed. He did recognize her from the television show but decided he wouldn't give her the satisfaction. "Never heard of it," he said.

"That's all right, Father. Our viewers have never heard of you either. That's why I'm here."

She was smooth, thought Oldman. Too smooth. Something wasn't right here. He decided to proceed with caution.

"Miss . . ."

"Ms. Keegan," she said. "Caroline Keegan."

"Well, Ms. Keegan, I really have no interest in being on television. I don't do charity work for fame; that's best left up to celebrities."

"Can we at least do a story on the mission? I'm sure some of the people here would love the opportunity to be recognized for the work they do."

"I don't think so," said Oldman, admiring the woman's persistence. "The work is reward enough. Now, if you'll excuse me, I have a floor that needs mopping."

"Would you be so interested in mopping the floor if I told you I've been in touch with Father Jean-Louis Trudel?"

Oldman looked at the woman for a long time. This was a bigger problem than he'd anticipated. Father Trudel had delved into Oldman's background several years ago after Oldman had refused to hear the confession of one of Trudel's parishioners. The priest had discovered several irregularities in Oldman's file, but had been miraculously transferred to Maine before he could investigate the matter further. At the time Oldman had thought, perhaps a bit foolishly, that that would be the end of it.

Obviously, it wasn't.

"If you wish to speak to me, we can do so in my office," said Oldman. "But no cameras!"

"All right, Father. No cameras for now."

Oldman nodded, "This way," and led her upstairs.

When they reached his office, it seemed hotter than usual for a midafternoon. Oldman ran a finger between his neck and the collar around it. His finger came back moist with sweat.

"Now," Oldman said. "What do you want?"

"Well, Father, I first became interested in the mission when I was going to do the story about Eddie Carver and Marjorie Watts's wedding, but you refused to marry them. . . ."

"I explained all that to Carver. It's been years since I've performed any of the sacraments—"

"Yes, I know," she interrupted. "Eddie told me all about it. Still, it seems strange. Considering the circumstances you'd think you would have been ecstatic about marrying the two of them."

Oldman didn't feel like defending himself on the matter anymore. He decided to get to the real reason why she'd come here, to call her trump. "You mentioned you had spoken to Father Trudel. . . . I hope he's well."

She seemed surprised by the change of topic but moved along without missing a beat. "Oh, he's very well, and just as interested in you as ever."

"Yes, he's quite a peculiar little man." Oldman found it hard to keep his contempt for the meddling priest from slipping into the conversation.

"He had some interesting things to say about you. . . ."

"Like what?"

"Well, for one, he said the only mention of you he could find anywhere in the records of the Catholic Church was where you were ordained." She opened up a small notebook on her lap. "A small town in Romania called Dacia in 1967."

"It was more of a village, really," said Oldman. "It was razed to the ground by the Ceauşescu regime in 1989."

"How convenient."

"I would hardly call the death of over ten thousand people in bloody civil warfare—*convenient*."

The room was silent for several seconds.

"The fact remains that there are no other records of you on file with the Catholic Church. No mention of where you attended seminary. Not as a member of any brotherhood. Not even a single record of you having performed a marriage ceremony . . . ever. It's pretty hard to believe considering how good the Catholic Church is about keeping records."

"Your point is, Ms. Keegan?"

"Well," she said in a huff, as if her point was painfully obvious. "I'm just wondering if you really are a priest—"

"I can assure you that I am." .

"And, I wonder what the hell is going on up in the Muir Woods at this cult compound you call a ranch?"

Oldman was shocked by the mention of the ranch. It wasn't something that was talked about around the mission. Those who knew about it didn't keep it a secret, but they didn't go around advertising its existence either. Either way, connecting Oldman's tenuous ties to the Catholic Church to the existence of the ranch could cause some real trouble, especially with a trashy tabloid show like *Inside Affair*.

"The ranch is merely an extension of the mission. It's a place that gives homeless people a chance to get out of the city and back to nature. A change of pace and surroundings."

"Could you take me there? Show me around?"

"I don't think that would be a good idea."

"Why not? Something to hide?"

"Don't be silly, Ms. Keegan. It's just that I don't think I'd like the kind of story you have in mind. Besides, it's a dangerous place." Oldman's face slid ever so slightly into its Glabro form, making it dark, foreboding, and perhaps just a little bit evil. "A city woman like you might get hurt in a place like that." He said the words slowly, his voice low and guttural.

"Are you threatening me?" she said.

"Not at all, Ms. Keegan. No more than someone might warn a friend not to step too close to a fire lest they should get burned."

"You're good, Oldman," she said, dropping the courtesy of calling him Father. "But you can't talk your way out of this." She got up to leave. "I'll find out what's going on up there in the hills, and when I do I'll be back . . . with cameras. And the police. Maybe even the FBI. We'll see how well you talk then."

She was shaken up, confused. That was good. The more she talked like this, the less likely it was that someone would believe her.

"You know where to find me, Ms. Keegan."

She let out an exasperated breath, spun on her heels, and walked out without saying another word.

Oldman went to his office window and watched her get inside the cab that had been waiting for her by the curb.

"Good-bye, Ms. Keegan," he said, trying to be flippant, but knowing full well that this was a problem that wasn't going to be taken care of with a shrug and a smile.

The door to Oldman's office burst open.

"Can *you* give me some answers?"

Oldman turned around. It was Holt, standing in the middle of the room with clenched fists at his sides.

Parker came through the door then, panting. "I tried . . . I tried to tell him to wait. . . . That we'd tell him when the time was right, but . . ." Parker swallowed, breathing deeply. "But he didn't care. The more he thought about what happened at Celeste's, the more he wanted to talk to you. . . ."

"Well, here I am," said Oldman. "Let's talk."

Oldman slid into his chair while Parker stumbled over to a chair across from Oldman and let himself fall heavily into the seat. Holt remained on his feet, pacing back and forth.

"What's on your mind?"

"I want somebody to tell me *exactly* what's going on. Today I get taken to see an 'adviser' that looks more like a bag lady. She turns into this werewolf kind of monster . . . and then she tells Parker I did well. This is getting a little too weird for me and I'm not sure I want to be part of it anymore."

Oldman looked at Parker. "Did he pass the test?"

Parker nodded, smiled. "With flying colors."

"There you go again. Passed what? What the hell did I pass?" He walked over to Oldman's desk and rested the knuckles of his fists on top of it. "Either you tell me what's going on . . . or I'm out of here."

"Well, Holt, one thing's for sure. From the way you're dancing around I'd say you've made a complete recovery." Oldman paused, waiting for the words to work on Holt, reminding him of the state he was in when he came to the mission just a few days ago. "I'll answer all of your questions if you just *have a seat and calm down!*" Oldman raised his voice for the last six words, making them sound like a command.

Reluctantly, Holt sat down next to Parker.

Oldman nodded. "Good. Now, I'm sure you have all sorts of questions, and rightly so, but rather than have you ask me a dozen different questions from a dozen different directions, let me tell you about me—and about you—for a little while. When I'm done, you can ask me any question you like. I promise to answer them as honestly as I can. How would that be?"

Holt's head bobbed up and down as if to say, "All right. Now we're getting somewhere." He looked at Oldman and said, "Sounds good."

Oldman took a deep breath and began. . . .

"You remember the night you came to the mission, the night the, uh . . . werewolf attacked you in the alley?"

"Of course I remember it. I'll always remember it. It still gives me nightmares."

"There's a reason why you remember it so well."

A look of skepticism crossed Holt's face. "Yeah, why?"

"You remember seeing the werewolf, first the one attacking you, then the one who saved you . . . because that's exactly what they were."

"What? Werewolves?" Holt said.

"That's right. The werewolf that attacked you was a former member of a pack that lives in Golden Gate Park. You were an unfortunate victim of his madness. He enjoyed killing, thought you were easy prey, but of course he was mistaken. You were strong and fierce, standing up to him. Fighting back." Oldman allowed a tinge of pride to creep into his voice.

Holt, sensing that pride, thrust out his chest, and smiled.

"And then the werewolf that saved you, that brought you here. That was . . ." Oldman paused. "That was me."

Holt shook his head. "You can't expect me to believe *that*. I know I've been seeing some strange things lately, and I know you've got the white hair and all, but c'mon. . . . What kind of a fool do you take me for?"

Oldman got up from his seat, stripped off his shirt, then quickly shifted the upper half of his body through Glabro into Crinos form.

A look of sheer terror crossed Parker's face before he managed to shield his eyes and turn away.

"One who isn't . . . too foolish not to believe his own eyes." Oldman struggled with the words. They came out sounding like grunts, but they were all comprehensible. He towered over Holt, glaring at him.

"Ho-lee shit!"

Oldman remained where he was, making sure that Holt recognized the features in his wolflike head—especially the shock of white hair and the salt-and-pepper shading around his muzzle that used to be his beard.

"It really is you, isn't it?"

Oldman nodded.

"Ho-lee shit!"

"Believe me now?"

"Yeah, uh . . . yes of course." He looked over at Parker ,who had his back turned to Oldman. "What's the matter with you? It's only Father Oldman. He won't hurt you."

"He can't look at me in my Crinos . . . uh, my werewolf form," Oldman said, changing slowly back into his Homid form.

"But I can?"

"Yes, you can," Oldman said. He turned to Parker. "It's all right, Parker. You can turn around now."

Parker pulled his hands away from his eyes and turned back around to face Oldman.

"Parker is human. If he were to look at me in my werewolf form he would immediately go insane."

"Why?"

"There are many reasons," said Oldman, putting his shirt back on. "But basically it's because the dependence of most humans upon rationality is so total they cannot accept the truth of what they are seeing. Their minds simply refuse to believe that they are seeing a werewolf, and therefore reasons they must be mad. We Garou call this phenomenon The Delirium."

He paused a moment, doing up his collar.

"That's why the sight of a werewolf can usually be explained by something very simple, such as a large dog or shadowplay on a wall. People would believe anything—no matter how ridiculous the explanation— rather than face the truth. We call that The Veil. It's the primary reason why werewolves are generally perceived to be creatures of myths and legends."

Holt's face was a mask of confusion, as if he were trying to understand some elaborate mathematical equation. "So you're saying that I'm not human?"

"No, not really."

"Okay, then what am I?"

"You are Kinfolk."

"I'm what?"

"Kinfolk. For all practical purposes you are a normal member of the human species, but there is some Garou blood in your lineage. That means you could be considered to be a Garou except for the fact that you did not receive the special gene which would allow you to make the change in form that I have just demonstrated."

Holt looked at Oldman curiously.

"So, I'm a . . . werewolf—"

"We call ourselves Garou," Oldman interjected.

"So, I'm a G-Garou," said Holt. "Except I don't get to do this fancy shape-changing stuff. What's the difference then? I might as well be human."

"No!"

The word came from Parker.

Holt turned to look at him.

So did Oldman.

"No, you're lucky not to be human. You've already lived your life as a human, lived among humans and ended up on the bottom rung of their ladder. Don't you understand what Father Oldman is telling you?"

Holt's face was a blank.

"He's telling you that you didn't fit into human society because you weren't meant to. It wasn't all your fault that you wound up homeless—you weren't living among your own kind. Now, he's offering you a new life, a truly *new* life." There was a touch of envy in Parker's voice as he talked about the thing he could never have. "You've found your real family. You'll be entering into a new world in which you'll be thought of as an equal member . . . always."

"But you're part of this thing too, aren't you?"

"Yes, in a small way," said Parker. "But because I'm human I can only be admitted so far into the world of the Garou. There are many places within it where I'm not allowed to go. You, on the other hand, will be welcomed into it . . . with open arms."

Oldman looked at Parker and sighed. The man wanted

so much to be part of the Garou world. It pained Oldman to know that it was something he could never have.

"It's funny, you know . . ." said Holt, fidgeting in his chair. "When I was a little kid I went to the zoo on a trip with the school and got lost from the rest of the kids. They found me at the end of the day sitting in front of the cages where they kept the timber wolves. I can remember sitting there for hours with this big gray wolf staring at me through the fence. It was pawing at the steel between us and letting out this soft whining howl. I remember feeling sorry for it at the time, a sort of . . ." Sudden realization broke across his face. "Kinship."

Oldman smiled. "It's possible then that your lineage is Lupus."

"What's that mean?"

"That one of your parents was a Garou of wolf origin."

"Are you telling me my father was a wolf? That he changed into a human . . . to be with my mother?"

"It's possible. What do you remember about your father?"

"Not much," said Holt. "My mother didn't talk about him too often. She said he worked up in the mountains. He came down a few times a year to see her and then he'd leave. . . ." Holt's words slowed as if he were coming to understand the full implications of what Oldman was saying.

"Do you remember his name?"

"Let me see. . . . He said his name was John. . . . His last name sounded Indian."

"A Native American name, you mean?" Oldman corrected him.

"Yeah, whatever. It sounded like one of those names."

For a moment Oldman wondered why Holt's father hadn't kept in touch—it wasn't like the Garou to lose track of a potential Garou child. It was definitely something worth looking into.

"Maybe I can find out something about him," offered Oldman.

Holt laughed under his breath. "My mom always said

he was a good man. Better than a lot of the other bums she brought home."

"I'm sure he was."

Holt's eyes dropped to the floor as he let out a sigh.

The conversation had come to a natural end. Holt looked exhausted, and rightly so. His world had just been torn apart, turned upside down.

He had plenty to think about.

His past.

His future.

Oldman wanted to give him all the time he needed.

"Why don't you take it easy for a while," said Oldman. "Take a walk in the park, lie down on your cot, whatever. . . . If you have any more questions, Parker and I will do our best to answer them for you. Fair enough?"

Holt got up. His legs looked wobbly. He looked at Oldman and nodded. "I think I'd like to go lie down now."

"Good, you do that."

Parker followed Holt out of Oldman's office. When he reached the door, Oldman called him back in. "Parker."

"Yes, Father."

"See what he's like in the morning. If he seems to be all right up here"—Oldman tapped his right index finger against his temple—"I want him moved up to the ranch as soon as possible."

Parker nodded and turned to leave.

"Oh, and Parker . . . thanks for your help with Holt. What you said about a new life did a lot to help convince him."

"I was only telling him the truth," said Parker.

"I know," said Oldman. "I know."

10

Holt got up early the next morning.

He hadn't slept all that much, and if he was going to be awake he'd rather be up and around than lying in bed.

His mind had been in turmoil throughout the night as he futilely tried to deny he was . . . what was the word? Kinfolk. But the longer he thought about it the easier all the pieces seemed to fit into place. His memories of childhood, his youth . . . adulthood, all seemed to make sense now that he was aware of his true identity. Now he understood why he never fit in well, never had many friends, why he couldn't keep a relationship going longer than a few weeks. There was a reason.

He belonged someplace else.

And considering how shitty his life had been up to that point, he couldn't wait to get there.

As he sipped his second cup of coffee of the morning, Holt watched the mission basement slowly fill up with hungry people looking for breakfast. As he looked at the faces of the homeless, he saw tired eyes surrounded by age lines that had been scored by time's sharpest knife. Unattractive, some might even say hideous, but he still felt an affinity toward them.

He was one of them.

Always would be.

Still, it felt good knowing that he was getting out.

"You're up early."

The familiar voice came from behind him. He turned around. It was Parker.

"I couldn't sleep."

"I'll bet." Parker pulled up a chair and sat down facing Holt. "Lack of sleep aside, how do you feel?"

"Not too bad. I think I've accepted the idea of being a Kinfolk." He shrugged. "I must have. . . . I'm already looking forward to my new life."

"Good, good," Parker said, placing a hand on Holt's knee. "Then what would you say to heading up to the ranch today, after breakfast?"

"I'd say, let's eat."

The Car.

It was a 1985 Chevrolet Chevette with a two-tone exterior of puke beige and puke green. It had over 180 thousand miles on the odometer and less than two thousand left in the engine under the hood. Oldman kept it parked in the alley behind the mission where it was more than once mistaken for a heap by the scrapmen who patrolled the neighborhood looking for steel.

"That's it?" said Holt.

Parker nodded.

"How far did you say we have to go?"

"Not that far. Just thirty miles or so."

"I hope a lot of that is downhill."

Oldman sat on the edge of his desk, one foot flat on the floor, the other dangling freely. He picked up the phone and dialed a long-distance number.

The phone was answered after several rings, but the person on the other end remained silent. Oldman waited a few moments to see if someone would speak, then knew who had picked up the other end of the line.

"Hot Eye?"

"Yes."

Hot Eye was the Gatekeeper of the Caern, a member of the Uktena tribe. He was born in Guatemala, but came to America when the change came upon him and he discovered his true heritage. During the seventies, he was part of the migrant workers' struggle for rights, where he met other members of the Sept like Celeste Snowtop and Able Heart, the Caern's Warder. His name was derived from the blood red eye he kept covered by a patch in all of his Garou forms.

"This is Wendel Oldman."

"Hello, Oldman. How are you?"

"I'm fine, and you?"

"I am doing well."

"Perhaps not," Oldman muttered under his breath.

Hot Eye was silent, waiting for Oldman to continue. He was probably the most careful listener in the entire Sept and rarely spoke unless spoken to. The only time he spoke first was in cases of emergency.

"Listen," said Oldman. "My assistant, Preston Parker, is on his way to the ranch this morning. There is a Kinfolk with him by the name of Kenneth Holt."

"Uh-huh," said Hot Eye.

Oldman continued. "I came across Holt while I was in Crinos form. When he didn't suffer The Delirium, I realized he might be Kinfolk. He's been checked out by Celeste since then, so there's no danger to the Caern. Both Celeste and I would like you to introduce him to the other members of the Sept, teach him the litany . . . you know, help to make him feel at home."

The line remained silent for a few more seconds, then Hot Eye spoke.

"This is wonderful news, Oldman," he said in a rare display of emotion. "I look forward to telling the others." But the joyful tone of voice didn't last very long. "Why then did you say 'perhaps not' when I said, 'I am doing well'?"

Oldman thought about denying he'd said anything, but knew Hot Eye could probably recite the entire conversation—including the muttered comment—verbatim.

"Well," said Oldman. "There *is* a problem. There was a reporter here the other day . . . a Caroline Keegan. She's with a television show called *Inside Affair*. She asked a lot of questions about me, asked about the ranch too. She thinks it's some sort of cult and she said she was going to find out what's going on up there. She might have been hysterical, or she might have been telling the truth. It's hard to say. She might be inside the Bawn already . . . or she might be on the other side of the world by now working on another story. Either way, I just thought I'd let you know."

"Thank you, Oldman," said Hot Eye. "I will tell the others."

The midmorning sun shone brightly on the surface of San Francisco Bay. The morning fog was almost gone, and the sky was clear and blue. The view from the Golden Gate Bridge was spectacular, one Holt had enjoyed while on foot many times before. He sat in the passenger seat of the Chevette waiting for its wheels to fall off or the engine to fall out, but it kept chugging right along, crossing the more than one-mile span of the bridge as quickly as all the surrounding traffic.

When they were off the bridge and driving along Bridgeway Boulevard in Sausalito, Holt breathed easier. The car sounded like it was running well enough, and Parker seemed to be unconcerned about its reliability, so Holt made himself as comfortable as he could in the cramped bucket seat and tried not to worry about it.

After a few more minutes of silence, he spoke. "So what's your story, Parker?"

"Pardon me," Parker said, his eyes never leaving the road.

"I said, what's your story? How did you end up needing Father Oldman's help?"

Parker continued driving, saying nothing.

Holt was about to ask him again when Parker took a deep breath and began talking.

"I was in the navy," he said, the words coming slowly. "We were docked in the Philippines for a twenty-four-hour

layover. Most of the guys were ashore visiting the broth-
els there. But a few of us who weren't into that kind of
thing stayed on board."

Holt looked at Parker, wondering what he'd meant by
"a few of us weren't into that kind of thing." When he
realized Parker was telling him he was gay, Holt was surprised that it didn't bother him. He'd always been
uncomfortable about that part of San Francisco but had
lived with it. Now it didn't seem to be a problem; he'd
come to respect Parker for the work he did, and knowing
he was gay wasn't going to change anything. For Holt,
Parker would always be just another guy.

"We were playing poker and it was getting late, we
were getting tired," Parker continued. "I had three aces
and was ready to pick up the biggest pot of the night
when one of the guys at the table accused me of cheat-
ing." Parker shook his head. "He wasn't really one of us,
he was confined to ship for some screwup during
maneuvers, so we felt sorry for him and let him in on the
game. Damned if he didn't pull a knife on me."

"Oh, shit," said Holt in long, drawn-out words. He had a
feeling he knew just what kind of trouble was coming up.

"He got up from the table and backed me up against a
bulkhead, insisting I had cheated and that he be given
the pot. But there was no way I was giving up the money,
there was over two hundred dollars there. But he kept
moving closer and closer . . . and the point of his knife
kept getting bigger and sharper . . . I had to do something, so I picked up a steel water pitcher and hit him
over the head with it."

"Serves him right," said Holt.

"Yeah, sure," said Parker. "Damned if he didn't fall to
the floor—dead."

"You're kidding?"

"Nope. I hit him in the head all right, but he died of
an aneurysm. The doctors said it had been in his head
for years just waiting to kill him." Parker inhaled a deep
breath. "I was cleared of the murder charges and it was
ruled self-defense, but the fact that I was gay came out

during the trial, and the navy used the incident as an excuse to discharge me. They let me go in San Francisco and I stayed, even tried to make a living as a lounge singer for a while. But even though I liked it here and felt comfortable in the city, getting kicked out of the navy put me in a state of mind that sent my life spiraling downward until I hit bottom and was homeless, broke, and willing to do just about anything for something to eat. Thank God for Father Oldman or else I'd probably be dead by now."

The interior of the car was silent for several long minutes as they turned west onto Stinson Beach–Highway 1 and followed the winding road toward the Pacific Ocean. When they turned north onto Shoreline Highway, Parker broke the silence.

"So, now you know my story. How about you?"

"Me?" Holt took a deep breath. "I was working in a factory where they made trucks, big trucks, you know . . . to pull semitrailers. One morning I left my apartment and was heading off to work when I stepped on a toy car a kid from down the hall had left on the steps. I fell down the stairs leading to the street and broke my neck in nine different places."

Parker cringed.

"I was practically paralyzed from the neck down for two and a half years. I was getting Supplemental Security Income when I came out of the hospital, but as soon as they got the brace off and I was able to walk around without it, they stopped payments—just like that." He snapped his fingers.

"So there I was barely able to walk, haven't worked for almost three years, and I'm supposed to go out and get a job when the only thing I'm trained for is heavy machinery mechanics. I did manage to get the odd job here and there, but I couldn't keep any of them for very long. So, I began drifting through the city, moving from shelter to shelter, scrounging for food . . . or money for the occasional bottle."

"How is your neck now?"

"Oh, it got better after a few years, but being on the street for so long is like being in a pit that keeps getting deeper and deeper. The longer you're in it, the harder it is for you to climb out."

Parker nodded. "I know exactly what you mean."

"So, like you said, thank God for Father Oldman or I'd be dead by now."

Parker took his eyes away from the road long enough to smile at Holt.

Holt returned the gesture, aware of the strong common bond, the kinship, between them.

They continued heading north toward Stinson Beach.

And for Holt, the inside of the car no longer seemed so cramped.

As they drove past the Muir Woods National Monument, Holt felt a strange feeling come over him, a kind of force stirring within him that he'd never felt before. He felt strong and powerful, primal. The feeling lasted for a while, then faded as they continued on past the woods.

The Muir Woods were surrounded by Mount Tamalpais State Park, almost six hundred acres of redwoods and trails. In the distance Holt could see Mount Tamalpais, "Mount Tam," the highest peak on the Marin Peninsula, rising majestically up from the park to a height of over two thousand feet above sea level.

"Is the ranch around here?" asked Holt.

"The Caern is in there, but the ranch is a little further north."

"What's a Caern?"

"You'll find out soon enough."

They continued north for a few more minutes, then turned right, taking a narrow dirt road that led straight into the forest. If Parker hadn't turned into it, Holt wouldn't have known it was there.

The road was bumpy and twisted through the woods like a snake, wending left to avoid this rock formation, turning right to miss that tree.

And then, just when it seemed to Holt that the ride

was never going to end, the forest opened up and they came upon a clearing.

"This is it?"

"Where? What is it?" Holt looked left and right but couldn't see anything other than forest.

"Look again."

He did, and slowly buildings and structures began to take shape. The scene reminded him of those prints street vendors sold down in Union Square. He once spent half an hour looking at one of those prints before he saw an image of a man and woman having sex appear in the midst of the squiggly, swirling lines.

"This is it," said Parker. "The Scott Ranch."

Holt could see the buildings clearly now and was aware of other smaller structures further into the woods. It had the layout of something like a military compound with, Holt guessed, a building for sleeping, another for eating, still another for recreation and meetings. But while the place was set up like a compound, it blended in with the surrounding woods so perfectly, so naturally, that it seemed as if the buildings had *grown* out of the forest rather than been built up from the ground.

Parker drove the car around back of one of the buildings where a garage was open, ready to accept the car and presumably hide it from view.

Inside the garage Parker turned off the ignition, and the car sputtered for about ten seconds before dying out with a rattling, wheezy sort of cough.

"Hey," Parker said. "You're a mechanic. Maybe you can take a look at it later."

"Sure," said Holt. "I'll take a look at it for you, but keep in mind, I'm a mechanic, not Jesus."

"Fair enough," said Parker, turning toward the center of the compound. "If I'm not mistaken there are probably a few people who are anxious to meet you. Come this way."

Holt followed Parker across the grass toward a big log building with a wide, gently sloping roof. When they entered, Holt was struck by a gust of warm air and the smell of fresh-cut pine and cedar.

The room was large, about the size of a high school gymnasium, with two large wooden posts rising up from the middle to support the roof's center beam. There were several people at the far end, gathered in an informal circle. Obviously this was some sort of meeting hall.

As they neared the group, they started getting out of their chairs. When they arrived, everyone was standing up, almost like a reception line at a wedding.

Parker nodded to the group. "This is Kenneth Holt," he said.

The group remained silent.

"Holt," Parker said, gesturing to the left end of the line. "This is Able Heart, Warder of the Caern."

Able Heart was a stocky, barrel-chested man of average height with brown eyes and close-cropped brown hair. There were several scars on his chest and arms, similar to Holt's. They shook hands; the man's grip was strong and firm.

The moved along to the next one in line. "Tim Rowantree, Guardian."

Rowantree was a large but gentle-looking man with heavy callused hands, long sandy blond hair, and blue eyes. He wore jeans and a tie-dyed T-shirt and wore his hair tied back in a ponytail.

"March Lion, Master of the Rite."

A small, wiry man with an air of determination about him, March Lion was a Native American with black hair and dark brown eyes. He looked old and tired. It was a look Holt had seen before in the face of Celeste Snowtop.

There were four more people waiting. Holt moved on down the line.

"Hot Eye, Gatekeeper."

Hot Eye shifted his walking staff from his right to left hand, then shook hands with Holt. He was another Native American, looking very tight-lipped and proud. There was a patch over his right eye.

Holt wondered what was underneath that patch, but considering Hot Eye's name, really didn't want to know. He shook hands and moved on.

"Sharon Morning Cloud, Keeper of the Land."

Sharon Morning Cloud was a slightly built young woman. Like the others she was Native American with long, dark hair and brown eyes. She was an attractive woman, and Holt looked at her closely. When their eyes met, she quickly looked away, as if she couldn't stand the scrutiny.

"Silent-Fist-That-Wins, Master of the Challenge."

Holt looked up. Way up. This Silent-Fist guy was huge, nearly eight feet tall with his head topped with short-cropped hair. He looked to be young, but his face and neck were covered by a road map of scars, new and old. He might *win*, thought Holt, but not always that easily. They shook hands, Holt making sure his grip was firm so his fingers wouldn't get crushed in the palm of the giant.

"And last, but not least," said Parker. "Sylvia Wood Runner, your Earth Guide."

"My what?"

"Your Earth Guide. She'll be showing you around, teaching you the litany and ways of the Garou. She will be your companion for the next few weeks."

Holt raised his eyebrows and smiled.

Sylvia Wood Runner was a middle-aged Native American, a few years younger than Holt. She was good-looking and shapely, but somehow seemed small and frail. Perhaps that was only because she was standing next to the Silent-Fist-Fighter guy, thought Holt. He could make Hulk Hogan look small.

He shook Sylvia's hand; it was as firm and strong as any of the others had been.

He looked into her eyes. They were a dark mixture of brown and green. Her hair was shoulder length and slightly curled, a lighter shade of brown, much like the color of the surrounding redwoods.

"Welcome to The Scott Ranch," she said in a friendly voice. She pulled him close and gave him a warm, heartfelt hug. "And welcome as well into the Sept."

The others gathered around.

"Welcome," they said, patting him on the back, giving him a hug or just brushing up against him.

It felt good, thought Holt. If felt like . . .

Home.

11

Holt spent the afternoon working on the Chevette, doing what he could with the limited tools available to make sure it would get Parker back into San Francisco or anywhere else he might want to go.

After Parker drove off, Holt spent the rest of the day walking the grounds, getting a feel for the place and the surrounding woods. In addition to the main compound there was a secondary one just to the north where, Holt was told, other homeless people were brought to continue their rehabilitation. It was where Holt would have gone if he hadn't been discovered to be Kinfolk.

By nightfall Holt was bushed and went to sleep in the bunkhouse just after eight.

The bunkhouse was the size of a single-room army barracks but was divided into several smaller rooms by wooden walls and doors. Holt's room was about ten-by-ten square and was furnished with an old squeaky bed and a solid wooden desk and chair, probably second-, maybe even thirdhand. The room provided him with a modicum of privacy even though the sounds of the others sleeping could clearly be heard coming through the cracks in the walls.

So, it was noisy.

Holt didn't care.

He could hardly remember the last time he had a room all to himself. He might as well have been in a palace.

He lay back on the bed and was asleep before his head hit the pillow.

Holt opened his eyes. It was still dark.

Someone was standing over him, a woman.

He blinked the sleep from his eyes, gave them a rub.

He recognized her now. Sylvia Wood Runner.

"Get dressed," she said. "We're going for a walk in the woods."

Holt wanted so much to set his head back down onto the pillow, to get just a few more minutes of sleep, but he knew he couldn't. He was in school now, and the classes started whenever the teacher wanted them to—like right now.

Groaning slightly, Holt got up, stretching his sleep-stiffened muscles and joints into action. By the time he was dressed, she was waiting for him out in the yard.

She was dressed in some kind of uniform, dark green pants and shirt, and a broad-rimmed hat—a park ranger. She looked petite standing there, almost frail.

Holt approached her and said, "Well, here I am."

"Good," Sylvia said. "We'll be going for walks every morning until you know your way around. I move quickly, so do your best to keep up."

Holt looked at her again, at her small, thin body that held up her clothing as if on sticks, and tried to picture her as a hardy woman hiking great distances through the woods. He couldn't see it. "You lead the way," he said, a trace of arrogance in his voice. "I'll be right behind you."

She stood there a moment giving him a look of disdain. "You think so?"

Holt nodded.

She turned and began walking, slowly at first, then faster.

Holt kept pace, his body hardly complaining about the strain. But, after they were about fifteen minutes into the woods, she rounded a large redwood tree . . . and vanished.

Holt walked around the huge tree twice but saw no trace of her. He turned back in the direction he'd come but suddenly wasn't sure which way that was. The forest looked the same in every direction.

All right, he thought. You've proved your point. Me and my damn big mouth. He made a mental note for the future—look, listen, and keep your big trap shut!

He sat down on a fallen log and waited. . . .

And waited.

It was over an hour before Sylvia returned.

"You've made your point," Holt said as she appeared out of the woods, as if by magic.

"Good," she said. Her voice had a tone of finality to it, as if the matter was closed. She was the teacher, he was the student. Period. End of discussion. "Now, eat."

She held out her hands. They were filled with berries and nuts.

Holt took them from her and ate them hungrily.

"It's not much, but it will tide you over until we return to the ranch for a proper breakfast."

"Why? What's for breakfast?"

"Rabbit."

Holt felt the inside of his mouth getting wet. "Then let's finish up our hike."

Sylvia began walking.

And Holt never let her out of his sight.

After breakfast, Sylvia brought Holt back into the woods, this time leading him south toward Muir Woods National Monument in the area around Mount Tamalpais.

The hike was fairly easy, not to mention scenic, as it brought them along well-groomed paths and trails through one of the most majestic redwood groves in the world. Some of the redwoods in the park stretched some 250 feet toward the sky and were over one thousand years old. Holt felt at peace here, the cool moist air invigorating him more than a hundred San Francisco sunrises ever could.

Despite it being early in the day, the woods were already getting congested with cars carrying hikers into the woods to enjoy its beauty.

"I didn't think all that many people came up here," said Holt, speaking for the first time since they'd set out. He was trying to save his breath and conserve his energy, not knowing how long this hike might last.

"It's a source of joy and sorrow for us," answered Sylvia, her long quick strides showing no signs of slowing. "We know that these people come here because they see the same beauty that John Muir did when he saved these woods from the axe in 1908. But we also know that the more people visit, the greater the chance the forests will be damaged in some way—either through pollution or by fire. We can only hope that the beauty will inspire people to preserve it."

Holt said nothing and walked on.

A half hour later Sylvia stopped. The abrupt halt caught Holt off guard. He'd taken that moment to glance at the ground, concentrating on keeping one foot in front of the other, and nearly walked right into her.

"Sorry," he said. "I didn't realized you'd stopped."

"That's all right," she said. "We're nearly there."

"Nearly where?"

"The Bawn . . ."

"The Bawn?"

"It is the boundary layer surrounding the Caern. A sort of buffer zone where mortals are watched."

Holt took a look around and for the first time realized that the forest had changed, grown quieter. Where before there were paved pathways and cleared trails, now there were narrow lanes that disappeared between the trees after just a few yards. Holt tried to remember the last time he'd seen someone other than Sylvia in the forest and realized he hadn't seen anyone for a long, long time.

"The guardians of the Caern are usually busy keeping track of who is near the Caern. Because of all the human traffic through the park during the day, the Bawn is structured in layers to prevent humans . . . and other enemies of our kind . . . from accidentally walking into the Caern itself."

"I didn't know humans were enemies of the Garou?" asked Holt, a little confused. Parker was human and he was no enemy. And Oldman had spent his life trying to help as many humans as he could.

"Most humans are good souls, but there are some who know of our kind and want nothing but to destroy us."

"And what about these 'other enemies'? Who might they be?"

"Mages seek the Caerns out to strip them of their aura, and minions of The Wyrm—a force of dark evil and decay—will sometimes corrupt Caerns in order to spread their sickness."

Holt felt like he did in school whenever the teacher talked too fast. It was all too much to keep track of. He told himself he'd learn it all in time, but how long that would take he couldn't be sure. Bawn, Caern, Mages, Wyrm, it seemed like so much. . . .

"When we entered the park we passed through the outermost layer of the Bawn. Our progress since then has been monitored by Kinfolk among the rangers and tourists."

"Kinfolk?" asked Holt. "You mean like me?"

"Yes, that's right."

Holt had been told that there were other Kinfolk, but he didn't know there were any so close by. It meant his new family, his new world, was bigger than he first imagined.

"We are presently at the next layer of the Bawn. Here there are a hidden series of paths that lead in a roundabout way to the site of the Caern. You can see some traces of the paths, but they are difficult to follow if you don't know the way, so I suggest you stay close behind me."

"Don't worry," said Holt. "I'm getting fond of the sight

of your behind. I'm at the point now where I'd follow it just about anywhere."

Sylvia ignored the comment and began to move.

Holt was no more than a step behind her.

The paths were difficult to follow, and more than once when Holt took his eyes off Sylvia to check his footing, she was out of sight by the time he looked back up, having made a sharp turn left or right that wasn't apparent in the layout of the path.

But at this point Sylvia was very forgiving, stopping to wait each time he fell behind. Holt got the impression that it was very easy to get lost in this part of the woods, even for Garou.

"Are we there yet?" said Holt, trying to hide his heavy breaths.

"Why, are you tired?"

"Well . . . it has been a while since I trekked for miles through some of the densest woods on the continent."

Sylvia smiled. "You've done well. We are almost there."

She turned to continue on her way, but stopped dead in her tracks. There was a woman standing in the path in front of them. She was tall, blond, and attractive. Behind her stood a man with a camera resting on his shoulder.

Sylvia looked shocked, but regained her composure quickly.

"Can I help you, miss?"

"My name is Caroline Keegan of *Inside Affair*." She gestured to the cameraman. "This is John Tersigni, my cameraman."

The man pulled his eye away from the viewfinder and nodded. "Videographer," he corrected her.

"Videographer, right. We're getting some footage for a story I'm doing on the National Monument," said the reporter. "Someone told us there were some pretty big redwoods in this area."

Sylvia stood up straight, thrust out her chest, and did her best to look both official and imposing. "There are, but . . . there have been reports of a renegade cougar in these woods, and we've been asked to turn visitors away from this section of the park."

"But it's important that we have those shots today, the story is supposed to air tonight . . . nationwide."

"I appreciate that, ma'am," Sylvia said, sounding more and more like a park ranger with each word. "But our concern is for the safety of the visitors to the park. If something happens to you, if you get mauled, or perhaps even killed by a hungry or sick cougar, no one will ever believe that I did everything in my power to persuade you to move on . . . to save your life. So, I'm going to have to ask you again to please turn around."

"But—" she protested.

Suddenly other rangers appeared behind Sylvia and Holt.

"Just spotted some fresh tracks a few hundred yards in that direction," one of them said. "They looked to be headed this way."

Holt looked at the rangers, then at the television reporter, and couldn't tell if the cougar threat was real or fabricated. One thing was for sure, it certainly *sounded* real.

"All right," Caroline Keegan said. Reluctantly, she turned around to face her cameraman. "I guess we can get some shots of the trees south of here. I suppose one tree's as good as the next."

Holt stood by Sylvia's side, watching the reporter and cameraman disappear into the woods. The surrounding rangers also disappeared, no doubt following the two until they were safely on the outer edge of the Bawn.

Holt remained silent, waiting for Sylvia to speak.

"Well, that's it for today," she said. "Tour's over. Time to head back to the ranch."

She turned and headed back in the direction from which they had come.

There was a gray cloud hanging over the morning now, and it seemed to take forever to cover the distance back to the ranch.

When they arrived at the ranch, Sylvia and Holt went directly to the meeting hall.

Several people working in the yard saw Sylvia walking toward the hall with haste and must have gathered that something was wrong. They stopped what they were doing and headed for the hall as well.

Hot Eye, Able Heart, and Sharon Morning Cloud were there inside the meeting room, as were a few of the others. After Sylvia and Holt entered, the door opened behind them and a half-dozen others flowed in.

"Is something wrong?" asked Able Heart, arching his eyebrows, which created several deep depressions along the scar lines across his forehead.

Sylvia spoke at once, hardly out of breath. Holt realized that if it wasn't for him she would have returned to the ranch in half the time they had taken.

"We were inside the third layer of the Bawn, near the Caern. I was about to take Holt inside when we met up with a woman, a television reporter named Caroline Keegan. There was a cameraman with her, too."

The room was silent enough for them to hear the gentle blowing of the wind outside. Everyone listened attentively, understanding that there was something important happening here.

"She said she was getting footage of redwood trees for a story she was doing on the park . . . but I didn't believe her. She had the look of one who lies."

"How is it possible that she could get so close to the Caern?" asked March Lion. "Especially when she was moving through the woods with a man carrying a camera?"

The room was silent.

Then Tim Rowantree stepped forward. He was dressed in a ranger's uniform. Holt recognized him now. He had been there in the woods when Sylvia had confronted the reporter.

"We were busy following Sylvia and Holt," Rowantree said, his voice stolid and impassive. It was obvious that the important thing right now was to gather all the facts.

If there was blame to be laid, it would all be shared equally—later. "But she couldn't have been walking through the woods like a regular tourist or we would have picked up on her and the cameraman. She must have been trying to stay hidden. Perhaps she was looking for something, possibly the Caern. I believe what Sylvia says to be true; I think her story was a lie."

March Lion was silent as he considered what Sylvia and Rowantree had said.

Holt took a look around, watching, listening, learning the ropes, and wondering if it would ever be his place to speak up in a meeting like this.

At last March Lion nodded. "Wendel Oldman said he'd been visited by this reporter and warned us that she could be coming our way. However, he also said she was interested in finding out about the ranch, and I think that is what she was mistakenly looking for inside the Bawn."

The tension inside the room began to dissipate as everyone took a collective sigh of relief.

"Still, she poses a threat," said March Lion. He turned to Rowantree. "Who is shadowing her now?"

"There were several of us following her as she moved south away from the Caern. I returned when she was safely outside the Bawn, leaving Wilson Fallingleaves and Dale Talons to keep watch over her."

"Good," March Lion said. "But perhaps we should keep an even closer eye on her, around the clock. I have a feeling she might prove to be persistent in her search for the ranch."

"I agree," Rowantree said. "Hot Eye, Fist-That-Wins, come with me."

The three of them left the meeting hall without saying a word, and the meeting appeared to have come to an end as fast and as informally as it had begun.

Holt looked at Sylvia, wondering just how serious a matter this morning's encounter had been.

"Is it really that important?" he said when the room had just about emptied out. "So she got close to the Caern, so what?"

Sylvia took a deep breath. "You wouldn't ask me that if we had entered the Caern and you had experienced it for yourself." And then her voice suddenly became edged with passion. "The Caern is our sacred place, like a human's church, temple, or synagogue. It's a site of worship, a spiritual meeting area, the final resting place for those too old to continue life's journey. Do you understand?"

Holt was taken aback by her subtle display of emotion. He'd had no idea the Caern was so important to the Garou. He'd thought he was just being shown around, like a visitor to a new city. Obviously he was being assimilated into the fold as quickly as possible.

"Yeah, I think I understand now," he said. "This Caroline Keegan could make trouble *for us.*"

Holt took a moment to think about what he'd just said.

For us.

Did I say that? Have I started thinking that way already?

"Yes," said Sylvia, flashing him a warm, friendly smile. "She could cause trouble. . . . For us."

Caroline Keegan sat in the motel room, the phone cradled in the nape of her neck, her hands busy massaging her sore and blistered feet.

"Sam? Caroline here."

"Well, what have you got?" asked *Inside Affair* assignment editor Sam Barlow.

"I'm not sure yet, but whatever it is I think I'm getting close. When I was in the woods today I came across a park ranger who chased me away with a story about a renegade cougar—"

"We didn't hear anything about that on the wire."

"That's what I thought. Whatever is up here must be big if the park rangers are in on covering it up."

Sam was silent, as if thinking the matter over. "All right," he said. "You stay up there as long as you need to in order to get the story. But I want you to keep me posted daily. I'll get a researcher looking into it down here. Maybe we can come up with something you can use."

"Thanks, Sam. You're a prince."

"Yeah, yeah. . . . Listen, you don't know much about these people. They could be dangerous, maybe even armed, so I want you to be careful. If it gets too hot I want you out of there, fast. There's no story that's worth getting killed for."

"I'll be the judge of that."

The line fell silent again.

"You will be careful, won't you?"

"Of course I will," she said. "Have you ever known me to be careless?"

"As a matter of fact—" Sam began to say.

Caroline hung up the phone.

12

Father Oldman was lying on his back shining a flashlight into the darkness. "It doesn't look good," he said.

"Why?" asked Parker, balancing the machine on two of its legs. "What's wrong with it?"

Oldman and Parker had been washing bedsheets in the ancient washing machine in the mission's furnace room when the machine suddenly stopped working and the room became filled with the sharp smell of ozone. The breakdown was an inconvenience more than a surprise. The washing machine had been obtained second-hand when the mission first opened, and its demise had been way overdue.

"It looks like the motor is burned out . . . practically fried."

"Perhaps Holt can take a look at it when he comes back from the ranch? He told me he used to work as a mechanic."

"He is pretty handy, isn't he?"

Parker nodded.

"All right, we'll leave the machine here for him to take a look at, but right now we have to wash the rest of the load. You'll have to take it down to the Laundromat, but bring them back wet if they aren't too heavy. At least the drier is still working."

"Right," said Parker, beginning to gather up the wet sheets out of the machine and bundling them up with the ones on the floor still waiting to be washed.

Then Oldman held the sheets for Parker, helping him tie the corners to make two large hobo sacks.

As they headed upstairs hauling a bundle each, they were met by police detectives Michael Garrett and Ben Chong.

Oldman recognized them right away. "Gentlemen," he said, puffing up the stairs with his burden held tight against his chest. "What brings you back this way?"

The two men backtracked up the stairs out of Oldman's way.

At the top of the stairs Oldman dropped his bundle onto the floor, where it landed with a soft thud.

Garrett hitched his belt up against his stomach, then moved his hands to the sides following the waistband of his pants. "We've got a suspect in the homeless murders," he said.

"What?" asked Oldman.

"Huh?" Parker said, just as incredulous.

"I said, we've picked up a suspect in the murders," Garrett said, rocking proudly back on his heels.

"Really?" said Oldman. "Then you must have given up on the wild dog theory."

"Yes!" Garrett said. "We actually have a *man* in custody."

Oldman still found it hard to believe. "Somebody from around here? From the Tenderloin?"

Garrett let out his breath in a huff. "No, he's from out of town. He was seen wandering in the area of the last murder around the time our forensic people estimated the murder was committed. He also fits one of the descriptions we have of the killer."

Oldman was impressed that they had made so much progress, but he didn't want to let on. "That's all you've got on him?" he said.

"We're trying to piece the rest together," said Garrett, a little defensively.

"So, why does that bring you here?"

Garrett was obviously getting tired of Oldman's questions. He opened his mouth to say something, but Detective Chong stepped forward and spoke before Garrett could get another word out. "Detective Garrett and I would like you to come down to the station and take a look at a lineup, see if you recognize this suspect. Maybe you've noticed him hanging out in this part of the city the last few weeks."

Oldman's curiosity had been piqued.

If they did indeed have Wingnut in custody, then he might do well to identify him as the killer. If Oldman hadn't scared the Garou off, maybe trouble with human authorities would.

And if they were off the mark and had hauled in an innocent man, the least Oldman could do was make sure that man wasn't unjustly charged with the murders.

Whatever the case, he wanted to see who the suspect was.

"Of course, gentlemen," Oldman said. "I said I'd help you out any way I could, and I meant it."

"Thank you," said Chong.

Garrett remained silent.

The two detectives drove Oldman to the San Francisco Police Department's Central Station on Vallejo near Stockton. It was situated in the northeast part of the city between North Beach to the east and Russian Hill to the west.

After winding their way through the halls bustling with police, criminals, victims, and innocent bystanders, the two detectives led Oldman into a small boxlike room. Its furnishings were spartan, with two chairs, a small round table, and a plain black telephone. For a moment Oldman wondered if he hadn't been brought there to be arrested rather than to look at some lineup.

"Wait here," said Garrett. "I'll just make sure everything's all ready in there. I won't be long."

Garrett left the room, leaving Chong alone with Oldman.

The stocky Asian pulled up a chair across the table from Oldman and smiled.

"Don't mind him," he said, referring to Garrett. "He's on edge lately because he's never had a case give him so much trouble. Every lead we get seems to bring us to two dead ends."

"I can imagine there's quite a lot of pressure on you to solve this case, especially when there's such a dangerously violent killer on the loose."

The room was silent except for the constant buzz from the fluorescent light overhead.

Finally, Detective Chong spoke. "You know, Father," he began. "I just wanted to tell you that I think what you're doing with the homeless people in the Tenderloin is fantastic."

The kind words caught Oldman off guard. His first thought was that this was a kind of good-cop, bad-cop ploy. But the detective's voice was too honest, too sincere to be telling anything but the truth. Oldman relaxed and enjoyed it.

"Thank you," he said. "We do our best at the mission with what limited resources we have . . . and we seem to be doing some good."

"No, you're doing *great*. I have a lot of relatives who live in the Tenderloin and every one of them talks about you like you were God, not just a local priest."

Oldman was genuinely flattered. It was hard for him to gauge what others thought about him because he interacted with very few humans. News like this was always welcome. He only wished Parker were here to hear it. "Why, thank you, Detective. Mission work is usually without recompense, but it can sometimes have great rewards, moments like these when you realize that what you're doing actually does make a difference. Thank you."

"Hey, Father, no problem," said Chong. "I'm just sorry I didn't get the chance to tell you the first time we met."

Oldman smiled broadly. "Thanks."

The door to the room opened up and Garrett stepped

in. "All right," he said. "We're ready. Father, would you come this way."

Oldman got up and followed Garrett out of the room with Chong bringing up the rear. They walked a short distance down the hall to another room, this one dark with one wall completely made of glass—the two-way mirror.

Garrett stepped up to a microphone sticking out of the wall on the left. "Okay, send them in."

A light came on on the other side of the glass wall showing spots for eight people and measurements in feet and inches in bold black numerals on the plain white back wall. A door at one end of the room opened up, and six men took their places against the wall.

They were all gruff-looking men, three of them dressed in the ragged clothes of street people, the other three dressed much better in clean pants and jackets, fashionable shoes, and neatly trimmed hair. They either had two descriptions of the killer or they'd filled out the line with whoever they had lying around at the station—maybe even a couple of police officers. Probably the latter, thought Oldman.

"Okay, Father, take your time," said Detective Chong. "Take a good look at each man and tell me if any of them look familiar to you."

Oldman looked at each one for a long time, studying them.

"Turn right," Garret said into the microphone.

All six men turned to the right, giving Oldman a clear view of their left profiles.

"Turn left."

They turned left, showing their right profiles.

"Straight ahead."

They all stood facing Oldman, giving him a good view of their faces and overall builds.

They were all roughly six feet tall, all with dark complexions. As Oldman walked down the line from left to right, he recognized two of the more scruffy-looking men as having visited the mission in the last month or two. The third street person looked totally unfamiliar to him.

Perhaps he was new in town, or else new to the streets. Either way there was nothing unusual about any of those three.

He moved on to the three better-dressed men. Two of them looked cool, flashy with NBA jackets and hats, baggy multicolored pants, and two-hundred-dollar high-tops. These men were probably dealers. He looked for their beepers, but if they'd had any when they'd come into the police station, the beepers were probably sitting in a bin somewhere along with their other valuables.

That left one more, a sharp, cleanly dressed man wearing dark dress shoes that matched the rest of his outfit. Clearly, this was the one who didn't belong in the Tenderloin, probably even the entire West Coast. He had an eastern look to him, New York or Boston, someplace like that.

This was the one who was most likely their suspect.

But there was something else about him . . .

Oldman stepped up to the glass.

"What is it, Father?" asked Detective Chong. "Do you see something?"

Oldman didn't bother answering.

He inspected the man closely, scrutinizing his features. There was something about him. . . .

Something familiar.

And then all at once he knew what it was.

"Ah, nothing," he said, shaking his head as he stepped away from the glass. "I thought I recognized one of them, but . . ."

"But what?" said Detective Garrett.

Oldman remained silent for a few moments. "But then I realized that the man I was thinking of had been one of the victims."

"Oh," said Garrett. "I'm sorry."

"That's all right," said Oldman. "I'*m* sorry I couldn't be of more help to you. If the killer is still out there, he must be caught."

"What do you mean?" asked Garrett.

"Well . . . I have a feeling you don't have the killer

here," said Oldman, trying to cover his tracks and wishing he hadn't.

Garrett nodded. "That's fine, Father. But we don't need your *feelings* about this case. What we need are facts that will help us find the killer."

"Yes, of course," said Oldman.

Detective Chong stepped forward then. "Thanks for all your help, Father. We have a few more people waiting to look over the lineup, but if you wait a while I could give you a lift back to the mission."

"No, thank you. Since I'm down here I thought I might run some errands."

"Then at least let me show you out."

"Sure, I'd like that. Thank you."

Oldman followed Detective Chong out into the hall, leaving Garrett behind to pace back and forth inside the room, always coming up against a wall no matter which direction he turned.

The afternoon was chilly, and Oldman found it difficult to find an inconspicuous spot to wait outside the police station. He ended up waiting across the street, close enough to a bus stop to make it appear that he was waiting for a bus, but not so close as to stop any of the buses along the route.

Oldman *had* recognized something different about one of the men in the lineup.

While they didn't have the killer in the lineup, they did have a Garou.

The well-dressed one from out of town had decidedly feral features: a long sloping nose and chin, thick and profuse body hair, sharp teeth clearly visible, and the unmistakable eyes of the wolf.

Oldman wasn't surprised that the police had brought him in. If they had a hazy eyewitness description of the killer looking something like a werewolf, or a man with somewhat wolflike features, this Garou fit the bill. And if he were anywhere near the murder scenes at the times of the murders, the police were probably right to have pulled him in.

But that still left a big question unanswered in Oldman's mind.

What was a strange Garou doing walking the streets of San Francisco's Tenderloin area allowing himself to be caught by police?

Oldman had to know.

And so he waited.

As Oldman suspected, the Garou exited the police station a few hours later, looking up and down Stockton Street wondering which way he should go.

He finally headed south.

Oldman followed, a half block behind.

The Garou seemed tireless, walking blocks of the city without once stopping to rest. He seemed to be looking for something, peering into shop windows, sniffing at the air. It seemed to Oldman to be a futile search, but he was content to hang back and wait for the Garou to stop of his own accord.

And then he did.

The Garou stepped into a coffee shop on O'Farrell Street called The Princess Café, a shabby little place where hustlers sometimes hung out.

Oldman entered the shop a few minutes later. When he saw the Garou sitting by the window, he ordered a coffee and sat down across the table from him.

The Garou looked at Oldman angrily, as if he were trying to scare the priest away, but Oldman ignored the sneer and smiled.

"I'm familiar with most of the Garou in San Francisco," he said. "So I was quite surprised to see you in that line-up today."

The Garou's sneer vanished, replaced by a look of utter surprise. "You were there . . . at the police station?"

"Yes, and I told them I recognized none of the six men under the lights."

"Thank you . . . uh . . ."

"Oldman. Wendel Oldman. I'm of the Children of Gaia."

"Randy Internet, a Glass Walker from Philadelphia."

Oldman was impressed. Philadelphia was a long way

for a Glass Walker to come just to stroll the streets of the city. He must be here on very important business.

Oldman sipped his coffee. "Of course you don't have to tell me if you don't want to, but I'm curious as to what brings you to the City by the Bay."

"No, I don't mind telling you," said Internet. "As a matter of fact, perhaps you can help me."

"If it is within my power to help you, I will," promised Oldman.

"I'm here looking for a boy, a cub, named Leonard Gateway. He is the son of Roland Gateway, the Don of the Philadelphia Glass Walkers."

Oldman had heard of Roland Gateway. A very powerful and influential Garou, not only in his hometown of Philadelphia but throughout the United States.

Important business indeed.

"The boy went through his first change two weeks ago and was so frightened by it, he ran away."

"Surely, he had been warned . . ."

The Glass Walker shook his head. "The boy is fourteen. The change came early. His father had never told him about his true heritage, thinking he didn't need to burden the boy with the knowledge for at least two more years."

The change would have been a frightening experience the first time through, especially if it came without warning. Oldman could picture the boy, out on the streets, alone, afraid, vulnerable. But he still didn't understand why he was so far away from home. "And you think he traveled all the way to San Francisco from Philadelphia because of the change?"

"He has some friends in San Francisco he met last summer at camp. There was a good chance he was going to stay with them, but I've checked with their families and they haven't heard from him yet."

"Then how do you know he's here?"

"A plane ticket to San Francisco was charged to his father's credit card two days ago. The airline said he got off the plane, so at least I know he's somewhere in the city."

"I see," said Oldman. "Then I will do my best to help you find him."

"Thanks," Internet said.

They talked for a while longer, each of them ordering a second cup of coffee.

When Oldman finished his coffee he glanced at the clock. It was getting late, time for him to leave. But before he did, there was something he had to ask the Glass Walker.

"Tell me," he said. "How does a Garou, especially an obviously street-savvy Glass Walker like yourself, manage to get himself caught by police?"

Internet laughed. "Wrong place at the wrong time, I guess."

"Really?"

"I was just walking along the street, and from out of nowhere two police cars pulled up in front of me. Four cops jumped out with their guns pointed at me yelling 'Freeze!' Sure, I could have changed form and run, but there were too many of them to make a clean getaway. I've been shot before and it's pretty damn painful."

Oldman nodded. That made sense.

"Besides, I knew I hadn't done anything wrong, so I figured it would be easier to be taken in and let go, rather than put up a fight."

"You did the right thing," said Oldman.

"I must have," said Internet with a smile. "I met you because of it, and Gaia knows I could use a friend in this town."

"So could I," said Oldman.

The night was cool.

Holt was hot.

First, he covered himself with a blanket, then uncovered a leg to cool himself down. Finally, he pulled the blanket off and lay on the bed in his T-shirt and shorts.

There was something on his mind.

Something on it, over it, in it, and under it.

He hadn't felt like having sex for a long time, certainly not since he'd been attacked by the Garou that night in the alley. Even before the attack he hadn't felt much of an urge. Surviving had been the main thing. Making sure he had food to eat and a roof over his head had taken up all of his time. Sex was something people had on television or in the movies, a fantasy.

Of course, he'd *thought* about it often enough, but it had always seemed to be something unobtainable, like a new car in a dealer's showroom, or a home in the hills with a white picket fence.

But that was then.

When he was living on the street.

Before the mission.

Before he'd been given a new life.

Now it seemed possible. His body had completely

healed, and he was fed, clean, fit, and trim. Healthy. The necessities had been taken care of: he could indulge in this other part of life, a part that had been lost to him for so long.

If only he had a willing partner . . .

Being so close to Sylvia Wood Runner the last few days had brought his desire into even sharper focus. They were together constantly, conversing in a mixture of serious and playful talk, interspersed throughout with plenty of innuendo and double entendre.

She was a beautiful woman, slim and shapely, with warm dark eyes and an inviting smile.

She showed him that smile often.

Holt hoped it meant something, but knew he was falling victim to wishful thinking.

How could a woman so young and alive be without a mate?

He didn't know.

But he could ask.

Holt rolled off the bed and put on a pair of long pants before leaving the room. Maybe she's up, he thought. Then again, maybe not. Even if she's not I can still do with a walk. Clear my head.

He padded down the hall toward Sylvia's room. When he got there he saw that her door was slightly ajar. Perhaps it's meant to be that way, he thought.

An open invitation.

He stopped outside her door.

He could hear Silent-Fist-That-Wins snoring in the next room.

Apparently he isn't always so Silent.

Leaning forward ever so slightly, Holt pushed the door open with an index finger. When it was open wide enough, he poked his head into the room. Although it was dark, he could see that Sylvia wasn't there.

Maybe she can't sleep either, he thought hopefully. Maybe she's up and around too.

He walked down the hall and went outside.

But Sylvia was nowhere to be seen.

With just a partial moon overhead it was difficult to see much of the forest. After a few yards into the woods, the trees and branches overlapped to create an impenetrable black veil.

Holt walked into the center of the yard, sat down on a picnic table, and looked up. Oh well, he thought. At least the night sky was pretty to look at. It was filled with a thick mat of stars that seemed to cover the earth like a glitter dome. It was the kind of view that was almost impossible to see inside the city because of the light pollution created by streetlights and store signs close to the ground.

He got up from the table and lay down on top of it. From that position he opened his eyes and was able to see the stars without craning his neck.

It was a magnificent sight.

He watched and admired it, unblinking, for a long, long time.

The view had a calming effect on him. He became lost in the stars, forgetting all of the day's tensions that had been keeping him awake. When he finally felt himself starting to fall asleep, he gathered himself up off the table to head back to bed.

As he turned toward the bunkhouse he noticed something dark dart through the outer-right portion of his field of vision. He turned to look, but by the time he did, it had disappeared into the woods, leaving a telltale branch waving in its wake.

Holt watched the forest for a while, looking for another sign of movement, but there was none. Whatever it was, it had gone as quickly as it had come.

He turned to head back to bed.

"Holt, wait!"

It was the voice of Sylvia Wood Runner.

He spun around on his feet and looked for her.

But no one was there.

And then she suddenly appeared out of the forest, wearing a long white cotton nightgown that pressed against the front of her body like a second skin. Her long dark hair blew gently in the breeze.

"I was out for a walk," she said. "I saw you here and thought you might like to talk."

"Talking would be nice . . ." he said, his words already shifting into double entendre mode. "But there's something else that would be a lot nicer."

She came closer.

Holt could see the outline of her body more clearly now, almost in silhouette through the thin white fabric. Her breasts were small and round, her hips were slightly curved, and her legs were long and shapely.

"A beautiful night, isn't it?"

"The night isn't the only thing." He almost grimaced after that one. *Do I* have to be so obvious? *I* sound like a damn teenager.

Sylvia took the compliment in stride, accepting it with a smile. "What brings you out?"

"Couldn't sleep."

"Too much on your mind."

"No, only one thing."

She smiled. "Really, what's that?"

"You."

She laughed. "I'm flattered." She sat on the picnic table, her bare legs dangling freely from the edge. She had a cunningly playful look about her, as if she were teasing him. "What is it about me that you were thinking of?"

She was definitely leading him on now, pulling him toward her with every word and gesture. She put her arms behind her and leaned back, the nightgown falling softly against her body.

"I was thinking about you and wondering if you had a m—" He was about to say man, but managed to correct himself just in time. "M-mate?"

She was silent, and the night was filled with the sounds of crickets and rustling leaves.

Holt was sure he'd asked a stupid question, spoiled the mood between them.

"There are very few suitable mates for me at the ranch," she said with a breathy sigh of disappointment. "Because of the deformities and madness that affect the offspring, Garou are forbidden to mate with other Garou." She looked up at him. "We are required to find mates from either wolf or human society."

"What about Kinfolk . . . like me?"

"You are basically Garou, but since you are missing the gene which allows the change, you are physically human."

Holt's face lit up. "You mean . . ."

Sylvia moved forward, spreading her legs slightly and placing her hands down on the table between them. She looked at him coyly, tilting her head to one side and smiling.

She answered him by nodding.

Holt moved closer to her, until he was standing at the edge of the table, his mouth and lips inches from hers.

"It means," she whispered, "that you are the perfect mate for a love-starved Garou woman."

Holt had been hard for a while, but now he was aware of his manhood against the denim of his jeans.

She took her arms off the table, grabbed him by the waist, and pulled him closer.

Their lips came together, hot and moist. She opened her mouth and her tongue touched his, sending waves of electricity coursing through his body.

For the moment Holt forgot everything else in the world and let his body be consumed by his desire. His hands roamed her body, feeling the long smooth curve of her back and the roundness of her hips.

Her hands were busy too, raking the length of his back through the thin fabric of his T-shirt, then squeezing the firm flesh of his buttocks, pulling him closer still.

"Do you want me?" she said.

"Yes."

"Have you always wanted me?"

"Since I first laid eyes on you."

"And now that you have me, what are you going to do?"

"Make love to you."

"Is that all?"

Holt realized his mistake. He could feel her passion, it was primal, carnal. They would be doing more than simply making love. "I'm going to fuck you," he said.

"Yes," she said, fumbling with the waistband of his jeans. "Do it to me . . . fuck me!"

She had his pants free and was sliding her hand up and down the length of his shaft, squeezing it, pulling on it, helping it to grow stronger, harder.

After so long without the touch of a woman, Holt was afraid he was going to climax too soon, but something deep inside him took over, putting off the inevitable in order to allow her to share in his pleasure.

He pulled at her gown, lifted it up and over her head, and cast it onto the ground, not caring where it landed.

Her body was magnificent. Lean and muscular like a female bodybuilder's yet still quite feminine. Her breasts were firm, the nipples standing stiff and erect in the cool night air.

He pulled his lips away from her mouth, kissed his way down her arched neck, and finally took one of the stiff nubs of flesh into his mouth. Holt tasted the saltiness of her flesh and smelled the sweet scent of redwood and pine. As he kissed and sucked on her nipple, she moaned a soft growl.

Her hand was working him harder, stroking him, fondling him, as if she'd never let him go. It seemed like she wanted him somewhere other than in her hand.

Holt cupped Sylvia's breasts in his hands and stood up straight, allowing his full length to jut out from his body. She took firm hold of the base of his shaft and leaned forward, allowing her lips to slide over it, covering it like a warm velvet sheath.

Holt moaned long and loud. He thought he might disturb the rest of the compound but didn't care. He didn't care about anything right now except for her. He had to have her, totally.

He eased her back down on the table, watching her writhe slightly in anticipation. Then she spread her legs, eagerly exposing the darkly swollen flesh of her sex.

Holt leaned forward and kissed her there, nuzzling his mouth up against the downy softness. She bucked against his touch, inhaling a gasp.

Holt stood up and took hold of his shaft and guided the plump head inside her.

Sylvia moaned, wrapping her legs around his body and pulling him closer, pulling him further inside.

Holt eased himself into her, then began moving back and forth, slowly at first, then faster and faster.

Sylvia shrieked and locked her legs around him, squeezing Holt with all the strength of a vise.

Holt was thrusting with abandon now, but wanted Sylvia even closer to him, feeling her hands caressing his body, her lips on his.

He took hold of her midsection and lifted her up so that she was off the table and hanging on to his body with nothing but her arms, legs, and sex.

Holt could feel the muscles roiling beneath her skin and patches of fur bristling up from the surface. She was consumed by passion. Their climax was imminent.

She must have sensed it too because she suddenly whispered into his ear. "Wait . . . wait . . ."

He eased her gently back onto the table and withdrew himself from her.

While Holt waited, she got off the table, turned her back to him, and leaned forward, resting the upper part of her body on the tabletop. Then she raised her buttocks to him.

"Now, give it to me," she said. "All of it. Inside me!"

Holt guided the tip of his shaft into her, then pushed the entire length inside with one long thrust.

"Wild me!" she cried, matching each of his thrusts, forcing back her buttocks to meet him in a hard slap of flesh.

Holt felt himself moving faster and faster.

He could feel the muscles writhing under her skin, and the patches of wolfish fur rolling down the length of her back in rhythm to his thrusts.

Hard, black claws raked the top of the table, then dug into the wood, holding her firmly in place.

Holt was shocked by what he saw, but was far too consumed by passion to think about it for more than a second.

Finally, she let out a long, howling moan. The sound of it was unlike anything Holt had ever heard before.

It was animal, primal, basic.

And it caused him to climax in a hot burst of pleasure.

He growled deep and loud until he was spent.

This time he was sure he had awakened the entire compound, but was pleased by the fact that he still didn't care.

"That was incredible," he said, his body numb and weak.

He wanted to touch her, hold her, ask her about what had happened, but she moved away from him almost immediately after it was over.

And now that her primal need had been taken care of, she seemed as distant as she'd been during some of their early days together.

Holt didn't know what to make of it. He wondered if this was a Garou trait, the way they expressed affection and emotion, or something specific to Sylvia's character.

"*Shh*," she said, placing a finger to her lips. "It's late, you need your rest and now you can get it. You won't have any trouble sleeping now."

"Not much," said Holt a little sarcastically.

He watched her walk over and pick her gown up off the ground. She seemed comfortable without clothing, perhaps even preferred it that way.

She slipped her gown over her head. "Good night, Kenneth Holt," she said, heading toward the bunkhouse.

"Good night," he said.

"Tomorrow is another day . . ." She paused a moment, and smiled. "And another *night*."

The look on her face was unmistakable. There was something there between them, something other than just sex.

Holt returned her smile, breathing easier. Relax, he thought. Just relax, settle down, and take this new life of yours as it comes.

She blew him a kiss and slipped into the bunkhouse, leaving Holt alone in the midst of Gaia, his eyes filled by the canopy of stars overhead.

14

The next few days at the ranch were uneventful.

Although *Inside Affair* reporter Caroline Keegan was still in the area searching for the ranch, she was well south of both it and the Caern. And while she was still being closely watched by Uktena and Kinfolk, as long as she was headed in the wrong direction there seemed to be little reason to worry.

Things between Holt and Sylvia were also going well.

They had made love twice since that first night under the stars—once in Sylvia's bed in the bunkhouse, and again during the day in a grass-covered clearing in the woods.

They had become so close in such a short time, thought Holt as he lay in bed waiting for the day to begin. Perhaps they had even fallen in love. Holt sometimes got the feeling that things were happening way too fast, but realized he was making up for lost time, for all the years he'd spent aimlessly wandering the streets of San Francisco when his true home was miles away in the hills overlooking the Bay. If he was falling in love, then so be it. He was quite prepared to sit back and let nature . . . let Gaia take her course.

There was a knock on his door.

He rolled over onto his back. "Come in."

The door opened. Sylvia stood there dressed in a light-colored T-shirt, matching shorts, and sneakers. On a hanger in her right hand was a freshly pressed ranger's uniform.

"I didn't know your size so I had to guess," she said, smiling. "But, I think I'm familiar enough with your body to pick out a pretty good fit." She tossed the uniform onto Holt's bed. "Get dressed. Today we're going inside the Caern."

Sylvia turned and left the room.

Holt's smile slowly ebbed from his face as a sort of nervous tension coursed through his body.

The Caern.

The sacred place of the Garou. The place where Garou come into contact with the spirit world.

Holt took a deep breath, knowing full well what this meant.

He was about to be fully accepted into the Sept.

The morning was crisp and cool and made the walk through the Bawn almost effortless.

As they reached the innermost layer of the Bawn, Holt could feel there was something special about this part of the forest. His body hummed with energy, a mixture of excitement and uneasiness. Instinctively, he knew that the Caern was close at hand.

He scanned the forest, looking for an entrance or a path that might lead into it, but could see nothing. He wasn't surprised. Sylvia had said the paths leading to the Caern were well hidden, and that appeared to be true.

"Here we are," Sylvia said.

"We are?" asked Holt, looking around. "There's nothing about this spot that sets it apart from a hundred other spots."

"I know. That's why the Caern is so well hidden."

Holt continued to look around, shaking his head.

The harder he looked for something, the less he saw.

"This way," said Sylvia, drawing her finger through the air to mark an imaginary line on the forest floor.

And then Holt could see it, a slightly worn path on the grass. The slight gaps between the bushes were also obvious now too. He kept his eyes on the path, knowing that if he looked away, even for a moment, he would probably lose sight of it.

They'd been walking along the path for less than a minute when they came upon a huge boulder in their way. The trees and bushes were thick on either side of the boulder, forming a barrier that was difficult to penetrate. There appeared to be no way around the giant stone.

"Great, now what do we do?" asked Holt.

Sylvia turned to him. "This boulder is the 'main gate' to the Caern, and is *always* guarded by a Garou in a ranger uniform."

Holt looked around. "I don't see anyone."

Just then there was a rustling in the nearby bushes. Holt watched the movement, tracking its progress through the woods until a park ranger appeared from out of the forest. He was a large man, probably of Native American descent. There was a rifle slung over his left shoulder.

"Jimmy Stopheart," said Sylvia. "This is Kenneth Holt. A Kinfolk."

Stopheart nodded.

"Pleased to meet you," said Holt.

"Kinfolk patrol the outer layers of the Bawn," said Sylvia. "But the entrance to the Caern is always patrolled by a Garou in ranger uniform—twenty-four hours a day, three hundred and sixty-five days a year."

"So are you a real ranger?" asked Holt, suddenly feeling uncomfortable in his uniform. "Or like me, just dressed up to look like one?"

"I'm for real," said Stopheart, adjusting the gun on his shoulder. "But don't worry, we can use all the help we can get up here."

Holt felt slightly better.

"May we pass the gate and enter into the Caern?" asked Sylvia, her voice solemn.

"Yes, you may," answered Stopheart, stepping aside.

Sylvia approached the boulder, then turned around to face Holt. "The top of the boulder is not flat. It has a steep face and a sharp top edge. To enter the path that leads directly to the Caern you must jump completely over the boulder in a single bound. If you don't feel up to it, we can turn around and try it another day."

Holt looked at the boulder, judged its height to be about four and a half feet, and decided he could do it if Sylvia could. "Today will be fine," he said.

Sylvia smiled at Holt, then looked over at Stopheart and nodded.

Stopheart returned the gesture and disappeared into the woods, returning to his post.

Sylvia was first to make the leap. After a run of about ten yards she took off on her left foot and soared over the boulder, clearing it by a good three inches.

Holt suddenly wondered if he was up to it. But, after taking a few breaths to calm himself, he decided there was no backing out now. He took a few steps back and charged the boulder. Like Sylvia he took off on his left foot, but didn't have quite the height she'd had. He was forced to place his hands on the lip of the rock and vault over the top.

He landed on both feet, but stumbled and rolled to a stop.

"You made it?" Sylvia said, a slight hint of surprise in her voice.

"You mean you doubted me?"

"Well, it is a feat only the more athletic should consider trying, and with the injuries you've sustained in the last few weeks I wasn't sure you were physically up to it."

"I've been fine for a while now," he said. "What I don't understand is that you said the Caern is the final resting place of those too old to continue the journey. If they're so old, then how do they get over the boulder in one bound?"

"You're a good student, Kenneth. Either that or I am well suited to the position of Earth Guide. Yes, it would be a considerable jump for an elderly human. But the longer you live among Garou the easier you will remember that we are not bound to our Homid form. A jump like that would be little more than a child's leap over a puddle to a seven- or ten-foot Garou in the Crinos form."

"Of course," said Holt. "What was I thinking?"

Sylvia ignored the remark. "This way."

Holt followed her down a path, this one slightly more apparent than the one leading up to the boulder had been.

They came upon a grove of very old redwoods.

"You mentioned those too old to continue the journey. Well, this place is called The Graves of Hallowed Heroes. Those marks on the trees . . ." She pointed at some scratches in the trunks of the trees several feet off the ground.

"They look like old bear markings to me," said Holt.

"Those glyphs signify who is buried here. There are about twenty graves in all. Every spring equinox a special Rite of Remembrance is held here attended by the entire Sept. The Rite lasts for three days and is filled with contests and stories of fallen heroes so the younger members of the Sept can learn about their ancestors."

"I look forward to the spring then," said Holt.

"It is a joyous time."

They lingered in the grove a few more minutes, then moved on. After a short walk they came upon a clearing spanning twenty-five or thirty yards. In the middle of it was a circle of five redwoods.

Holt looked at the trees in awe. He'd seen taller trees in the forest, but none so perfectly placed.

"They are about eighty-five years old," Sylvia said, looking up at the treetops. "They were planted by the Children of Gaia when they assumed control of the Caern."

"But I thought your tribe, the Uktena, controlled the Caern?"

Sylvia sighed, as if the subject was one close to her heart. "This Caern has been here for a long time. . . ."

"It's a beautiful place."

"Its history is long and rich."

"I'd like to hear it sometime."

"I will tell it to you." Sylvia gestured for him to sit. "Right now."

Holt found a comfortable place on the ground—the student. Sylvia remained standing—the teacher.

She began the lesson.

"The Caern was created by an Uktena Garou named Hawk-Sees-the-Sun long before the white man came to California. He chose this spot because it was obvious to him that these majestic redwoods were sacred to Mother Earth.

"The Uktena tribe and their Kinfolk among the Ohlone Indians tended the Caern for centuries . . . there are even stories of meetings between Uktena and Sir Francis Drake when the explorer stopped near here in the winter of 1579.

"Then the white man began to arrive and the Uktena began casting powerful magics, the purpose of which is unknown. Most believe they were wards against the coming invaders, while some others believe they were divinations for the future. Whatever the reason they were cast, the magic went wrong . . . causing a great Cataclysm.

"About the Cataclysm itself I can't say much, and even if I could, you wouldn't understand. Suffice to say it caused a tremendous earthquake that forced coastal mountain ranges to break apart, creating San Francisco Bay and the Golden Gate, the strait which is now spanned by the famous bridge."

Holt's eyebrows arched in surprise. There was a lot more to this Garou culture than wolves and fangs.

"Our tribe has never divulged the nature of the Cataclysm, not even to the Children of Gaia within the Sept. Since we hold the Cataclysm at bay with secret rites and fetishes it is no concern of theirs."

She paused for a moment. "Do you understand so far?"

Holt felt awkward, like he sometimes had in school when everyone in the room except for him seemed to understand what the teacher was saying. He'd never asked a question then for fear of looking stupid or foolish. Ah, to hell with that, he thought. "No," he said. "I don't really get it all."

Sylvia looked at him, a look of understanding on her face. "Of course you don't, it's too much for you to comprehend all at once. All that is important for you to understand at this point is that this place, the Caern, is supremely important to the Garou."

"*That* I understand."

"Good." A pause. "Now, you asked me before about the Uktena controlling the Caern. The Uktena did control the Caern at one time, but there was a dark period in our history—from about 1750 to 1910—when the Uktena and their Kinfolk's hold on the Caern was severely weakened. Missionaries came, claiming souls. Farmers and ranchers came, claiming the land and hunting down the natives like animals. The Sept tried to defend and assist its people, but there just weren't enough Garou to stop the onslaught, especially when too much energy had been spent healing the damage done by the Cataclysm.

"The Uktena needed help.

"So, early in the nineteen hundreds the Sept held its final moot . . . a meeting where they invited the Children of Gaia to help them hold the Caern and maintain peace with the humans."

Holt nodded, beginning to understand a little more about the inner workings of Garou culture.

"It is an arrangement that has worked well for us," said Sylvia. "The Children of Gaia have worked within the system to protect the Caern, creating a network of environmentalists who managed to preserve much of California's wilderness and establish many parks . . ." She extended her arms and turned around appreciatively. "It was the influence of the Children of Gaia, as well as powerful Kinfolk like John Muir, that ensured that this Caern site remained protected.

"Today, Children of Gaia like Wendel Oldman provide us with numerous Kin to protect the Caern, leaving us Uktena free to concentrate on its spiritual affairs."

"I see," said Holt. "That's where I come into the picture."

"Yes."

Holt was silent, thinking back on everything that had been said. Finally, he spoke. "This Cataclysm you talked about . . . What is it?"

"I can't tell you," Sylvia said, a hint of an apologetic tone in her voice. "Uktena cannot share the secret with anyone outside the tribe."

"But it's a bad thing, right?"

"A very bad thing," she said. "If our hold on it was ever lost, it would mean the end of the world as we know it."

Holt exhaled a long sigh, then sat there saying nothing. He tried to think of the Caern in terms that he could understand, but for the moment he could only think of it as the rough equivalent to the Gates of Hell. That, or a neutron bomb—if it ever fell into the wrong hands it would mean the end of everything.

He shook his head. It was such a beautiful place, so calm and peaceful . . . A holy place. For a moment he imagined it gone and felt a deep and terrible loss. And then he knew that he must work like the others to preserve its sanctity.

"I'll do my best to protect it from our enemies," he said, rising up off the grass.

"Good," said Sylvia. "Then our purpose in life is one and the same."

Holt looked at her, not just at her face but deep into her eyes, and realized he'd just crossed another bridge into the world of the Garou.

Perhaps it was even the final one.

They came together in an embrace, remaining that way for a long, long time.

The boulder at the main gate to the Caern was easier to get over on the way out. Holt and Sylvia climbed up the sloping face and eased themselves down onto the path that would lead them away from the center of the Caern.

As they headed up the path, Holt looked around for Stopheart, but couldn't spot him in the dense mat of trees and bushes. Still, he knew the Garou was there, could feel him there, guarding the entrance to the Caern.

"Bye, Stopheart," said Holt.

He waited a second.

"Good-bye, Holt," came the reply. The voice sounded as if it was a few feet away, and Holt turned expecting to find Stopheart's face peering at him from somewhere deep in the bush. But still he could see no one.

"C'mon," Sylvia said. "It's time that we should be getting back."

Holt nodded and followed Sylvia up the path out of the inner layer of the Bawn. When they were in the second layer, Sylvia stopped abruptly, signaling Holt to do the same.

Holt stopped, unsure about what was going on, but knowing enough not to ask questions.

They stood there still and silent.

Off to the left was the sound of trees rustling, twigs snapping, and voices speaking in conversational tones.

Sylvia looked surprised at the sound. They were still too close to the Caern to come across the casual tourists, and Uktena and Kin wouldn't be so obvious in their travels through the woods.

The sounds grew louder and the movement amid the trees more pronounced.

And then, all of a sudden, there she was.

Caroline Keegan.

Holt was unsure about what to do in this situation. The last time their paths had crossed Sylvia had been dressed as the ranger and Holt was able to stand by and observe. But today he was the park ranger and Sylvia was the visitor. It would be up to him to scare the reporter off. It was a job he was totally unprepared for.

"Hello, ma'am," he said, trying to sound confident and in control. "Can I help you?"

"No, I don't think so."

"Ma'am, if you're in this part of the woods, you've

obviously lost your way on the trail. That's what happened to this young lady," he said, gesturing to Sylvia. "Perhaps it's best that I escort you all back to the posted paths."

Caroline Keegan stood her ground. She squinted her eyes, looking closely at Holt, then at Sylvia. "These woods are open to the public . . . I don't see any signs prohibiting access to this or any other area. I'm not moving."

The cameraman behind her took the camera off his shoulder and set it onto the ground.

Holt was at a loss as to what to say next. He was always able to solve a problem given enough time, but he was never very good at thinking fast. "There are no signs posted because the fire just started an hour ago and has already been contained. But there's still a danger of incidental fires starting up in the area so we're keeping it clear to let the firefighters do their job."

It was the best Holt could come up with under the circumstances. He looked at Sylvia, hoping for a nod of approval, but her face remained a blank. Obviously there were some problems with his story.

"What fire?" asked the reporter. "I don't see any smoke, I don't smell anything burning."

"The main fire is out now and—"

"And if firefighters are in the woods, why didn't we hear them driving through? Certainly they must have had their sirens going at some point during the drive in."

Holt looked to Sylvia for help.

"It's up over that ridge," she said. "It was burning real good for a half hour before the firemen put it out. There were ashes and cinders flying all over. Luckily the wind is blowing in the other direction now or this whole grove would have gone up in smoke by now."

Holt looked at Sylvia with a touch of admiration. She had spoken so well that he almost believed her.

Caroline Keegan, however, remained skeptical. She continued to look at Sylvia long after she'd finished talking.

"You," she said at last. Her right index finger shot up, pointing at Sylvia. "I've seen you before . . . in these woods."

"No, I don't think so," answered Sylvia.

"Yes," she paused, thinking. "I remember now. It was a couple of days ago, only you . . . were the park ranger." She looked at Holt. "And he was . . ."

"I'm sure all the rangers begin to look alike after a while—"

She cut him off. "You're part of it, aren't you—"

"Pardon me?" said Holt.

"This cult that's living up here in these woods. You're in on it too. The park rangers are helping to protect the cult from being discovered . . . which means I'm getting closer."

"I don't know what you're talking about ma'am, but the only thing you're close to right now is getting killed in a forest fire." Holt's voice had become surprisingly strong, commanding. "And if you don't move out of this area, I'm afraid I'm going to have to escort you out."

Just then several other rangers stepped onto the path. A few, like Jimmy Stopheart, held weapons in their hands.

"Oh, I'm leaving, all right," she said. "But I know you're hiding something here, something big. I can *feel* it. I'm leaving for now, but I'll be back, and I'll keep coming back until I find out what you people are hiding."

She turned around and pushed aside her cameraman as she made her way down the path on which she'd come. The cameraman panned the gathered rangers and then turned around, following Caroline Keegan out of the woods.

Several rangers followed the two down the path to make sure they didn't double back.

"I'm sorry," Holt said when the reporter and most of the rangers were out of sight.

"For what?" asked Sylvia.

"I don't think I handled that very well."

"Don't worry about it, Holt. There was nothing you could have said or done that would have changed what just happened here."

"What do you mean?"

"Well, most humans feel the forces present in the

Caern and that feeling is usually unsettling enough to keep them out of the area. It frightens them and makes them want to stay away. But this one, this reporter . . ." She shook her head. "Even though she said she *felt* something here, it seems to be drawing her closer instead of pushing her away. I guess you could call it news sense. . . . Whatever it is, it's probably one of the things that makes her such a good reporter."

"Do you think she's good?"

Sylvia looked at Holt a long time. "She is on the verge of discovering an entire society of werewolves secretly coexisting with human society. A story like that . . . provided she could get anyone to believe it, would rock the world. Whether she knows the magnitude of the story or not doesn't matter, she senses there's a story here somewhere and she's vowed to get it. That's her job and she's good at it, so yeah, I think she's a good reporter."

Holt was silent a moment. "What does that mean for us? For the Sept?" He paused. "And for the Caern?"

"It means we're in a shitload of trouble."

Father Oldman slipped into his pajamas in preparation for bed.

The day had been full of a dozen little problems, from a fight in the mess hall to an overflowing toilet plugged with paper. It was one of those days he was glad to see come to an end.

He pulled down the sheets and switched on the light on his night table, hoping that a half hour of light reading might help him fall asleep.

He had just lain back down on the bed and opened up his paperback when the phone rang.

Oldman got out of bed, trudged over to his desk, and picked it up. "Scott Mission, Father Oldman speaking."

"Oldman, this is Able Heart."

"Yes."

"I've just got off the phone with Celeste. We're calling an emergency meeting of the Sept for tomorrow afternoon."

"What's the problem?"

"A reporter," said Able Heart. "Caroline Keegan—"

"I understand," said Oldman.

"Good. Celeste is in the city right now, so I ask that you give her a ride."

"I will."

"You *and* Parker . . ."

"Parker?"

"Yes, this is a meeting of the entire Sept of the Western Eye. Celeste and I consider him to be as much a part of the Sept as anyone."

Oldman was silent for a moment. Non-Kinfolk like Parker had never been invited to a meeting of the Sept before. Apparently the problem was far more grave than he'd first thought.

"All right," he said. "*We'll* be there."

15

Parker was sitting in the mess hall eating a slice of toast and sipping his morning coffee when Oldman pulled up a chair next to him and sat down.

"Morning, Parker," said Oldman.

Parker turned around. "Morning, Father, sleep well?"

"Not really. I got a call late last night from Able Heart. There seems to be a problem near the ranch with that reporter Caroline Keegan."

"Oh?"

"He and Celeste have called a meeting of the Sept for later today, so I'll have to be heading up there soon."

"The car has been running well since Holt took a look at it. It should get you there without any problems."

"That's good."

"And things seem to be under control here, so if you want to stay up there overnight, even for a few days, I can handle things for you."

Oldman looked at his assistant and smiled. Such a good man, he deserves to be part of the Sept even if he isn't Kinfolk. "Able Heart was very specific in his instructions to me. He asked that I give Celeste a ride up from the city . . ." Oldman's voice trailed off, making the moment last.

"And?" asked Parker.

"He asked that you come along as well."

Parker was speechless, looking at Oldman for a long time. "Are you kidding?"

"No, he said that he and Celeste considered you to be part of the Sept and they *wanted* you to be there."

Parker cracked a smile and held it for a short time before it faded. "The problem must be serious."

"Apparently," said Oldman. "But don't think about that now. I know how much this means to you so just enjoy the moment."

"All right, I will." The smile returned to Parker's face.

"We'll be leaving around ten."

"I'll be ready."

"I'm sure you will be."

The car ran well, growling like a contented pup as it carried its three passengers across the Golden Gate Bridge heading out of San Francisco.

Oldman sat in the backseat catching glimpses of Parker's smiling face as he drove the car with Celeste Snowtop by his side. It was a proud moment for Parker, and for Oldman too—one of the few true rewards he'd had for running the mission all these years.

"I'm glad I'm making the trip with you, Celeste," Parker said as they exited the bridge and headed north on the Marin Peninsula. "I just hoped it would have been under better circumstances."

"That's all right, Preston. The Sept has had this kind of trouble before and I'm sure we'll have it again. The only difference this time is that this Caroline Keegan woman is a television personality, a celebrity, and that makes the situation a little more delicate. But it's still something I'm sure we can handle *peaceably* if we put our minds to it."

Oldman leaned forward and looked at Celeste. From the way she'd said *peaceably* it sounded as if she were prepared to handle the situation *forcibly* if she had to.

"And what if a peaceful resolution isn't possible, Celeste?" asked Oldman.

"If that's the case, there are members of the Sept who

could solve the problem quickly—once and for all." The interior of the car was silent for a few moments. "But that is what we're hoping to avoid by calling this meeting. Nobody wants anyone to get hurt if we can help it."

It wasn't like Celeste to consider violence as an option; the Children of Gaia were peacemakers, not savages. But Celeste was leader of the Sept and as such was bound to consider *all* her options.

Oldman leaned back in his seat and watched the trees flow past; his mind was suddenly busy trying to think of a way to save Caroline Keegan's life.

Parker kept his eyes fixed on the road, saying nothing.

Oldman wondered if he was thinking about the very same thing.

As they neared the ranch, Oldman looked longingly at the great redwoods on either side of the road. After running the mission for so long, he'd come to have an even greater appreciation for the majesty and glory of the Wyld.

"It's beautiful up here," he said, not caring if anyone heard him.

"John Muir did well to save these woods from the axe," said Celeste. "We can only hope we can do as well to preserve it for the human and Garou generations to come."

Parker drove the car into the clearing where several other cars were already parked. Garou and Kinfolk Sept members from throughout the Bay Area had already begun to gather for the meeting.

After shutting down the car, Parker ran around to the other side to open the door for Celeste. She was getting on in years and was said to be looking for someone to take over her position. As Parker helped her out of the car, a crowd of Garou gathered close by to welcome her to the ranch. Hot Eye was there, as well as Tim Rowantree, Sharon Morning Cloud, and March Lion.

As Celeste was greeted by the group, Oldman got out of the backseat to little fanfare. As he looked up to say hello to the other Garou, he saw them walking away from him, escorting Celeste into the meeting hall.

"She's the leader of the Sept," said Parker. "You've got to expect her to get a little star treatment."

"I know," Oldman said, smiling. "But I come up here so seldom, it would be nice if someone said hello."

"Hello," said a voice.

Oldman turned around. Kenneth Holt stood there, a strong young man looking fit enough to take on the world.

"Well, look at you," said Oldman. "The ranch certainly agrees with you. I can't believe how much you've changed . . ."

"It's like you're a whole different person," said Parker.

"Thanks," said Holt, seemingly humbled by the compliments. "It's nice up here. I like it."

"Care to show me around?" asked Parker.

Holt looked at him a moment, then turned to Oldman.

"Able Heart and Celeste Snowtop have asked that he attend today's meeting. . . . They've allowed him into the Sept."

Holt smiled, knowing what this meant to Parker. "That's great," he said. "I'm new here myself, but I'd be honored to show you around."

"Let's go," said Parker.

Oldman watched the two men walk away, Holt's arm around Parker's shoulder as if they were brothers.

And his heart filled with pride.

The trip up here was already doing him some good.

It was late in the afternoon, and the woods were beginning to fill with long shadows and darkness.

Father Oldman walked slowly between the trees, drinking in the surroundings, feeling Gaia give under the weight of his feet, feeling the branches bending to let him pass. The air was clean and fresh, smelling of wood and grass, earth and rain.

It was walks like these Oldman missed most living in the city. While the work that he did was necessary to the Sept and gave him satisfaction, it was the feel of Gaia under his feet and against his skin that gave him the greatest amount of pleasure. For here Gaia was still strong and powerful, wild and untamed. Just being here in these woods gave him a feeling of strength as a sort of revitalizing energy coursed through his veins.

He continued walking for several minutes, then stopped dead in his tracks.

A large gray-white timber wolf stood in the path, its teeth bared and its body tensed to jump.

Oldman did not move.

Neither did the wolf.

They remained that way for several long seconds, neither willing to make the first move.

Finally Oldman crouched down on one knee and held out his hand.

The wolf slowly came forward, sniffing first at the air, then at Oldman's outstretched hand.

Oldman remained still as the wolf continued to sniff at his hand. Only when the wolf began to lick at his fingers did he move, grabbing the wolf by the scruff of its neck and playfully kneading his fingers into the thick coarse fur.

The wolf leapt up, putting its forepaws on Oldman's shoulders. It opened its maw then too, making soft growling sounds like a dog might make chewing on a meaty new bone.

Finally the wolf bowled Oldman over and they rolled around on the ground, two friends at play.

The meeting hall was full of people, the air warm and heavy with the scent of bodies. Practically every member of the Sept had shown up for the meeting, bringing together the Uktena and Children of Gaia of Homid and Lupus background as well as their Kinfolk for a gathering that was truly unique. Despite the urgency that prompted the meeting, the room was filled with something akin to a party atmosphere.

Parker and Oldman stood silently by in a far corner of the room, Parker content just to be present for the proceedings and Oldman knowing that the matters concerning the Caern were best taken care of by those whose job it was to do so. Oldman would have little to say on the

matter, but his presence, like Parker's, was necessary
should a vote need to be taken.

Just before the meeting was scheduled to start,
Oldman saw Holt enter the hall. He took a seat near the
back, but his Earth Guide, Sylvia Wood Runner, grabbed
his hand and led him closer to the front.

Oldman beamed with pride at the sight. Holt was
being assimilated into the Sept faster and more easily
than he'd ever thought possible.

A few minutes later a door at the side of the hall
opened up and Celeste Snowtop entered, followed by
Able Heart, Hot Eye, and Tim Rowantree. They stepped
up onto an elevated platform—something used out of
necessity rather than for pomp or ceremony—and took
their places behind a table.

Moments later the room fell silent as Celeste moved
to the front of the platform.

"First of all, let me say that despite the nature of this
meeting, it is wonderful to see so many members of the
Sept in one place at one time. Welcome all."

There was a small amount of applause, but it died out
quickly as people realized there was no time or reason to
cheer.

"Now, no doubt all of you are somewhat familiar with
what is going on near the Caern, but before we can discuss the matter I would like to call on Guardian Tim
Rowantree to give us a full explanation of recent events."

Celeste returned to her chair.

Rowantree got up from his.

The room remained silent.

"About a week ago a television reporter named
Caroline Keegan approached Wendel Oldman in San
Francisco to ask about his credentials as a priest and
about the nature of our business here at the ranch.
When Oldman told her nothing, she began to suspect
that this ranch was operating as some sort of cult."

A slight wave of laughter washed over the room.

"Of course this was bad for us. After what happened in
Waco, Texas, any mention of the word 'cult' sets off alarm

bells in people's minds, and that's doubly true for reporters. A couple of days after her meeting with Oldman, Caroline Keegan was up in the Muir Woods. While she was looking for the ranch, she did come close to the Caern. She was turned back, but vowed to return. Sure enough, she was caught even closer to the Caern yesterday. We turned her back again, but she is persistent and *will* be back, perhaps even with authorities.

"Although she doesn't quite know what she's looking for, I believe she will not stop looking for it until she finds something. That means she will eventually find the Caern and do her best to divulge the secret of our existence to the rest of the world.

"Obviously, she must be stopped."

Oldman listened in silence. He knew what was going on, and had even suspected as much would happen when he first met Caroline Keegan at the mission. He'd tried to warn her, but anything more than the little he'd said would have been taken as a death threat, which would mean more trouble for Oldman than it was worth.

Others in the crowd who were hearing this story for the first time weren't taking it so well. Oldman could feel the powerful undercurrent of rage flowing through the room.

Having finished talking, Rowantree returned to his seat. His place at the edge of the platform was taken by Able Heart, who would be conducting the next part of the meeting.

Before he spoke he unstrapped the klaive from his back. It was a two-handed curved weapon made of silver with matching leather handles. He held it casually in front of him, his symbol of strength and power, and used it to bring the room to order by banging it hard onto the floor of the platform.

"All right, now," he said, holding the klaive waist-high with both hands. "The reason we called you all here tonight is to help us decide the best way to handle Ms. Caroline Keegan." A pause. "We'll take a few minutes before we entertain suggestions. . . . And might I remind you that this is a very serious matter and we'd appreciate it if you make your suggestions accordingly."

Able Heart sat down, and the room erupted in a dozen simultaneous conversations, some of them quite heated.

Parker turned to Oldman. "So, Father. What do you think?"

Oldman looked down, his eyes sweeping the floor. "I think . . ." he said, his voice sounding like a heavy sigh, "that Caroline Keegan is a dead woman."

The blood suddenly drained from Parker's face, and his skin looked a deathly shade of white. "Do you really think so?"

"My head tells me that this will be the case, but my heart hopes that we will be strong enough to find another alternative."

Parker nodded. "I hope so too."

Able Heart rose from his chair and the room fell silent once more.

The rage filling the room was stronger than ever.

"Now that we've all had a chance to consider the problem, I'd like to begin hearing some suggestions."

A dozen arms shot up into the air, each one of them standing straight and unwavering.

Able Heart looked over the crowd to make sure he would be entertaining suggestions from younger members of the Sept first in order to give older Garou the chance to have the last word.

At last he pointed the sharp end of his klaive at a young woman in the center of the room. "Yes, Brings-Green-To-Grass."

Brings-Green-To-Grass was an Uktena who worked as a clerk in the park office.

"Perhaps we could do nothing . . ."

There was an immediate outcry from the rest of the crowd.

Able Heart stamped his klaive onto the floor of the platform until silence was restored. "Let her speak," he said. "And I promise all will have a chance to voice their opinions."

The crowd settled down.

Able Heart nodded to Brings-Green-To-Grass to continue.

"Like I said, perhaps we could do nothing. . . ." She paused as if expecting a similar outcry. When there was none she continued. "Television reporters are busy, well-paid people. She can't possibly remain here much longer without a story. If we keep repelling her she will eventually move on to another story somewhere else."

Able Heart was silent for a few moments. "Although Rowantree mentioned her persistence and her avowal to learn our secret, we will consider your suggestion."

Brings-Green-To-Grass turned to look at those around her, a proud smile on her face.

"Someone else?"

Eight hands rose up above the heads of the crowd, one taller than all the rest.

"William Skytoucher," said Able Heart.

William Skytoucher was a tall and lanky Garou of the Children of Gaia. He worked at a filling station at the entrance to the park and played an important part in monitoring who entered and left the park and when.

"We could make sure she was without her camera and then isolate her in the park, preferably late at night. Then several of us could appear before her in Crinos form, ensuring that she went mad from The Delirium. That would not only scare her off, but would also make her forget all about the cult she *thought* was up here."

Heads in the crowd began bobbing up and down in agreement. It really was a good plan, thought Oldman. The Delirium was a powerful weapon and would prove effective on a number of levels—including making her story so outlandish that no one would ever believe her. It wasn't surprising that Skytoucher had suggested it. The Garou was said to have ventured into Sausalito on occasion to scare tourists in the middle of the night. Oldman tried to picture Skytoucher in his eleven-foot Crinos form jumping out from darkened alleys and howling "boo," but it was just to comical for him to envision.

"Very good, Skytoucher," said Able Heart. "We shall consider your suggestion. Anybody else?"

No more than three hands went up.

"Yes, Adam Stargazer," Able Heart said. "What have you to say?"

Adam Stargazer was an old Garou who, as his name suggested, had spent much of his life studying the stars. He was small, just over five feet tall, and frail. But he was as wise as he was old—a Garou whose words were never meant to be taken lightly.

The room fell silent, and he began to speak, carefully measuring each of his words.

"With all due respect to those who have spoken before me . . ." he said in a gravel-throated voice. "I think none of the suggestions we have heard have addressed the root of the problem. . . . Caroline Keegan is a human who likes . . . correction, whose job it is to poke her nose where it doesn't belong. . . . Hoping that she goes away, and scaring her off aren't satisfactory solutions because they aren't permanent."

"Yes!"

"Here, here," others said in support.

"The only way to deal with a problem like Caroline Keegan . . ." Stargazer continued. "Is to get rid of it. . . . And that means getting rid of her."

More and more of the people in the crowd threw their support to Adam Stargazer. If order wasn't restored soon, the gathered Garou might storm out of the hall, track down Caroline Keegan, and kill her in cold blood wherever they found her.

"Settle down," shouted Able Heart. "Settle down!" He pounded his klaive against the platform for several beats until the mood in the room had calmed. "This Sept has never accomplished anything by acting without thought. Stargazer's suggestion will be considered and voted upon like the others."

Stargazer waved his knotty, twisted walking stick in the air, helping to restore silence, then resumed speaking.

"I'd like to add something . . ." he said. "Her death need not be violent or cruel. . . . It can just as easily be painless as filled with agony. . . . And . . . it could be made to appear to be the work of a bear or mountain lion . . . giving the area comprising the Bawn a reputation for being a dangerous place . . . and helping to ensure that future visitors stay well away."

Able Heart nodded to Stargazer. "Thank you, we will consider it."

Oldman thought about it a moment. While no one really wanted to kill the human, Stargazer's suggestion seemed to make the most sense of all. Unless she were dead there was no guarantee that she wouldn't be snooping around in another month or two. And if her death was made to look like the work of a wild animal, it would likely keep people out of that area of the park.

Oldman decided he'd vote for that suggestion when the time came. He looked over at Parker, wondering how he would vote. He was about to ask him, but decided against it in case their talk might change Parker's mind. He was a full member of the Sept now, thought Oldman. He can make up his own mind.

Able Heart scanned the group slowly. There were three suggestions to be considered. There didn't seem to be any more need for discussion, but he asked if there were any more suggestions as a matter of course.

"Anyone else?" he said, then quickly turned away to prepare for the vote.

A lone hand rose up over the crowd.

Oldman craned his neck to see who it was and was surprised to find that it was . . .

Kenneth Holt.

Celeste Snowtop gestured to Able Heart that some-one wished to speak, and the Warder turned back around and pointed his klaive at Holt.

Holt stood up, visibly shaking under the scrutiny of the entire Sept.

"I, uh . . . "

"Speak up!" said Able Heart.

Holt cleared his throat and turned around to face the group. "I think, uh, our take on the situation is wrong."

Several people gasped, no doubt at the audacity of the new member.

"All we've been talking about is how to eliminate the

problem of Caroline Keegan, but there would be a lot more to be gained by turning what is currently a negative into a positive."

"The Moon-Calf suffers The Delirium. . . ."

"He's in the Thrall of The Wyrm. . . ." came the mumbled words of the group.

"Silence!" ordered Able Heart. "Kenneth Holt is a member of this Sept and has as much right to be heard as anyone." He looked at Holt. "Go on."

Holt nodded thanks to Able Heart. "Television reporters are powerful people in today's society. Their words reach millions of people in the blink of an eye. Just think what a television reporter like Caroline Keegan could do in the fight against The Wyrm, or for the preservation of Gaia, if she were only befriended and became an ally of the Sept."

The room was filled with an excited buzz.

Oldman sat up in his seat, eager to hear more.

"Caroline Keegan wants to know what's going on here at the ranch, and she wants to know what we're hiding inside the Caern. Well, instead of killing her, I propose that we show her. We can give her a tour of the ranch, take her inside the Caern, and explain to her who we are and what that place means to our kind. Then . . . if she remains unconvinced about who we are, or she still wants to divulge our secret to the rest of the world, we can make her insane with The Delirium or even kill her. . . . At least then she will have played a small part in deciding her own fate."

The room was silent a moment, then broke into applause.

"Despite the fact that it goes against The Ways by bringing a non-Kinfolk inside the Caern," said Able Heart, "your suggestion is a good one. One which I recommend to the members of the Sept."

Able Heart turned around to consult with Celeste Snowtop, then returned to face the gathering.

"We shall put it to a vote. First, all those in favor of Kenneth Holt's suggestion to try and befriend Caroline Keegan, raise your hands."

Roughly a third of the hands in the room went up.

"Perhaps I should rephrase the suggestion," said Able Heart. "All those in favor of eliminating Caroline Keegan"—he gave a respectful nod to Adam Stargazer—"should an attempt to befriend her fail, raise your hand."

Everyone in the room raised their right hand, including Oldman, Parker, and Adam Stargazer.

"Very well, then, it's agreed that that is what we shall do. We will begin making plans upon the conclusion of this meeting."

People began shifting in their seats and getting up to stretch, but before the assembly was too broken up, Celeste Snowtop stood and stepped up to the front of the platform.

Seeing their leader standing before them, the members of the Sept returned to their seats and sat quietly in expectation.

"Before we go our separate ways, I'd like to formally express appreciation to one of our members on behalf of the Sept. This Garou has worked tirelessly over the past six years to rehabilitate humans and give them a new lease on life. Several Sept members here tonight and countless other Kinfolk and non-Kinfolk alike who work to help protect the Sept from its enemies owe their very lives to the work being done by this Garou. And while the rewards bestowed upon him have been few and far between, we would like to rectify that here tonight before the largest gathering of the Sept in many years."

Oldman felt his face get hot.

He looked to Parker and suddenly realized why his presence had been requested.

"Wendel Oldman, we sing your praise."

The gathering rose up from their seats as one and turned to face him. Obviously no one there had any trouble bestowing this honor upon Oldman.

Celeste began the howling Hymn of Praise, and was quickly joined by the others in the group.

Oldman felt his heart gather up in his throat. He'd always thought that his work at the mission had gone unnoticed within the Sept. Now, the sudden recognition of his work as being invaluable to the group was touching. He held back the tears for a while before one slipped through the net, leaking out of the far corner of his right eye.

In addition to the gratification brought by the Hymn of Praise, there was also a political matter to be considered. The Hymn of Praise gave Oldman a certain amount of renown within the Sept, paving the way for him to move up within its ranks. Oldman had never been all that ambitious in regards to the Sept, but now it was definitely something to think about.

When the Hymn of Praise ended, dozens of Garou and Kinfolk came by to congratulate Oldman on the honor and thank him for the job he'd done for the Sept.

Finally Holt came over to speak with Oldman.

"Congratulations," said Holt. "From what I've been told the Hymn of Praise is quite an honor."

Oldman nodded, finding it more awkward to receive such an accolade than he'd thought. "I was just doing my job."

"Well, speaking as one of those in attendance who owes his life to you, the honor couldn't have been bestowed on a more worthy recipient."

Oldman smiled. "Thanks," he said. "And what about you? That was a great suggestion you made. I have to admit I would have been a little nervous about making it had I been in your shoes."

"I know I would've been too scared to," commented Parker, who was standing by Oldman's side.

"Well, I figured someone's life was at stake. It was the least I could do."

"You've done well," said Oldman.

"I've had good teachers," said Holt.

They made small talk for another minute or so before Sylvia Wood Runner joined them.

"Excuse me, Wendel," she said, then turned to face Holt. "Celeste, Able Heart, and some of the others want to speak with you about your plan," she said. "Now."

Holt looked at Parker and Oldman in turn. "If you'll excuse me, I think I've just suggested myself into a whole lot of work."

16

Despite there being no shortage of volunteers for the job, it was decided that Holt and Sylvia Wood Runner would be the ones to escort Caroline Keegan inside the Caern. Holt had never imagined that he'd be the one to implement his suggestion, but he was more than eager to start doing his part for the Garou.

Caroline Keegan and her cameraman had been under constant surveillance for days. This morning she was being watched by a half-dozen Uktena, each in contact with the others by radio.

When she entered the Bawn, the Uktena formed a loose circle around her, keeping their distance and remaining hidden from sight. They also contacted the ranch, informing Holt and Sylvia of the reporter's progress.

"All right," said Holt. "This is it."

"Before we head out," said Sylvia, "I just want to remind you that if this doesn't work she was probably going to be killed anyway. Her death won't be on your hands. You're giving her a chance . . . no one else was willing to do that."

Holt nodded. "Thanks. Try and remember to tell *her* that if and when the time comes."

"I will."

They set out from the ranch dressed in light clothes and hiking boots, which allowed them to move quickly through the woods. Holt carried a rolled piece of paper in his hand tied with a bright red ribbon.

After a few minutes they entered the Bawn, then came upon a Uktena member forming part of the loose circle surrounding the reporter.

"Raven Head!" Sylvia said softly, recognizing the Garou by his long thick mane of black hair.

Raven Head turned around and placed a finger to his lips. He pointed in the direction of Caroline Keegan.

Holt nodded.

They moved north in a wide arc bringing them to the top of the circle. They waited there for the Uktena. In a few minutes Tim Rowantree appeared out the woods, coming toward them.

"They are about fifty yards behind me," Rowantree said.

"Good," said Holt. He stepped past Rowantree and entered the circle, leaving Sylvia behind.

Trying to be as silent as possible, he ran through the forest toward the reporter. When he saw her through the trees, he noticed she was walking ahead of her camera-man, who was several yards behind her, struggling to carry his heavy equipment through the woods.

"Perfect," Holt mumbled softly under his breath.

He maneuvered slightly to the left so that he was directly in her path, then tied the roll of paper to a branch so it hung down in the middle of the trees. He stayed there for a few more seconds to make sure that she'd seen it, then darted off into the woods before she could spot him.

Caroline Keegan's feet ached. So did her legs. In fact just about every part of her body was sore. She'd started on this trek into the woods with visions of a half-dozen different awards dancing about in her head. Now she dreamed of an easy celebrity interview by the poolside of some Vegas hotel.

She would have given up the ghost days ago if it hadn't been for the strange, creepy feeling she got whenever she came near a certain part of the woods. There was nothing visibly different in the trees or bushes, but there was definitely *something* there, and it made her anxious to find it. There was a big story in these woods, and if someone was going to report on it, Caroline Keegan was going to make sure that she was the one to do it.

She stopped a moment to rest and turned around to check on the progress of her cameraman, John Tersigni. Apparently he had fallen behind . . . again. As she waited for him to catch up, she realized her search must be doubly hard on him, carrying that heavy equipment through the forest day after day.

She decided then and there to give up this wild-goose chase and head back into San Francisco after dinner.

She turned back around and saw something hanging from the trees. It looked like a roll of paper tied to the tree by a bright red ribbon. Obviously it had been put there for her to find, but by whom? She looked through the forest and saw no one. She hadn't heard anyone either, which was surprising since the paper was hanging from a tree less than ten yards away. The thought of someone being that close without her knowing it sent a chill down her spine.

She moved toward the roll of paper, untied it from the tree, opened it up, and read it.

MEET ME HERE
AFTER DARK
ALONE

Suddenly all of her body's aches and pains were forgotten as she became filled with a powerful and intoxicating rush of adrenaline, the kind of thing she usually experienced only while reporting on a major fire or earthquake.

This story was hot again.

And it was hers, all hers.

Sure it would be dangerous, but even so, she didn't have to think about it twice.

She'd come back after dark.

Alone.

She heard something rustling through the woods behind her. Her cameraman. Quickly, she folded the paper into quarters and slid it into her pocket, leaving the ribbon wrapped around the fingers of her right hand.

"Don't bother waiting up for me," he said between tired gasps. "I can carry this camera up and down these hills all day long. . . . So what if we don't actually film anything." The sarcasm in his voice was unmistakable.

He set the camera down and placed his hands on his hips. He stood there for a few minutes catching his breath.

"You're right, John. I'm sorry I've put you through this." The cool tone of her voice betrayed little of her excitement. "We've been through these woods so many times I'm not even sure that we haven't walked this path already."

"No, no, no," he said, waving his hands in the air. "This path is different from the rest of them. This one has *big* trees. . . ."

"Okay, okay, you win. Let's call it quits for today. You enjoy yourself tonight. If I don't come up with anything by tomorrow, we'll head back to San Francisco tomorrow evening."

He was silent for a moment. "Are you sure? The last time I spoke to Sam he seemed pretty set on getting this story. I know I'm complaining a little, but I'll keep looking with you if you want. I'm racking up all kinds of overtime up here."

"No, I've had enough. Let's go back to the motel and have some lunch. I'll buy."

"All right," he said a little reluctantly. "I can't argue with that."

They turned around and headed back in the direction they'd come, out of the woods and toward the road.

After a few minutes on the path, Tersigni spoke. "Hey, what's that ribbon you got there?"

Caroline looked at her hand, saw the ribbon wrapped

around her fingers, and realized how noticeable its color was against the backdrop of leaf greens, red wood, and brown earth. She had to think fast.

"Oh, this?" she said, waving her hand in the air nonchalantly. "It's a little something to remind me to buy you a big draft to wash down your lunch."

"Well, all right," he said, a slight spring finding its way into his step.

It was just beginning to get dark out. The night sky was clear, the air cool and fresh.

Oldman stepped out of the meeting hall and onto the porch. Parker was sitting there reading a paperback. "It's beautiful up here, isn't it, Parker?"

"It sure is," said Parker. "I'm glad we were able to stay the night. It's good to get out of the city."

Oldman walked to the edge of the porch, took a deep breath, and rubbed his palms over his chest and stomach. "I think I'll go for a walk," he said. "Don't wait up."

"Don't worry, I won't."

Oldman stepped off the porch and walked through the yard. He stepped into the forest, shrouded on all sides by darkness and the faint glow of moonlight.

As he walked along a path he undid his shirt, took it off, and hung it on the branch of a tree on the edge of a small clearing. He took off his pants as well, laying them neatly over the branch. He stuffed his socks inside his shoes, then tied the laces together so they hung on the branch, keeping his clothes from blowing away in the breeze.

He stood there for several moments . . . naked.

He arched his back, raised his head, and let out a long high-pitched howl that was somewhere between The Call to Hunt and the Anthem of War.

When he finished, he waited.

A pair of glowing yellow eyes appeared in the bushes nearby, then another, and another.

The first wolf stepped into the clearing, moving toward Oldman with a cautious gait.

When the wolf was close enough, Oldman extended his hand.

The wolf sniffed the hand, then continued sniffing his leg and groin. And then the wolf suddenly reared up on its hind legs and put its front paws affectionately on Oldman's chest. The wolf howled loudly, duplicating the call Oldman had made just minutes before.

The rest of the pack stepped into the clearing, playfully rearing up on their hind legs and leaping a few feet in the air. As the wolves came down on all fours, they would playfully nip at the heels of other wolves in front of them, sending them jumping into the air.

Oldman bent over with his hands out and began the change, spending a few seconds in the Glabro, Crinos, and Hispo forms until finally settling into the majestic Lupus form of the wolf.

Oldman was a beautiful wolf with a distinctive streak of white running up from his muzzle, over his head, and down the thick fur of his back where it faded into a coat of light gray.

He howled once, telling them he was ready.

The leader, a huge white wolf with a large head and powerful muzzle, howled a variation on the Anthem of War and bounded into the brush.

The rest of the pack followed . . . including the large white-streaked wolf that was Oldman.

Running through the forest and into the night.

17

Holt and Sylvia Wood Runner remained at the ranch until the night's darkness was total. As they stepped out of the bunkhouse, Holt looked up at the slight sliver of moon cutting through the fabric of the night like a curved blade. Good, he thought. It will give us just enough light to find our way, and the faint glow will make the Caern look spookier than hell.

They headed into the woods, their route dotted with Uktena who were guarding it to ensure nothing would interfere with the smooth undertaking of the night's operation.

When they neared the designated meeting place, they were greeted by Tim Rowantree, who had a rifle over one shoulder, a radio over the other.

"She's been waiting there for about five minutes now," said Rowantree, matter-of-factly.

"Is she alone?" Sylvia asked.

"As far as we can tell she is. We tracked her in from well outside the Bawn and there was no sign of the cameraman. I think he's spending the night in town."

"That's good," said Sylvia.

"Perhaps she can be trusted, then," Holt said hopefully.

Sylvia and Rowantree looked at him as if he'd just said something stupid.

"Okay, okay, so I'm being a little too optimistic," said Holt. "Let's get going."

They left Rowantree behind and moved closer to the meeting place. When they had Caroline Keegan in sight, they stopped one last time.

"If you want to call it off," said Sylvia, "this is the time to do it."

Holt just looked at her. "You know I couldn't call it off now, even if I wanted to."

"Yeah, I know. I was just asking."

"All right, then. Let's go."

They turned toward Caroline Keegan and stepped into the clearing.

When the reporter saw them, she let out a gasp, but quickly recovered from the sudden loss of composure by crossing her arms over her chest in a dramatic fashion.

"Caroline Keegan?" asked Sylvia.

"You were expecting someone else?"

"Very funny," said Holt, his voice as deadly serious as he could make it. "This is Sylvia Wood Runner, and I am Kenneth Holt."

"Pleased to meet you," she said a little sarcastically, having already met up with them twice before.

"You wanted to know what we are hiding here in these woods," continued Holt. "Tonight, we are going to show you."

"What about cameras?" Caroline asked, waving an 8mm palmcorder in her hand.

"No cameras!" said Holt.

"Forget it, then. I'm a television reporter. There's no story for me without any pictures." She spun around on her heels and began to walk away.

Holt looked at Sylvia as if to ask her what he should say next, but her face was just as blank as his was. "Wait!" he said, giving himself an extra few moments to think.

"We'll show you what's here tonight. If you still want

to report on the story, we'll let you come back tomorrow with your cameraman."

Sylvia looked at him.

He gestured to her that it was all right, that he knew what he was doing. . . . So what if he didn't? What did it matter? He could promise her anything right now. If she still wanted the story tomorrow, the others would see to it that she wasn't alive to get it.

Caroline Keegan stopped, then slowly turned around. "How can I know you're telling me the truth?"

"You can't," said Holt. "You'll just have to trust us."

She hesitated on the path, then slowly came toward them.

Holt looked at Sylvia with a slight smile. "So far so good," he muttered under his breath.

Sylvia didn't answer.

It was a pleasure to run.

It was a special pleasure to see Gaia from a few feet off the ground, from the unique vantage point of the wolf.

Oldman ran with mad abandon, the rage built up from months of city life ebbing from his body with each powerful bound. But while his body dispensed with its rage, it was similarly filled with another feeling.

Hunger.

It wasn't enough for Oldman just to run with the wolves. He wanted to hunt with them too. He wanted to feel his fangs sinking into hot red flesh, to feel his teeth tearing at fresh meat, to feel his jaws snapping bone.

He let out a howl to let his feeling be known to the others. The cry was answered by a chorus of similar howls. Apparently the majority of the pack was feeling the same way.

Six wolves remained on the hunt.

They were led down to a meadow and ran across it. When they came upon a fence, the leader of the pack hunched down and crawled beneath the bottommost wire, then lifted it up with his back, allowing the rest to run under it unhindered. When all were through, the wolf hunched down once more and crawled forward.

They were inside the fence now, six wolves . . .

And a dozen cows.

The white wolf, the leader of the pack, howled a short Call to Hunt, advising the pack that they were to only take down a single cow. When the howl ended, the leader set off at a half-run, chasing the cows in a long circle around the edge of the enclosure.

Waiting . . .

Until one of them fell behind. The wolves continued the chase for a while longer until it was obvious that they'd isolated the weakest cow from the rest of the herd.

The leader was first to attack, leaping high up on the cow's throat, clamping its jaws into the meaty flesh and hanging on for a second before falling away with a piece of meat still clenched firmly between its teeth.

When the white wolf fell away, the cow overbalanced and stumbled. It seemed to lie on its side for the longest time, trying to get up before the second wolf dove in on its haunches. The cow let out a scream before a third, then fourth wolf descended upon its body.

Oldman was the last wolf on the cow, sinking his fangs into the meaty part of the animal's back. As he bit into the flesh, he felt hot blood spurt into his mouth, sending him into a frenzy. He jerked his muzzle from side to side until it came away from the body, filled with a steaming gobbet of meat.

The flesh slid easily down his throat, taking the edge off his hunger, but not slaking it completely. He chomped down on the body once more, tearing the meat off the carcass more slowly this time, enjoying the sensation of chomping on the hot live flesh with his teeth and sending it sliding down his gullet.

In minutes the wolves' most acute hunger pangs were gone. The pack remained over the body a while longer however, lapping at the blood that continued to leak from the still steaming body.

Oldman licked the blood from his muzzle, looking at

the terrified eyes of the other cows as they watched one of the herd being eaten alive by the pack.

He felt sorry for them, sorry too for the rancher who had just lost one healthy head of cattle. But he consoled himself with the knowledge that the latter would be compensated for his loss by the Sept, and the former would soon be suffering the same fate, except in their case their flesh would be cooked before being eaten.

The Tenderloin.

Wingnut cruised the grimy underside of San Francisco looking for easy pickings. His arm was growing back quickly; the long thin stump was a pale shade of pink now, and the dull stubs of two fingers were ever so slowly growing up from the end. If he was lucky the two fingers would turn out to be his thumb and forefinger, giving him the use of a pincer-type claw before the rest of the hand grew back.

As he walked along Eddy Street, he moved right to avoid three large men coming down the sidewalk toward him. As he moved aside, one of the men bumped him, sending him stump-first into the side of a building.

Searing pain shot up his arm like fireworks, forcing him to cry out.

People nearby turned around to look at him for a second . . . then quickly returned to their business, wishing they hadn't looked.

As he stood there massaging his throbbing stump with his good left hand, he vowed to double up the revenge he intended to take this evening.

Tonight's victim wouldn't be just any homeless person. No.

Tonight's victim would be a friend of Wendel Oldman's.

Wingnut took a few moments to let the thought sink in.

And then he laughed a long satisfied Howl of Mockery, his moist eyes glowing red from the light shining down from the neon signs hanging over the sidewalk.

They neared the Caern. A park ranger with a rifle in his arms stood along the path. As they approached, the ranger stood aside, stepping off the path and disappearing into the forest.

"What is this place anyway?" asked Caroline Keegan as they neared the boulder leading into the Caern. "It's giving me the creeps."

"Patience, please, Ms. Keegan," Sylvia said, not bothering to turn around. "All will be revealed to you in time."

Caroline said nothing more.

Sylvia ran ahead, gaining speed. She leaped over the boulder in a bound, leaving Caroline standing on the path with Holt behind her.

Holt had wondered how they would escort the reporter inside the Caern, and now it was obvious. If Caroline Keegan wanted to know the truth, she'd have to break a sweat to get it.

"Your turn," said Holt.

Caroline turned around, looked at him as if gauging him, then turned back around to face the boulder. Without another moment's hesitation she was off, running down the path. Holt watched as she vaulted over the boulder with ease.

Holt was impressed, and a little dismayed. Great, he thought. Watch me be the only one to have trouble getting over. He took a deep breath to prepare himself, then started off. His foot didn't feel right as he leaped off the ground, but he managed to recover from the bad footing and cleared the big rock with an inch to spare.

He spent a moment straightening his clothing, smiling to himself. That's one hurdle gone, he thought.

Sylvia was waiting for them on the other side of the rock. After Holt landed, she wasted no time moving deeper into the Caern.

"I'm not feeling so well," Caroline said.

She looked pale. Holt wondered if his idea had been such a good one after all. Too late for that. "It will pass," he said.

They walked on for a short distance and came upon the circle of redwoods surrounding a small clearing.

"Here we are," said Sylvia.

"What?" shouted Caroline. "What do you mean here we are? This is just another part of the forest."

"No, Ms. Keegan. That's where you are wrong. This is our Caern."

"Your what?"

"Our Caern."

"Looks like a nice place to have a picnic, but—"

"I wouldn't be so flippant, Ms. Keegan." Sylvia narrowed the gap between them. "In fact, you should feel honored. You are one of only a half-dozen humans who have ever been allowed to enter here."

"But this is a public park. . . ."

Holt stepped forward. "Maybe it would be better if you explained to her the nature of the Caern and what it means to us."

Sylvia looked at Holt for a few seconds, then turned to face the reporter. "Sit down," she said. "This might take a while."

Caroline looked around for a place to sit, then decided on a short log that had fallen onto its side.

"All right, let me begin. . . ."

Sylvia began by explaining the nature of Gaia to her and told her stories about the Garou's fight to protect Her from The Wyrm. She talked about the Sept of the Western Eye, not as a collection of Garou but as a group dedicated to the preservation of Gaia. Then she explained how Father Wendel Oldman's mission helped recruit new members to aid in the fight, and how the ranch north of the park was an extension of that recruitment. . . .

As Sylvia talked, Holt tried to gauge Caroline's reactions to what was being said. She either had an open mind or was doing a good job at hiding her true feelings. Her face was a virtual blank.

Sylvia then began talking about the Caern, beginning with Sir Francis Drake and the Ohlone Indians and moving on through to the alliance formed between the Uktena and Children of Gaia tribes.

At this point Caroline looked to be losing interest. As

Holt had feared, the history of the Garou and the Caern were too much to take in all at once. From the look on the reporter's face she probably felt that they were both out of their minds.

Finally Sylvia's talk came to a end.

". . . So you see, Ms. Keegan. We aren't trying to *hide* the Caern from the outside world as much as *protect* it. This is a holy place to our kind. It is as sacred to us as a church or synagogue might be to humans of Christian or Jewish faith."

Caroline was silent for long time. Finally she spoke. "We?" she said. "Our Kind? Garou?" She looked at Holt and Sylvia in turn. "You two don't look any different than anybody else in California. If this isn't a cult, then what the hell is it?"

Holt stepped forward, nodding to Sylvia.

Taking her cue, Sylvia stepped out of the circle of redwoods, stripping off her clothes as she walked.

"While we have every outward appearance of being human," said Holt, including himself in the *we* for the sake of simplicity of explanation, "let me assure you that we are not."

"Yeah . . . right. Now you're going to tell me you're an alien or something."

"No, I'm not," said Holt, his voice unwavering.

Sylvia entered the circle again, her naked flesh a pale white in the faint moonlight that filtered in through the trees.

"What the hell is going on?"

"Our words don't seem to be convincing you, Ms. Keegan," said Holt. "Perhaps a demonstration is in order."

Sylvia continued to walk toward the reporter.

"We are Garou, Ms. Keegan," said Holt. "Or what humans might call *werewolves*."

"This is getting too weird," she said. "I'm getting out of here."

Just then Sylvia began the change into Glabro form, gaining six inches in height and more than doubling her body mass.

The light in the clearing was dim, and Caroline probably didn't perceive the full extent of Sylvia's change. She stepped closer, giving the reporter a better look at her long sharp claws and teeth.

"Oh, my . . . l-lord," she said, her body suddenly overcome by a series of shuddering spasms. She placed a hand over her heart, then moved it in front of her mouth.

Sylvia stopped where she was and remained there, letting the woman view her Glabro form closely.

"No, it can't be . . ." she said, moving her head wildly from side to side.

"Ms. Keegan," said Holt, "you are a reporter, I expect you to be skeptical, but not when seeing something with your very own eyes."

"There . . . are n-no such th-things as w-were . . . wolves."

Sylvia took a step forward and bent over the cowering woman. "Oh, but there are," she growled, shifting into Crinos form.

Caroline's eyes widened in sheer terror, then suddenly relaxed.

For a moment Holt was sure that he'd seen it in her eyes, the realization that all they'd said was true.

Caroline looked calmly at Sylvia's hulking form for another few seconds before her eyes rolled over and she fell victim to The Delirium.

Oldman padded leisurely through the forest. He'd left the pack behind and was now being escorted back to the ranch by a single gray-brown wolf.

They both looked tired, their tongues lolling loosely to the side after the night's long run and short hunt.

When they arrived at the ranch, the two wolves stopped at the edge of the woods. Oldman turned back toward his companion and made a few soft growls. The second wolf put together a similar string of howls, then turned and headed back toward the pack.

Alone now, Oldman stepped into the clearing. The

dark splotches of blood on his paws, neck, and haunches were clearly visible under the pale light of the moon.

He padded across the compound slowly, showing more of the toll the night had taken on his body now that the other wolf was out of sight.

He thought about changing back into his Homid form and spending the night in his bed in the bunkhouse, but he was still enjoying his Lupus form and, truth be told, was too exhausted to make the change.

He crouched down on all fours and squeezed under the bunkhouse porch.

There in the dark, quiet stillness he curled himself into a tight circle on the ground and closed his eyes.

He let out a long, contented sigh.

He was at peace.

And asleep in seconds.

Wingnut stood in the mouth of a darkened alley a few doors down the street from The Scott Mission. It was long after dinner, and those who wouldn't be sleeping overnight inside the mission would be heading out to wherever they intended to crash.

He let the first few men who exited the mission pass him by; they were all too young and strong. Then he saw an old man stumble through the front doors and onto the sidewalk.

Perfect.

"I can't believe I ate the whole thing. Hut! Hut! Hut!" said the old-timer, walking down the street as if he hadn't a care in the world. "Two all-beef patties. Hut! Hut! Hut!"

Wingnut had to laugh. What an idiot, he thought. Just the kind of nobody Wendel Oldman would take a shine to.

He stepped out of the alley and followed the man.

"Betcha can't eat just one. Two. Buckle my shoe. Hut! Hut! Hut!"

Just the kind of nobody Wendel Oldman would miss most.

"Ice cream you scream. Hut! Hut! Hu-tahh!"

18

John Tersigni shifted his camera from his left shoulder to his right, but it didn't do much to help relieve the ache. He'd been carrying his camera for days, following Caroline Keegan on some wild-goose chase to find some nonexistent cult she'd convinced herself existed somewhere in these woods. Hopefully, today would be his last day in this park. He'd talked to Sam Barlow earlier in the day, and the assignment editor wanted them back in San Francisco *with* a story, any story, by tonight.

Of course, heading back into the city all depended on whether or not Caroline was ready to give up the ghost.

But before he could find that out, he'd first have to find Caroline, and that wasn't going to be easy.

She'd been out all night.

He didn't know where she'd gone or spent the night, but he had a good idea where he might find her this morning—the spot in the woods where they kept meeting up with the park rangers. Even if she wasn't there, he could ask the ranger who would be there if he'd seen her.

As he neared the spot, he started to feel that same queasiness he'd felt before. It was like this part of the woods was haunted or something.

He slid his hand under his shirt and placed it over the

Saint Christopher medal his mother had given him as a child. Then he pulled the medal out from under his shirt and let it dangle freely on top of his clothes.

He started to get the chills and decided it might be better to go back to the hotel and wait for Caroline there.

As he turned around to head back, there was a sound behind him. A rustling sound, like a few pairs of feet stomping through the woods.

He turned back around and was startled by the sight of three park rangers standing there with rifles in their hands.

"Are you John Tersigni?" one of them asked.

"Y-yes."

"Are you looking for Caroline Keegan?"

"Yes, is she all right?"

The park rangers simply looked at him. Then the tall one on the left said, "Come with us. We will take you to her."

Tersigni hefted the camera on his shoulder and began moving slowly along the path. The rangers moved quickly through the woods and were waiting for him to catch up after less than a minute.

"Would you like one of us to carry that camera for you?"

"It's a very expensive piece of equi—" he began to say when the biggest of the three took the camera from him and tucked it under his arm.

They started off again.

And he still had trouble keeping up.

Oldman opened his eyes.

It was still dark.

A moment later he opened them again, this time taking a look at his surroundings. The immediate area around him was dark, but further out the sun was shining brightly.

And then he realized where he was. . . .

And what he was.

He was still under the porch of the bunkhouse, and he was still in his Lupus form.

Slowly, he got up off the ground, coaxing the stiffness out of his body. He crawled out from under the porch, stretched his back and legs, and gave one final yawn of his long, feral maw.

Then he proceeded to change form, moving through Hispo, Crinos, and Glabro before settling into his familiar and most comfortable Homid form.

He stood there a moment, feeling the warmth of the sunlight against his naked body. Then he turned around and headed up the bunkhouse steps, looking forward to having a long, hot shower.

He took a quick look at himself as he walked across the porch. Gaia knows I could use it, he thought.

His arms, face, and neck were covered with blood.

Caroline Keegan stirred.

It was a good sign. She'd been motionless most of the night, and The Delirium had shown little sign of wearing off. She moved again and let out a sigh, as if she'd just had one of the most peaceful night's sleep of her life.

Slowly she opened her eyes . . .

And let out a scream.

Ringing her bed were half a dozen people: two park rangers, a short Native American man, a black woman with a head of snow white hair, and the two she remembered from the night before—Sylvia Wood Runner and Kenneth Holt.

It was a scene right out of *The Wizard of* Oz, except in this version, Dorothy was still a long way from home.

"What are you doing here?" Caroline said. She took a look around. The surroundings were totally unfamiliar to her. "What am I doing here?" she said. "W*here* am I?"

"You're in a guest room inside the bunkhouse of The Scott Ranch," said Holt.

"The Scott R-Ranch . . ." The name sounded familiar, but that was about it.

"Sylvia and I brought you here last night after you passed out in the woods."

She tried to recall that, but couldn't.

Sylvia leaned in closer over the bed. "You have experienced something we call The Delirium," she said, taking over for Holt. "Normally, you wouldn't be able to recall anything about what happened to you last night, but I am going to try and help you remember some of it. It's very important that you remember . . . more than you can even begin to imagine. You must remember! Do you understand?"

Caroline nodded.

"Good," said Sylvia. She placed a small, flat fetish stone in the palm of her hand and then placed her hand on Caroline's head with a movement that was meant to look like a comforting gesture. The stone would help her to remember. "Now, you set out last night from your motel to meet Kenneth Holt and me. We took you inside the Caern, the clearing in the circle of redwoods. . . . Do you remember that?"

The Caern. Another familiar word. "I think so."

"I explained to you what the Caern was, what it meant to our kind. Do you remember that?"

Caroline desperately tried to recall the previous night. It wasn't easy, but more and more of it was coming back to her as if holes were being punched in the translucent curtain that had been draped across her memory. *Sitting in the woods talking about the Garou . . . The Caern is a holy place, a temple. . . . A boulder, a big boulder to jump over. . . . It needs to be protected. . . .*

Caroline nodded. "I remember . . . It's a holy place. It needs to be protected."

"Good," said Sylvia, nodding her head approvingly. "Excellent."

The words were echoed by the others surrounding the bed. Particularly impressed were the Native American and the elderly white-haired woman, both of whom up until now had been watching with blank expressions on their faces.

"Do you remember anything else?"

Caroline tried to remember, but everything was still pretty hazy.

"Do you remember watching me change my shape? Do you remember seeing me change into the other forms of the Garou? Do you remember seeing . . . a werewolf?"

She closed her eyes and thought about it. Suddenly she felt uncomfortable, frightened. Her heart raced. Her skin dampened. Her breathing grew short and rapid.

"I think so. . . ."

"Good," said Sylvia, taking her hand away from Caroline's head. "We'll leave it at that. Any further recollection might bring on The Veil."

Caroline breathed easier, happy to let the image of the beast fade from her mind.

"Would you like something to drink?"

"Yes, please. Juice if you have it."

Sylvia nodded. There was movement elsewhere in the room. A moment later a frosty glass of apple juice was placed in Caroline's hand. It was cold and fresh and soothed her parched throat.

"I'm sorry if I had you people figured out all wrong," she said.

"That's all right," said the white-haired woman. "We understand that you were only doing your job. Now that you know who we are and why we exist, I hope that we can be of mutual help to each other."

"How could I help you?"

"A television reporter is a very powerful person in today's society," said the short, stocky Native American.

"I've been called a lot of things in my career, but I've never heard anyone call me *powerful* before."

"Any report you broadcast is seen by millions of people across the country, maybe even the world. If that isn't real power, I don't know what is."

"What Able Heart is trying to say," Sylvia interjected, "is that if you spread the word about the glory of Gaia . . . sorry, about the glory of Mother Earth and the beauty of nature, more people will hear the message than if all of us stood on a soap box in Union Square and shouted it from now until the end of time."

Caroline sipped her juice.

"We're asking you to help us," said Sylvia. "And in turn we offer to help you in any way we can."

Caroline said nothing. There *was* a story here, a good

one. The only problem with it was that it was the kind of
story that would only ever make it onto the front page of
the *Enquirer* or *Weekly World News*. Even if she got pictures
and on-camera interviews with these people, the chances
that anyone would ever believe her were slim. So, in the
end the big story was a nonstory. She thought about
helping them and receiving whatever help they could
offer her in return. Their help might not amount to much,
but still . . . the thought of having a pack of werewolves as
close personal friends was far too enticing to pass up.

"All right," she said at last. "I'll help you. I don't know
how, but I'll give it a try."

A collective sigh washed over the room. Everyone
seemed relieved to hear the words.

"We were hoping you would," said Holt.

"I can see that," said Caroline. She paused a moment,
wondering. "Just out of curiosity, what would have happened to me if I had refused to befriend you, if I still
wanted to do the story this morning? Would you have let
me come back with my cameraman?"

Holt looked around at the assembled Garou, then
looked at Caroline. "Probably not."

"I didn't think so." She paused, still thinking. "What
would you have done to me?"

"You don't want to know."

Caroline looked at him a long time, imagining what
kind of carnage these werewolves, these Garou, were
capable of doing to a human body. "You're right," she
said at last. "I don't think I do."

It was late in the afternoon when Oldman finally
caught up with Holt.

"You're a tough man to track down," Oldman said.
"Even for the keen senses of a Garou."

"Well, things were pretty hectic the last day or two."

"I bet," said Oldman. "I hope everything has turned
out all right."

"I think so. Caroline Keegan seems to understand who
and what we are, and she said she would help us, but

only time will tell if she truly intends to make good on that promise."

Oldman looked at him strangely. "Since when did you become so wise?"

Holt smiled. "Since I started hanging out with you."

Oldman let out a laugh, then said, "Have you got a minute? I want you to come and walk with me."

"Why? Are you leaving already?"

"No, not quite yet. I want to take you somewhere. There's someone I'd like you to meet."

"Sure, whatever you say, Father."

"Good, let's go."

They set off into the woods, heading east. After walking at a brisk pace for fifteen minutes, Oldman stopped at the edge of a small oval clearing. Then he cupped his hands around his mouth and let out a long soft howl.

They waited at the edge of the clearing for a few minutes until a small gray wolf appeared at the opposite edge. The wolf howled once, then began moving toward them.

After a few steps the wolf began to change shape, shifting from Lupus into Homid form.

"What's going on?" cried Holt.

Oldman realized Holt had never seen the full gamut of shape changes and thought that perhaps he should have been warned about what he was going to see. Then again, he was Kinfolk, and if he intended to remain among the Garou, he would have to be exposed to it sooner or later. Might as well be now.

At last the change was complete, and an elderly woman approached them. She had long gray hair and a short stocky body. Holt felt a little embarrassed by her nakedness, but she didn't seem to care, so he did his best to ignore it.

"Kenneth Holt," said Oldman. "This is Faster-Than-Fox."

Holt nodded hello.

Faster-Than-Fox smiled, revealing a dirty row of stained and broken teeth.

"She knew your father," said Oldman.

Holt looked at Oldman, then turned to Faster-Than-Fox. "Really?"

Faster-Than-Fox nodded. "He was a good Garou. He died bravely. . . ."

Oldman turned and headed back to the ranch, giving the two of them the chance to talk.

"So, Parker," said Oldman, "did you enjoy attending your first gathering of the Sept?"

Parker tossed their two travel bags into the back of the car, then closed the hatch.

"I really did, Father," said Parker. "It was a great experience. One I hope to repeat sometime soon."

"I'm sure you'll be up here again. I always felt bad coming here by myself and leaving you behind, but now that you're a member of the Sept there's no reason why we can't make more regular visits together."

"That would be wonderful, Father. I'd like that very much."

They got into the car. Parker was about to turn the ignition when he stopped. "Isn't Celeste coming back with us?"

"No, she gets to missing this place as much as any of us. She's decided to stay here for a week or so."

"I don't blame her," said Parker, starting up the car. The motor rumbled softly, like a purring cat. He shifted it into drive. "Are you ready for the city?"

"Not really," said Oldman. "But then . . . is the city ready for us?"

John Tersigni had been told to "Wait Here!" more than an hour ago.

"Here" was a hard wooden bench set against one wall in a small room in what looked to be a ranger station. No, he thought, it was more than that. From what he could see of it through the window, it looked to be more like a training camp for the park rangers for all of California's state parks.

He'd thought of getting up and taking a look around plenty of times, but the ranger who had told him to "Wait

Here!" had been a huge man, nearly eight feet of solid muscle, and Tersigni figured it might be best just to do as he said.

He got up off the bench, stretched his arms, rubbed his sore rear end, and paced the room. That done, he sat back down and felt an ache beginning to come to life way down in the lower part of his back.

Just then the door opened and Caroline Keegan stepped into the room. She looked like shit.

"Where the hell have you been?" he asked, not really expecting to get much of an answer besides her usual shoulder shrug and slight flip of her head.

"I went out walking last night, and wouldn't you know it . . . I wound up getting lost," she said. "The rangers picked me up around midnight and I spent the night here."

"Oh-kay." Tersigni nodded, skeptically. It was the longest explanation he'd ever received from Caroline Keegan about anything.

He wanted to ask her for the truth, but knew he wouldn't be getting it no matter how hard he tried. "So," he said. "What's up for today?"

"Well, my good friend Silent-Fist-That-Wins—he's the big, tall park ranger—will be driving us back to the motel. After that we'll pack our things and head back to San Francisco. We should be there in time for dinner."

"What about your story?"

"What about it?"

"I talked to Sam this morning and he said he didn't want you coming back without one."

"Well, there's no story up here," Caroline said with a shrug of her shoulders and a slight flip of her head. "I had it wrong from the start. It happens. Not often, but it happens."

"When Sam sees you and hears you haven't got a story for him he's going to go apeshit . . . wilder than a mad dog."

Caroline looked at him and smiled coyly as she shook her head ever so slightly. "Believe me," she said, "after what I've seen he could get as crazy and as wild as a whole pack of mad dogs—it wouldn't scare me in the least."

Tersigni looked at her for the longest time.

And for some reason, he believed her.

PART III

Before you two battle, I remind you that one of you will die. I ask you if this act is the legacy you wish to leave to the world that gave you birth. Would you see us go screaming to Malfeas because the Garou people are torn by self-disembowelment? Or will you summon the courage of your ancestors and find the inner strength to place Gaia's wounds above your wounded pride?

—Selesti Calm-Bringer
Children of Gaia Philodox

19

Oldman wasn't inside the mission for more than a minute before things began to get hectic.

"Have you heard?" Alcina Williams asked. She looked as if she'd been waiting impatiently for their return.

"Hello to you too, L.C." said Oldman. "Heard what?"

"The Homeless Killer struck again last night."

"No!" said Parker.

Oldman just stood there in shocked silence shaking his head. It couldn't be. It's impossible. Please don't let that be true.

"Yes," she said. "And the worst part is who the victim was."

"Tell me!" ordered Oldman, the first hints of his powerful Garou rage creeping into his body.

"Maybe you'd better sit down first," she said.

Parker did as she suggested, taking a seat by the wall.

"Tell me!" repeated Oldman, anger flaring in his voice.

"It was . . . the General."

Parker gasped, and then his head fell forward and his eyes swept the floor.

Again Oldman found himself too shocked to speak. He couldn't believe it. Not the General. Not while he was off in the Muir Woods running wild and free . . . enjoying himself. No!

Oldman inhaled deeply. "Where . . . where did it happen?"

"On Eddy Street, not more than half a block from here."

Oldman nodded.

Eddy Street. The very same street the mission was on. He understood now.

This wasn't a random senseless killing by a Garou in the Thrall of The Wyrm. This was a killing to strike back at Oldman. Not against him in any physical sense, but against his Children of Gaia heart. Wingnut knew that killing one of his flock would hurt him far more than any amount of physical harm.

He wondered how he would handle the Garou this time, but knew that another confrontation between them could only end with one of their deaths. And Oldman wasn't about to become a cadaver.

"All right," said Oldman, a strange feeling of calm overtaking his body. "I'll be spending the afternoon in my room. Parker—"

"Yes, Father," Parker said quickly, no doubt sensing Oldman's inner rage. "I'll let you know when the sun sets."

Oldman looked at Parker. The man's eyes were moist with tears.

Wingnut had caused enough pain. The General's death would be avenged, and the killings would be stopped— once and for all.

Without saying another word, Oldman went quietly to his room and locked the door behind him.

Oldman tried to get some rest, but of course he couldn't.

He was too full of rage to even close his eyes and ended up lying awake staring blankly at the ceiling.

The killings had stopped for so long he'd thought he had taken care of the problem, convinced himself that he'd sent Wingnut running away with his tail between his legs. But Oldman realized now that he should have known better. If Wingnut was truly in the Thrall of The Wyrm, what was the temporary loss of an arm going to do to stop him? All it had done, he realized now, was give him a painfully embarrassing wound. Just enough to stop the killings while he healed. Then he'd be healthy enough to kill again, this time killing to exact his revenge against Oldman.

It seemed so simple now, but he couldn't see it at the time. When they'd first met, Oldman had been a little too filled with compassion and pity for the mongrel. Now he had nothing but contempt and rage for him.

Now, even the mercy of a swift and painless death would be too good for him.

He deserved to die . . . in agony.

Oldman was up and sitting on the edge of the bed when Parker knocked on the door.

"Thank you, Parker," he said before Parker could tell him that it was getting dark out.

Parker knocked on the door again.

"Yes, Parker. What is it?"

The door opened slowly and Parker stuck his head inside the room. "I just thought you'd like to know, Father. The radio has had stories about the Homeless Killer all day long. The police say they will be increasing the number of cars patrolling the Tenderloin tonight."

The Homeless Killer.

He even had a name now.

"Thanks," said Oldman. "That's good to know."

"There's something else."

"Come on in."

Parker stepped into Oldman's office. Oldman got up off his bed and came into the office, sitting down on the couch facing Parker.

"The return of the killer is bringing more people into the mission," said Parker. "L.C. says she's running low on food stocks and other provisions. She has enough to last three or four more days provided we don't get too many more people knocking on our door."

"How many meals were served tonight?"

"Almost fifty."

Oldman sighed. The mission usually served about twenty-five meals at supper time and never had more than fifteen sleeping in the dormitory. If things continued on like this, they'd be cleaned out of food and filled up with bodies in less than three days. "All right," he said. "I'll see what I can do."

Parker nodded and got up to leave. "Good luck," he said. "I've been able to get through the day by thinking that the killer is going to get what he deserves."

"He will," said Oldman. "If I have anything to do with it, he will."

Seemingly satisfied, Parker left the room.

So, thought Oldman. The mission is running high on demand and low on supplies. He'd have to try and procure some food. Not an easy task considering the police would be out in force tonight. He wondered if added police protection would make a difference. It might make the citizens of the Tenderloin feel safer, but it wouldn't do much to dissuade Wingnut. The Delirium affected policemen as much as anybody.

Oldman got up from the bed, stripped down to the waist, and shifted into his Glabro form. Then he walked down the hall to the back door of the mission. He stepped outside and stripped off his pants, shifting into Crinos form as he did so.

The change didn't feel as good as it had in the forest surrounded by Gaia, but it still felt good to flex his powerful muscles. They felt especially strong tonight, full of rage.

He drew his claws over the ground, listening to them click and scratch against the hard pavement. Then he held his right hand up to his face to take a closer look at the talons.

They were long, sharp . . . and deadly.

He set off down the alley.

The hunt had begun.

Again.

The Tenderloin seemed quiet.

Even the extra patrols promised by the city's police force seemed to be nonexistent. Oldman saw the odd officer on foot, a patrol car here and there, but nothing out of the ordinary. There may have been added police officers out on the street, but Oldman couldn't see any evidence of them in his travels.

Oldman covered Eddy Street twice from Van Ness Avenue to Powell Street, then went south to Turk and searched that street before doubling back on Golden Gate Avenue heading west.

Nothing.

He moved north covering the same amount of pavement along Polk Street and then finally went west along Geary Street.

Again, nothing.

The streets were empty.

Not a pusher, pimp, prostitute, or homeless person in sight.

Oldman took a rest standing atop a building at the corner of Geary and Polk Streets, and for a few moments he imagined that the darker elements of society weren't out in force tonight because they simply didn't exist anymore. Gone were illicit drugs and illicit sex. Unknown were unemployment and poverty. And society was full of safety and rehabilitative nets that propped people up when they faltered. . . .

And then a gunshot brought him sharply back into reality.

It came from somewhere south of his position, judging by the sound of it, no more than a couple of blocks away.

He headed south across the rooftops, covering huge spans of distances with each bound. When he reached O'Farrell he clambered down onto street level and ran the rest of the way through back alleys and yards.

By the time he reached the scene of the shooting two police cars were there and a crowd of people gathered around. Oldman got as close to the scene as he dared and listened carefully to a conversation between a police officer and an eyewitness.

"He said he was going to kill him for what he did to her," said the frightened young Hispanic woman. "He took his gun out of the closet and went down the street to shoot him. That's when I called the police. . . ."

Oldman turned away from the scene.

It was probably some sort of domestic violence, or drug deal gone bad, nothing he could help with and nothing to do with the reason he was out on the street.

He crept back into the shadows and wandered south toward Eddy Street and the mission.

When he was just past Ellis Street he heard a strange howling sort of scream. If he wasn't mistaken, it sounded like The Call to Succor—a howl used by the Garou to call their pack for aid. It was an embarrassing call, sounding a lot like puppies crying for their mother.

Oldman ran down the street toward the curious cry. Halfway between Ellis and Eddy he turned down an alley, following the cry to its source.

He came upon that source in the back lot of Penn's Fender and Body Shop.

A young boy, perhaps even a teenager, had his back to a fence while three punks taunted him by taking turns lunging at him or pretending to punch and kick him.

It seemed innocent enough to Oldman, nothing kids didn't do every day in the city. The scene seemed normal, but The Call to Succor he'd heard had put a strange twist to the situation. He crossed his arms, leaned up against a wall, and watched. Perhaps he could learn something.

"Gimme your jacket!" one of the punks demanded.

The boy who was wearing a fancy NBA team jacket with the team crest of the Philadelphia 76ers on it, said, "No!"

"And what if I take it from ya? You gonna stop me?"

"Maybe."

The middle punk stepped forward and connected with a solid kick to the boy's chest. The boy flew back and hit the wall, howling in pain.

Oldman stood up straight.

The boy's howl had sounded very much like that of a wolf.

"I said gimme your jacket!"

The boy, on the verge of tears, remained defiant. "Fuck you!"

"Whoa, tough man!"

"You gonna start crying now?"

"Your momma know you talk like that?"

"Go to hell, you . . . you . . . *monkeys.*"

The alley suddenly became silent.

"What did you say?" asked one of the punks.

Oldman wondered about what the boy had said too. While two of the three punks were black and would certainly take the word *monkey* to be a derogatory term about the color of their skin and their racial heritage, Oldman knew the real context the word was being used in. The young boy being tormented was Garou and had used the word as a vulgar term for all humans.

Perhaps it was an appropriate expression from the Garou's point of view, but it was the wrong thing to say considering the situation.

The alley's silence was suddenly broken by the sound of a switchblade *snicking* open.

Oldman could see the long blade glinting in the moonlight.

The show was over. It was time for him to act.

He leaped through the air and landed on the ground directly behind the three punks.

The young boy against the wall saw him in his Crinos form but did not cower or suffer The Delirium—further evidence that the boy was Garou.

Oldman quickly grabbed the hand of the knife-wielding punk and forced the knife blade through the palm of his other hand. Without a sound, the punk released the knife's hilt and looked at it sticking out from his hand like something to hang a coat on. Then he screamed long and hard as the excruciating pain finally registered in his brain.

The other two punks turned to look at Oldman. Their mouths dropped open in surprise as little more than terrified squeaks escaped from their quivering lips.

He grabbed them both by their collars, lifted them up off the ground, then snarled loudly in their faces, finishing off the scare tactic by snapping his massive jaws together within an inch of their noses.

The two punks fell unconscious from The Delirium.

Oldman continued to hold them, propping them up for a few moments to allow The Delirium a chance to wear off. Then, after they regained consciousness, he set them down and let them sprint out of the alley, their friend following close behind trying desperately to remove the knife blade embedded in his now bloody hand.

Oldman watched them leave, then turned to console the Garou.

"They're gone now," he said. "You can relax."

The young Garou took a deep breath, but his body was still racked with fear and uncontrollable shakes.

Oldman waited a minute for him to settle down, then spoke again. "Where are you from?"

The Garou looked up. There was still fear in his wide wet eyes, but also relief. "Philadelphia," he said.

Although Oldman had suspected as much, the final piece of the puzzle fell into place. This was the runaway Garou from Philadelphia the Glass Walker had been looking for. Oldman did his best to mask the relief he felt over having found the cub and shifted into Glabro form to make speech a little easier.

"Philadelphia? That's a long way from here."

"Yeah."

"Were you trying to get *to* something, or were you running *away* from something?"

"Running away . . ."

"I see."

"My father never told me that . . ." He looked up. "That I was like you. I got scared. . . ." He looked down. "I got stupid."

"Well, you're still quite young," said Oldman. "I don't think your father expected you to grow up so fast, or for the change to come so soon."

"Do you know my father?" The boy's face suddenly brightened.

"No . . . not exactly. But I do know that he's concerned about you and has people looking for you right now even as we speak."

"Really?"

"Yes, really," Oldman nodded. "I'll tell you what. Why don't you come and spend the night with me, and tomorrow I'll get you started on your way back home. How's that sound?"

"I'd like that very much. I miss my father."

"And I'm sure he misses you. C'mon."

They started out of the alley, but the young Garou fell behind, weak from his travels and sore from his ordeal with the punks.

"Hop on my back," he said. "I'll give you a lift."

"Thanks . . ." The boy's voice trailed off.

"Wendel is my name, Wendel Oldman. How about you?"

"Leonard Gateway, but all my friends call me Lenny."

"Pleased to meet you, Lenny."

"And I'm glad to meet you, Wendel."

Oldman reached back over his shoulder with his right hand and they shook.

"Could you do me a favor, Wendel?"

Oldman nodded.

"When you talk to my father, please don't tell him I was afraid of those three boys. I mean, I wanted to change into Crinos form and scare them off, but I just couldn't make it happen."

"You were probably a little too scared," said Oldman. "Shape-changing takes some time to master. . . . But don't you worry, as far as I'm concerned, you scared off those boys all by yourself."

"Thanks," said Leonard, wrapping his arms around Oldman's neck and pulling them tightly together in a hug.

As Oldman shifted into his Crinos form, his lips pulled back to reveal a smile full of sharp teeth and fangs.

Then, after taking a few seconds to fine-tune his form, he padded out of the alley and headed back to the mission.

Lenny held on tight.

20

Oldman opened his eyes and blinked until the numbers and hands on the clock on his night table came into focus.

It was ten after nine.

He rolled over onto his back and looked at the ceiling as he thought about last night. It had been a good night considering he'd found the runaway Glass Walker boy from Philadelphia, but there was still a gnawing feeling in the pit of his stomach. He'd found the boy, but hadn't found Wingnut, and that meant the Garou would have been free to kill last night, and would be free to kill again tonight.

Tonight and every night.

Until he was caught.

Well, Oldman thought, sitting up in bed. There's nothing to do about it until nightfall. In the meantime there's a boy who needs to be reunited with his Kin.

He got out of bed and got dressed.

When he went downstairs, the last few slow eaters were just finishing up breakfast. The young Garou, Leonard Gateway, was sitting at the table closest to the kitchen. Parker sat next to him, chatting.

"Well, Parker," said Oldman, pulling up a chair of his

own. "I see you've met up with the mission's newest guest."

"Sort of, Father," said Parker. "Actually he found me this morning, asking me where he could get something to eat."

"That's great," Oldman said. "Did you know Leonard . . . sorry, Lenny, is a Glass Walker from Philadelphia?"

"He mentioned something to that effect," said Parker, giving Lenny a wink. "He also told me about a certain someone who took care of three unruly punks last night."

"I wonder who that could be?" It was Oldman's turn to give Lenny a wink.

Lenny was grinning from ear to ear, loving every minute of it.

"The only certain someone I know who scared off some punks last night was Lenny himself."

"That's not what he said." Parker looked at the two of them, confused.

"Well, that's *my* story and I'm sticking to it." This time, Oldman gave Parker a wink.

"Oh . . . okay." Parker turned to Lenny. "Well, I'm impressed."

Lenny continued to grin as he wolfed down a milky bowl of cereal.

Oldman leaned close to Parker and said. "How was he this morning?"

"He seemed a little frightened, or perhaps just wary of everybody." Parker kept his voice low as well. "He's awfully hungry . . . That's the third bowl of cereal he's had, not to mention a couple of slices of toast." Parker then raised his voice dramatically so Lenny could hear him. "I'd tell you about the half pound of bacon he's had, but L.C. doesn't know about that and I'd be happy to keep it that way."

Parker was obviously exaggerating because the smile on Lenny's face broadened, then broke into laughter.

"What?" said Parker. "What is it?"

Lenny looked up.

And Parker turned around.

"Oh, hi, L.C.," said Parker. "How long have you been standing there?"

"Long enough to know where I can find an extra pot-washer without having to ask."

Everyone at the table laughed . . . including Oldman.

Oldman searched the messy pile of papers on his desk muttering under his breath.

"I know I left it here somewhere. . . . Where could it be?"

After turning over every paper on the desk at least twice, he interrupted his search and gazed at the ceiling with squinted eyes. A few seconds passed before his index finger suddenly shot up into the air as if to say "Eureka!"

He opened the top right-hand drawer of his desk.

And there on top of a ramshackle collection of pens and pencils was a single scrap of paper with a telephone number scribbled on it.

"I knew I put it somewhere," he said, picking up the paper.

He tucked the receiver into the nape of his neck and dialed the number.

"Hello."

"Internet?"

"Yes, this is Randy Internet. Who's this?"

"This is Wendel Oldman, we met—"

"Oh yes, yes, how are you?"

"Fine and you?"

"Not so good . . . " Internet's voice trailed off. Obviously he was depressed over not being able to find the runaway.

"Well, then, I just might have some news that will cheer you up."

"Yes." He said the word sharply, with great anticipation.

"I found Leonard last night."

"Really? How is he?"

From the way the question was asked Oldman was sure Internet expected his next word to be *dead*.

"He's scared, and he wants to go home."

Internet let out a long sigh. "That's great. Where are you now? When can I pick him up?"

"I'm calling from The Scott Mission, but I'd prefer that you meet us in Union Square. Do you know where that is?"

"Don't worry. I'm sure I can find it."

"This afternoon at two, then."

"I'll be there."

Oldman had hardly hung up the telephone when there was a knock on the door.

"Who is it?"

"It's L.C. I'd like to talk to you."

"C'mon in."

The door opened a crack. L.C. stuck her head into the room, then slowly slid in through the open door.

She sat down hesitantly, still uncomfortable about being in Oldman's office after working at the mission for more than four years. The familiar cigarette butt was between her fingers, extinguished. "I didn't want to bother you with this downstairs, you know . . . in front of the boy and the others, so I thought I'd come up here where we could talk in private."

"All right, what's on your mind?"

"Food," she said.

"Pardon me?"

"Food, Father. It's food that's on my mind."

"All right, what about food?"

"We haven't got any," she said, matter-of-factly. "I mean, we've got some, but not much. We're *really* low on supplies. So low that I'm going to have to start seriously rationing soon, and you know what that can lead to."

Oldman nodded.

Fights often broke out whenever the mission ran short of things like food and beds, and it looked as if both those commodities would soon be in short supply.

"All right, I've got other business to attend to, but I'll go out and make some rounds this morning and see what I can find," he said. "How would that be?"

L.C. nodded. "That'll be fine with me, Father. But just

remember whether there's food or not, I won't be the one going hungry."

"I get the message," he said.

"Good," she said, getting up to leave. "Now if you'll excuse me, I've got to go downstairs and see what I can *scrape* together for lunch."

Oldman sighed. From the way she said the word "scrape," it sounded as if she'd meant it literally.

Oldman had just enough time before his meeting with Internet to make a quick run to Mr. Kim's and some of the other grocers in the area. But even so, he took some time out to make a special trip to the City Lights Bookshop.

When he got to the store, he crept up to the window and looked inside, making sure Bongos was nowhere to be seen. Then he slipped into the store and headed straight for the poetry section. When he found the three copies of Bongos's book, *The Rage Pages*, on the shelf, he reached inside his shirt and pulled out his own copy, the one he'd bought years ago when he first learned it contained the work of a Garou.

Then, making sure that no one was watching, he placed the book on the shelf.

It was a subtle form of revenge, but Oldman was immensely pleased with himself. This was the kind of thing that would hurt Bongos deeply, a blow right at the center of his heart. Oldman's only regret was that he wouldn't be there when Bongos found out that one of his books had been *returned*.

That done, Oldman hurried back into the Tenderloin to begin his rounds of the grocery stores.

His first few stops were pretty unsuccessful. People living in the Tenderloin had recently been stocking up on food, deciding to stay indoors until the killing spree had ended.

By the time he got to the Kim's grocery store, he had just a single bag of donated food. If his luck didn't change, L.C. would be one disappointed cook.

He shuddered to think about it.

The bell tinkled over the door as he entered Jackson's Fruit and Vegetables. Mr. Kim was in his familiar spot behind the cash register, his wife close by his side.

"How's business?" Oldman asked.

"Too good."

Oldman looked at the man for a long time. His usually jovial smile and joking manner were gone. This was a side of the grocer he'd never seen before, the side he might expect to see around tax time or whenever he was paying the bills.

"What do you mean too good?" asked Oldman. "I didn't think I would ever hear you say something like that."

"Look!" he said. "Look at my shelves!"

Oldman turned around and looked at the shelves that normally held rows and rows of canned goods and other nonperishable items.

Empty.

He looked around to other parts of the store, and all the shelves were noticeably bare.

"Everybody wants to stay inside," said Mrs. Kim. "No go out anymore."

"But you've sold so much stock, you must have made a killing this week . . . uh, no pun intended."

To Oldman's surprise Mr. Kim didn't crack a smile. Neither did his wife.

"No, I don't make killing. I almost get killed."

"What?"

"A crazy man came in here looking for cans of food. I told him I have no more. He say I no sell to him because he is black. But that's not true, I don't have any more to sell, not to black, not to white. He come around counter and punch me, then run out of the store."

Oldman shook his head.

"Don't worry. No happen again." He lifted a shotgun off the counter in front of him. He tried to crack a menacing smile, but it was obvious that he was uncomfortable with having the gun in his hands.

He'll be lucky if he doesn't kill himself, thought Oldman.

"Do you have anything in the back room?"

"Everything old," said Mrs. Kim. "But you take a look."

Oldman nodded and headed to the back of the store. There wasn't much there, certainly not as much as he'd found in the past. There was a bag of old turnips and some cabbage. Oldman picked them up and gave the rest of the stuff a quick scan. He decided to leave the rest there. It was too far gone even for L.C. to save.

Oldman went back to the cash register. "That's all," he said showing them the bag of turnips and cabbage.

"Sorry," said Mr. Kim.

"You have *no* food?" asked Mrs. Kim.

"We have some, but more people are staying with us because of the killings and we only have enough food for another day or two at the most."

Mrs. Kim looked at him. "Wait a minute," she said.

She walked over to the door that led into the store's basement and went downstairs. A few moments later she came back with a carton of macaroni and cheese boxes.

"Take this," she said. "For the mission."

Mr. Kim's eyes opened wide. Obviously giving away new stock didn't sit well with him. He opened his mouth to speak, but his wife cut him off with a wave of her hand.

"You quiet!" she told him. "People need to eat." Then she turned to look at Oldman. "With everything we sell this week we can afford to give some away."

"Thank you very much," said Oldman. "The next time I come in I'll bring you a receipt so you can deduct it on your taxes as a charitable donation."

"Never mind," said Mrs. Kim. "This is a gift for you. You a good man and I want to help."

Oldman nodded, then looked to Mr. Kim. "I'll bring you a receipt," he said softly.

Mr. Kim gave a little nod. . . .

And smiled.

Oldman had set up the afternoon meeting in Union Square because it would give Lenny a chance to see some of San Francisco's sights. After spending the morning with Parker, the young Garou went with Oldman, first walking east along Eddy to Powell, then taking the Powell Street Cable Car north to Union Square.

Union Square was a park situated near the center of San Francisco and was the closest thing to a cross-roads the city had. It was filled with chess players, lovers, panhandlers, brown-baggers, soap-box speakers, flocks of hungry pigeons, and, best of all, many beautiful flowers.

After walking casually through the park, munching on bags of popcorn bought from a vendor, Oldman found Randy Internet sitting at the base of the Naval Monument, a gray column of concrete that had been erected to commemorate some 1898 victory during the Spanish-American War.

"Uncle Randy!" Lenny cried when he saw the familiar face of Internet. He ran from Oldman's side and gave Internet a long, tight embrace.

They were still together when Oldman arrived at the Monument. "Glad to see him, are you, Lenny?"

"Not as glad as I am to see *him*," said Internet, a smile on his face for the first time since Oldman had met him. "And not half as glad as Mr. Gateway is going to be when he's back safe at home."

"When are we leaving?" asked Lenny.

"Our flight leaves tonight after dinner."

"Can we have pizza?"

"You bet," said Internet. After a few moments' silence, he turned to Lenny and handed him a bag of feed. "Here, Lenny. Go feed the pigeons for a minute or two. I want to talk to Oldman here in private."

"Sure, okay."

The two of them watched Lenny walk away.

"He's a good cub," said Oldman. "He'll make a fine Garou some day."

Internet nodded absently.

"What is it you wanted to talk to me about?" asked Oldman.

"I just want to thank you again for finding Lenny. How in the name of Gaia did you do it?"

"Just lucky, I guess. . . . I was out for a walk and happened to run into him. No big deal, I'm just glad I could help."

"Well, Mr. Gateway is going to want to thank you for what you did. What can I tell him you'd like as a reward?"

"Reward?" Oldman laughed. "I don't want any reward. Seeing your reunion and knowing there's an even greater one coming in Philadelphia is reward enough for me. Just tell Mr. Gateway it was my pleasure to be of assistance."

Internet shrugged. "All right, I'll tell him, but you should really think about it. Mr. Gateway is a powerful Garou with a lot of connections in both the Garou and human worlds. He could do a lot for you."

Oldman smiled, trying to be polite. "I'll keep it in mind," he said. "Thanks."

After saying good-bye to Internet and Lenny, Oldman went straight back to the mission. He'd been tired out by all the running around he'd done that day and needed some rest. Procuring food and sending Lenny on his way had been necessary distractions, but his number one priority was still finding the killer Garou and getting rid of him.

When he arrived at the mission, there were several new faces milling about the upstairs hallway, obviously new guests forced inside by the threat of the Homeless Killer.

He walked by them without saying a word and went downstairs to check on L.C. She was in the kitchen standing over a huge pot of boiling water.

"How are you doing?" he asked.

"Not too bad," she said, her face slick and wet from the steam rising up from the pot. "I can do a lot with macaroni and cheese dinners. That carton you brought in will do us for two meals, maybe two and a half. After that it's the same old story—we're running low on everything except hungry mouths to feed."

Oldman sighed. He'd expected as much. This food shortage problem wasn't going to go away until the killer did.

Tonight he hoped to solve the problem—once and for all.

21

Oldman had become accustomed to the nightside of the Tenderloin. He was aware of its rhythm and beat, the sounds it made while some of its people slept and some others came alive.

Tonight, like other recent nights, the Tenderloin was a quiet place, cowering under the stars like a child under the sheets afraid of the monster hiding under its bed.

Oldman, in his Crinos form, made the usual rounds, across Geary, O'Farrell, Ellis, and Eddy, and up and down Jones, Leavenworth, Hyde, and Larkin, but he didn't hear or see any evidence of the killer. Nor did he see any evidence of any other crimes going down, which surprised him.

There hadn't been one night that he'd been out on the street when he didn't witness a crime of some kind, but tonight it seemed that everyone had been pushed indoors. No doubt the crimes were still going on—the prostitutes were probably working the donut shops and restaurants, and the drug dealers were staying close to the crack houses—but the streets looked safe enough for a family stroll.

The emptiness of the streets suited Oldman just fine. If Wingnut couldn't find easy pickings on the streets of the Tenderloin, he might be prompted to just stop the killings.

Oldman shook his head. Purely wishful thinking.

Wingnut was still out there looking for an easy victim to kill in order to exact his revenge.

He was somewhere out there . . . killing.

But where?

Oldman searched the Tenderloin, rooftop to rooftop, alley by alley until five-thirty the next morning.

When the sun began to rise up over San Francisco Bay, he reluctantly headed back to the mission, hoping to Gaia that someone hadn't been murdered in the night.

It was almost light out.

But it was still dark inside . . .

Inside was an empty husk of a building that used to house a bank. When the bank pulled out, the building remained, and then the homeless moved in.

Tonight, the werewolf followed them inside.

As Wingnut stepped through the door, he could hear the rhythms of their sleeping breath . . . long and deep.

The floor of the building was strewn with trash and debris, broken glass and rat droppings. The werewolf carefully stepped over the mess, making sure not to make a sound or disturb anything that might topple over.

He found her lying under a teller's counter, curled up in a tight little ball, dirty money bags propping up her head and neck. She was an old scraggly-looking woman; her skin was brown and dirty and in need of a wash. Her hair was silver-gray, and the lines on her face were many and deep. She was somebody's mother, somebody's grandmother.

He watched her sleep, thinking it would be a pity to disturb her.

So without a sound he slashed his claws across her throat, tearing out a chunk of her neck, breaking it in the process.

She opened her eyes, still glazed over with sleep, and

looked at him. As blood poured freely from the ragged rent in her throat, something like recognition flashed across her face. Then The Delirium set in and she fell back unconscious.

Blood gushed out from the hole in her neck for a few more seconds, then the torrent slowed until the dark oily liquid oozed out in a regular but ever-weakening pulse. When the last of the blood was gone from her body, she let out a long sigh; the air as it passed her vocal chords created an eerie-sounding moan that escaped from the blood-soaked wound in her neck.

Wingnut sat there, absently licking the wet tips of his claws.

The kill had been too easy.

It had served his purposes of revenge, but it hadn't been any fun. There had been no thrill to the kill.

Just then he heard the sound of someone else's breathing.

It was a loud snore, quite possibly that of an older man. Wingnut listened closely. It was coming from the back of the bank, from the vault.

He was about to get up and check it out when he remembered something. He tore his claws against the outside of one of the money bags under the woman's head. As he suspected, it was filled with crumpled news-paper rather than bills.

Oh, well, he thought. Worth a try.

He got up then, padded over to the vault, and peeked inside.

There was a bald-headed old man asleep on the floor covered by a ragtag set of dirty blankets and old coats.

Wingnut let out a long high-pitched howl, then stepped back from the entrance to the vault.

The old man snorted, then woke from his sleep. "What the hell is going on out there?" he said.

Wingnut snarled and snapped his jowls, sounding as ferocious and menacing as he knew how.

"May?" the man said nervously. Then after a long pause, "May? Is that you?"

He stepped back into the entrance to the vault, blocking out the dawning light filtering in from outside and creating an imposing silhouette of bristling fur, bulging muscles, and razor-sharp claws.

"M-May . . ." the old man said, his voice beginning to crack.

"I'm not May," said Wingnut.

Now *this* was going to be fun. . . .

Oldman awoke to the sound of commotion outside his room.

He sprung out of bed, slipped on a pair of pants and a white undershirt, and opened the door to see what was going on. The hallway was filled with people, all huddled around the small television that had been rolled out of Parker's office.

"What's happening?" Oldman asked the young black man in front of him, someone he'd never seen before.

"It's the Homeless Killer," the young man said. "He killed again last night. They're reporting it now on the news."

Oldman felt his heart fall deep into the pit of his stomach. He pushed his way forward through the crowd, denying that what he'd been told could possibly be true.

When he got close to the television and saw the look on Parker's face as he stood there watching the screen, he knew it was true.

The Homeless Killer had struck again.

"Despite the fact that people in the Tenderloin heeded police warnings to stay indoors after dark," said the voice of the television reporter, "the Homeless Killer has killed again, claiming the lives of two of the area's transients."

"*Two* of them?"

"Oh no!"

"Did he say who they were?"

"Early this morning police found an elderly woman and man dead inside this abandoned bank building on O'Farrell Street," continued the television reporter. "According to police the woman had been killed by a single blow to the throat, while the man suffered numerous wounds to the head and body. Names of the victims are being withheld until next-of-kin can be notified."

Then Detective Garrett appeared on screen, Detective Chong by his side, but Oldman didn't care to hear what the two policemen had to say. He turned his back on the television and headed back to his room, closing the door behind him and locking it tight.

He lay down on his bed and felt the sickening feeling in his stomach starting to spread throughout the rest of his body. A Harano, a feeling of inexplicable gloom.

Two more of the flock had died because he'd been unable to save them, because he'd not gotten rid of the problem when he'd had the chance.

He couldn't let it happen again.

He *would not* let it happen again.

When the news report about the Homeless Killer ended, Parker unplugged the television set and began to wheel it back into his office. As he did, the crowd gathered in the hall began to complain. . . .

"I want to see more," said one.

"Try another channel," said another.

"Leave it out here. There's a game on tonight."

Parker didn't want to leave his television out in the hall; who knew what might happen to it if he did. But as he looked around at the angry faces before him, he realized he didn't have much choice in the matter.

He turned around and plugged the television back into the wall, then walked through the crowd to his office. When he was inside, he closed the door behind him and locked it.

Things are starting to get out of hand, he thought. And Father Oldman's too busy to spend his time keeping things under control.

I need help.

He reached for the phone and dialed a long-distance number.

———

It was four in the afternoon when Parker knocked on the door. Oldman was lying on the couch in his office, staring at the ceiling, waiting for night to fall.

"What is it?" he said, not taking his eyes off the ceiling.

"It's me. Parker. I'd like to speak to you a minute."

"Come on in."

The handle twisted several times. "I think it's locked."

"Just a minute." Oldman got up, went to the door and unlocked it, then returned to the couch.

Parker hesitantly stepped into the room, followed by Holt.

Oldman's eyes widened in surprise at the sight of Holt, but his expression quickly turned into a smile. "What brings you here?"

"I did," said Parker. "The mission's getting crowded and you're busy with other things, so I thought he might be able to help me keep things under control for the next few days. I hope you don't mind."

"Of course not," said Oldman. "Holt will always be welcome here at the mission. Who knows, maybe he might even be able to help *me*."

"Anything I can do . . ." offered Holt.

Oldman glanced at Parker, then turned to Holt. He was about to speak, telling Holt all about the Homeless Killer when Parker cut in.

"Uh, before you get too far into it, there's something I need to discuss with Father Oldman."

"Of course," said Holt, finding himself a seat.

"What is it?" asked Oldman.

"Well, I was downstairs and . . ."

"And let me guess," sighed Oldman. "L.C. is saying we need more food, or fewer guests."

Parker said nothing for a moment, then nodded. "I've been on the phone most of the day. The food banks are all down to nothing. I called Frank at the St. Vincent de Paul Society, and the best he could do was give me a couple of supermarket vouchers, but he can't get them to me until tomorrow. . . . They have to be signed by the vice-president as well, and she's out of town."

Oldman was silent, breathing deeply in and out.

"We could start turning people away," Parker suggested.

"No," said Oldman. "If we do that we'll be giving the city and the state an excuse to cut off what little funding we get as it is."

"What do you suggest, then?"

"I'll get something to hold us over until the vouchers arrive."

"How will you be getting it?"

"Don't ask."

Parker nodded. "Okay, I won't," he said, turning to leave. At the door, he turned and said, "Excuse me, gentlemen."

Both Holt and Oldman nodded to Parker, then began talking business. "The werewolf that attacked you," said Oldman, "his name is Wingnut, but they call him the Homeless Killer now. I thought I'd scared him off, but he came back with a vengeance. . . ."

Oldman continued talking.

Holt listened with great interest.

Oldman stepped into the alley behind the mission and slipped into Crinos form. He didn't like changing form during the day, especially on days in which the sun shone brightly, but he had no other choice. The mission needed food, and with the help of The Delirium, he could easily be able to procure enough food to get L.C. through another day.

But he didn't like stealing what he needed. In addition to going against everything he'd worked for in establishing the mission, he'd be stealing from honest, hardworking people. Furthermore, stealing wasn't in keeping with the general spirit of cooperation the Children of Gaia had adopted in regards to humans. And finally, it even went against one of the Ten Commandments.

Oldman consoled himself with the thought that, if such a thing were possible, stealing food to feed hungry people was a noble crime. Even so, it didn't sit right with him, and he wanted to get it over with as quickly as possible.

He ran out of the alley and west along Eddy to Larkin Street.

He tried to stay close to the shadows, more so than at night because of the strange sensation of having the hot sun beat down on his fur. It made his fur feel hot and clammy, as if it were a second layer of skin rather than his only one.

He also tried to stay out of sight to avoid relying too much on The Delirium. If too many people saw a werewolf that day, a few of them might report the sighting to the authorities. That could cause a whole new scare, or add fuel to the current one.

When he reached Larkin Street, he crossed it and turned up the alley behind the stores and restaurants facing the street. Already his nostrils detected the delicious smells of *goong mae naang* simmering in big clay pots, *shabu shabu* broiling in broth, and prawns and other delicacies stir-frying on high open flames.

Half the population of the Tenderloin was Southeast Asian, and restaurants dotted most of the streets, Larkin especially, selling exotic foods prepared in delicate spices.

An abundance of restaurants also created an abundance of food, for both the paying customer who entered these establishments through the front door and for the nonpaying ones who entered through the back.

Today, Oldman would be one of the latter.

He passed the back doors of three restaurants before he found one that had been left open.

After taking a deep breath and reminding himself why he was doing this, Oldman ran into the restaurant, which he recognized from the interior as being the King Palace.

He moved slowly through the tight rear hallway, lined on each side with cases of soda and boxes of produce and other supplies. When he reached the end of the hall he turned right—the kitchen.

There was a window in the center of the door, but it

had long ago been covered over by layers of dirt, grease, and steam. Oldman pushed the door open slightly and peered in through the crack. There were several waiters in the kitchen, as well as a potwasher and cook.

He eased the door closed. Too many people.

He turned around to leave, but heard movement in the kitchen, plates rattling, and a door on the other side—the side leading into the restaurant—opening up.

He peeked into the kitchen again. This time there was only the cook and potwasher, one standing over a giant wok, the other with his arms elbow-deep in soapy water.

Oldman pushed his entire body through the doors and stood for a moment inside the kitchen, looking at the two men in turn.

He could only guess what went through their minds at the sight of a nine-foot werewolf suddenly appearing in their kitchen, but whatever it was the thought didn't last long as The Delirium affected them almost immediately. They dropped to the floor like falling redwoods, their muted shrieks falling with them.

Oldman moved fast. He had a few choices of food in the kitchen but wanted to make sure that whatever he took would go the furthest in feeding a large number of people.

He settled on the whole fresh chickens hanging by their feet above the stove. L.C. would be able to make soup stock out of them, then use the leftover meat in some other dish. Oldman grabbed four of the chickens by their necks, tucked them under his left arm, and ran out of the kitchen.

As he stepped outside into the alley, he could hear the high-pitched voices of the waiters as they came back into the kitchen to find the two men lying on the floor unconscious.

Oldman smiled, wishing he could have stuck around to watch the scene and listen to the cook and potwasher explain to the others how they came to end up on the floor. While he didn't understand Cantonese, he had a feeling he wouldn't have had to.

As he ran down the alley he noticed another smell in the air—fresh bread. Up ahead a cube van from the Yet Wah Bakery was turning out of the alley onto Larkin Street.

He passed the back door of another restaurant and stopped. A full sack of buns had been left out on the step next to a smaller bag of fortune cookies.

Oldman put the chickens inside the sack and tossed the whole thing over his shoulder.

Then, without another moment's delay, he ran out of the alley and back toward the mission, his cache of goodies bobbing up and down behind him.

As he ran down Eddy Street, he tried to envision what he looked like with a bulging sack of bread over his shoulder and a shock of bright white hair atop his head.

And then he wondered if anyone seeing him would report to the police that they'd seen a werewolf, or Santa Claus.

Dinnertime at The Scott Mission.

Curtis Richards sat at a crowded table slurping a bowl of potato soup. It wasn't much of a meal, but at least it was warm and halfway filling. Still, he could do with something more to eat.

Richards looked to his left and saw an older man sitting there, gray scraggly hair and a beard to match. On the table between them was a slice of white bread. It looked inviting to Richards, calling him to pick it up and eat it.

The old man would never miss it, he thought.

Casually, he reached over and picked up the bread, then quickly dunked it into his soup. As he ate the soggy bread, the old man began looking around the table.

"Where'd it go?" he said.

Richards ignored him.

"Who took my bread?"

Richards did his best to eat the bread slowly, but found himself stuffing it into his mouth more quickly.

"You!" said the old man. "You took it."

"Take a hike, old-timer," said Richards, his mouth full of sopping-wet bread.

"I'll take a strip out of your hide is what I'll do." The old-timer threw his elbow into Richards's chest. The blow was surprisingly strong, knocking Richards backward out of his chair. He hit the floor with a heavy *thud* and took his time getting to his feet.

When he did finally get up, there was a knife in his hand. "You shouldn't have done that, you old fuck," he said, waving the knife menacingly before him.

"Why not, Richards?" said a voice behind him. "What are you going to do? Steal his bread, then kill him when he complains?"

Curtis recognized the voice—it was Kenneth Holt's. He could also feel the tip of Holt's knife poised against the small of his back and knew the man wasn't afraid to use it.

"Seeing as Father *Old-man* runs this mission, one of the rules we live by in here is that you respect your elders. Obviously you haven't learned that one yet, so I suggest you don't come back until you do."

Curtis felt a little pressure on the knife and began moving forward, up the stairs and toward the front door.

Oldman had been lying on the couch in his office for over an hour, but sleep was only just coming to him now.

L.C. had been happy to receive the chickens and bread from "a wealthy resident of Nob Hill" and said she could feed the mission for more than two days on it.

Oldman had been glad to hear it, but the pleasure had been short-lived.

So what if they had enough food for two more days. What if they had enough food for the rest of the month? The year? Until the end of the century?

The killer was still out there.

It was a lot like treating the symptoms of a cold. Get rid of the cough, the running nose, the aches and pains and what have you got? A body that was still infected by a virus.

He tried not to think about it, closed his eyes, and waited for sleep to wash over him.

There was a knock at the door.

Oldman remained silent.

Another knock.

"Go away," said Oldman. "I'm trying to sleep."

"It's Parker, Father. There's a phone call for you. Long distance from Philadelphia. . . . It's Roland Gateway."

Oldman's eyes opened sharply at the mention of the name. He rolled off the bed and headed for the phone on his desk. "I'll take it in here," he said. He picked up the phone and waited for Parker to hang up the other extension. At last he heard the click. "Hello."

"Hello. Is this Wendel Oldman?"

"It is."

"This is Roland Gateway, of the Philadelphia Glass Walkers."

"How are you?"

"I'm fine, thanks." There was a pause, and Oldman could hear what sounded like Gateway puffing on a big fat cigar. "But never mind about me, I'm calling to thank *you*. I picked up my son at the airport last night. He says you saved his hide in some back alley of that town of yours."

"Is that what he told you?"

"Yes."

"Well, it wasn't all that much really. I just lent a hand. He seemed to have the situation pretty much in control."

"Don't try to be modest with me, Oldman. I've been talking to some people and I know you've been awarded some renown in your time. And talking to my son, I don't wonder."

Oldman felt himself starting to blush. "Thank you," he said, realizing Gateway wasn't interested in him being humble.

"Now, I want to show you how much I appreciate what you did for me, and I want you to tell me what you need over there."

"Your thanks is more than enough reward, Gateway."

"A*pe*shit!" said Gateway. "You run a mission there for homeless people, right?"

"Yes."

"And you mean to tell me you don't want anything for the mission? There's got to be something you need."

"Well, we've been short of food the last week or so. I suppose we could use some potatoes."

"Done," Gateway said. "What else?"

Oldman thought about it for a moment, then decided— what the hell, it's worth a try.

"Do you know anybody in Maine?"

"Yeah, lots of people. Garou and human."

"Do you know anybody in the Catholic Church?"

"Oldman, you'd be amazed by how many people I know." Gateway's voice had become soft, serious. It was obvious to Oldman that this was the kind of favor he had in mind.

Oldman sat down at his desk, made himself comfortable, and told Gateway all about the persistent priest in Maine, Father Jean-Louis Trudel.

22

Oldman and Holt sat in Oldman's office talking about the night's search for the killer.

"I've been prowling the streets and back alleys of the Tenderloin for the last couple of nights," said Oldman. "But I haven't seen a trace of the killer Garou, or very many homeless people for that matter."

"I'm not surprised," said Holt.

"What do you mean?"

"Well, if I was still homeless and I knew there was a killer stalking the streets at night, I sure as hell wouldn't be sleeping outdoors—I'd probably find some hole to crawl into where no one would find me until I was dead for a week."

"So you think I should be looking indoors, abandoned buildings . . . places like that?" Oldman had suspected as much, but it was still good to have Holt confirm his suspicion.

"If you want to catch him, I do."

"Right," Oldman nodded. He walked over to his desk, took out a folded map of San Francisco from one of the drawers, and laid it out on the top of the desk. "You probably know the streets better than I do. Where do you think he might strike next?"

Holt moved around next to Oldman and began scanning the map. There were a half-dozen abandoned and condemned buildings in the Tenderloin in which homeless people spent their nights, and it was up to Holt to figure out which buildings suited the killer best.

After a few minutes Holt decided there were really only three buildings they had to worry about.

One of them was an abandoned building on Golden Gate Avenue near Market Street. At one time it had housed a small Italian supermarket owned by the Commisso brothers. But when the Asian immigrants moved into the Tenderloin in the seventies and opened up dozens of little grocery stores, the brothers closed up shop and moved their operation north to California Street on the border between the Tenderloin and the highly affluent neighborhood of Nob Hill. The move had left a big building boarded up and empty, the perfect place for the homeless to bed down for the night to get out of the wind and rain.

The old store was a possibility, but Holt figured it was a little too far south to be a real hunting ground for the killer.

That left two other places, an abandoned Victorian home on Ellis Street called *The Candle in the Window* and the old Driftwood Community Center on Hyde.

"I think there are only two buildings you really have to worry about," Holt said at last.

"What are they?"

"Have you ever heard of *The Candle in the Window*?"

"I think so. It's an old house on Ellis, isn't it?"

"Yeah, that's it."

"What's the other one?"

"The Driftwood Community Center on Hyde."

Oldman looked at Holt for what seemed like a long time. "There's two places, and there's two of us . . ." he said, his eyebrows arching suggestively.

"I'll check out *The Candle in the Window*," said Holt.

Oldman nodded. "Sounds like we have a plan."

———

It was a short walk for Holt from the mission to Ellis Street, and in a few minutes he was standing in front of the old weather-beaten house.

The Candle in the Window.

Holt spent a few minutes just looking at the house, recalling the nights he'd come here looking for shelter. It somehow looked older to him now, more rundown, a fact Holt attributed to the recent improvement in *his* situation.

Now, looking at it, Holt realized the home had done quite well to remain standing all these years, through earthquakes and tremors and the usual fires that ensued. But although it was still standing, the house still looked as if it might fall down at any moment. The outside of the building was an earth brown color, a far cry from the "painted ladies"—Victorian homes that had been well preserved and elaborately painted in a variety of decorative colors—that dotted the residential areas of the rest of the city. The windows had all been boarded up with unpainted plywood, except for the plywood covering one of the top windows, which had a candle and curtains painted onto it. As a result of that single feature, the home had been called *The Candle in the Window* and was known among the homeless as a place where they could go to be indoors.

Holt stepped up to the darkened alcove and pulled on the door handle. Of course, the door didn't open. Then he tried swinging it to the left, and the door slid sideways, swinging on a nail in the top left-hand corner. He slipped through the tight opening, careful not to catch his clothes on any of the exposed nails jutting out from the wood. Almost immediately, he was overcome by a foul stink of sweaty bodies and refuse.

Holt found it hard to believe he could have felt at home in a place like this. Still, he had some fond memories of his nights spent in this building, and that made the smell a little bit easier to take.

Holt made a quick inspection of the inside of the house, being careful not to make too much noise on the stairs as he went up to the top floor. There were half a dozen people lying around, some asleep, the rest just staring blankly at the ceiling as they tightly clutched the bags containing their few worldly possessions.

He went back downstairs and looked for a spot in what used to be the living room, where he could keep a close watch on the front door. He pushed aside the garbage on the floor with his foot and made himself comfortable on the bare floor.

Then he reached into his jacket pocket and felt the knife in his hand, making sure the blade was sharp and his grip was firm. . . .

And then he sat back and waited for the killer to arrive.

Searching for food during the day and the killer at night was taking its toll on Oldman.

He was in his Crinos form, stalking the back alleys and shadows of the Tenderloin, but he felt weak, tired . . . *old*. Instead of feeling rage and the power of Gaia coursing through his veins, charging his muscles with energy, he felt lethargic, lead-footed, more man than wolf.

He was glad to have Holt's help, but if he didn't find Wingnut tonight, he'd have to get even more help—Able Heart, March Lion, or Silent-Fist-That-Wins, maybe even ask for the help of the Bone Gnawers themselves. He shook his head at that last thought. As far as they were concerned, this renegade Garou had been blackballed and therefore did not exist. If they tried to find or stop him, they would be ignoring their own rite and fetish. In the minds of the Bone Gnawers Wingnut was already dead.

And even if they could be of some help to him, Oldman would hate to be indebted in even the smallest way to Bongos and his pack. If he ended up needing help, he'd stick to the members of the Sept. Hopefully, it wouldn't come to that.

Oldman made a cursory search of the Tenderloin from the rooftops of some of the tallest buildings in the area. He didn't expect to find Wingnut that way, but he wouldn't have felt right continuing the search on the ground if he hadn't first taken a look from above.

That done, he headed for the community center.

The Driftwood Center was a fairly large brick building on Hyde Street midway between Geary and O'Farrell. For years it had served as a focal point to the people of the Tenderloin, providing rooms for them to meet in, either for neighborhood meetings, club gatherings, or for young people's dances. An old building, it had finally fallen victim to the earthquake in 1989. Although the Tenderloin went virtually unscathed in that quake, the tremors had been just enough to knock the building off its foundations.

It was condemned by the city, but had never been demolished, leaving it as a place for a forgotten sector of the population—namely the homeless—to call home.

Oldman entered the building through the half-open door at the back. He could hear and feel the presence of more than a dozen people inside, but they were well scattered throughout the building, creating an impression that the place was empty and barren.

This was where the killer would come for his next victim, Oldman was sure of it. He went up a flight of stairs looking for a place to sit and wait. There was a small meeting room off to the right, but that already had two men in it. There was a washroom across the hall, but that was still being used and smelled like it.

There were other rooms on the main floor, but all of them were too far away from the building's only entrance. Oldman padded down the stairs into the basement. There was a woman in one corner sleeping behind a wall of plastic bags that had been set up as if to act as some sort of buffer between herself and the rest of the world.

Then he turned around and saw that there was a wide-open space under the stairs. It was close to the entrance and almost black with shadows.

Perfect.

He could remain there unnoticed all night.

He crouched down and moved into the space under the stairs. Then he made himself comfortable and waited.

And waited . . .

And waited . . .

Until exhaustion set in and his eyes became heavy and he slowly drifted off to sleep.

The front door of *The Candle in The Window* slid open, and the faint light from the night outside filtered in through the small triangular-shaped opening.

The hair on the back of Holt's neck stood on end as he watched the silhouetted figure crawl through the opening into the house. He grabbed firm hold of his knife, his muscles tensed and ready to spring into action, but when the door slid back and the inside of the house was returned to darkness, he could see that the figure was just another homeless woman looking for a place to sleep.

He eased his hold on the knife yet again. It was the fifth time someone had entered the house, someone other than the killer.

Holt took a fresh look around. There were twice as many people here now, all bunched closely together, each within sight of the next.

There were *too many* people, he thought. Wingnut needed a place with some privacy and dark shadows, especially since some of his killings were long, drawn-out affairs in which the victim's agonized screams could be heard blocks away.

There was strength in numbers.

Holt realized that the people here were safe.

And that left only one other place, the Driftwood Community Center.

Holt scrambled to his feet and headed for the door.

"Hey, buddy!" a voice said. "That's my spot."

Oldman felt something poking him in the chest. He opened his eyes, still fogged over with sleep, and saw the rounded end of a broom handle hovering inches away from his nose. "Get lost," he said, in the low throaty voice of his Crinos form.

"No fucking way," the voice said. Oldman looked up out of the shadows. The voice belonged to a middle-aged man dressed in dirty green fatigues with an American flag sewed onto one of the arms. He had shoulder-length black hair, a stud in his left ear, and a full mustache and beard. Oldman didn't recognize him, but guessed that he was a Vietnam vet.

"Get lost," Oldman said again, this time grabbing the broom handle and biting off the end of it with a powerful snap of his jaws.

The vet pulled the broom handle out of the shadows and looked at the broken end and the hairy clawed-hand still holding on to it—and his eyes grew wide with terror.

Oldman snarled at him, then let out a long, low growl.

"But, if you want to sleep there tonight," he said, peering into the darkness at Oldman, but seeing nothing, "hey, it's all right with me, pal. Enjoy!"

Without another word he turned around, scrambled up the stairs, and ran out of the building.

Oldman held his breath, listening to the sound of the man's scurrying feet as they slowly faded in the distance.

And then he heard a scream.

It was a muted cry coming from somewhere deep inside the building. If he hadn't had the sharpened senses of his Crinos form, he might never have heard it. Yes, he thought, and if I hadn't fallen asleep I might have heard the killer enter the building.

He crawled out of the alcove under the stairs and ran up the steps to the main floor in search of the source of the scream. He stopped at the top of the stairs, listening. There was a faint whimpering sound coming from the next level up.

He ran up another flight of stairs toward it.

There were four rooms on the second floor, all of them with their doorways covered in some way, either with an old broken door or by some sort of debris. Again Oldman stopped to listen, and again he heard a faint sound. This time it was a whimpering cry, as if someone was suffering in great pain.

Like a homing device, Oldman tracked the sound— along with the strong scent of the Garou—until he was sure it led to the room down the hall on the right. Then he bolted toward the room, smashed down the door, and found *him*.

Wingnut.

The Killer.

Holt ran down Hyde until he came upon the front of the community center. He ran up the steps to the front door and tried opening it. He managed to open it a crack but couldn't squeeze through the narrow opening. Even if he could he'd never be able to get past the debris piled up against the inside of the door.

And then he remembered there was another way in around the back. He let go of the door, flew down the steps, and hurried around to the rear of the building.

Wingnut was crouched down next to an elderly woman, killing her slowly, cutting her up with his claws and making her beg for her life. He was even in his Glabro form, just to make sure she wouldn't be affected by The Delirium and would remain conscious to suffer the full extent of his torture.

The thought of it turned Oldman's stomach.

"You!" he snarled.

Wingnut stopped himself in midswipe of his one good clawed-hand and turned around.

Recognition flashed in his eyes, as well as a bit of fear.

"Oldman," he said, in a surprisingly calm voice. "Imagine finding you here."

"Get away from her," Oldman said.

"Temper, temper," Wingnut said, pointing his stump at Oldman like an admonishing finger.

"Step aside!"

"Oh, angry, aren't you? Perhaps I've done something to make you mad? Let me see now. . . . What could it be?"

"Last time you got away," said Oldman, struggling with the words. "This time death will be your only escape!"

Wingnut continued on with his own end of the conversation as if he hadn't even heard Oldman.

"Perhaps you're upset a touch that I killed your friend. What was his name . . . the General, wasn't it?"

Oldman's lips pulled back from his fangs and the hair on the back of his neck bristled as if charged with electricity.

"You know what he said when he died, Oldman? When I took the last dying breath from his body?"

Oldman just stood there, seething.

"He said, 'There's no place like home. . . . Hut . . . Hut . . . '" A pause. "'H-hut . . . ' And then he died." Wingnut quickly shifted into Crinos form, his grin remaining constant throughout.

Oldman was blind with rage. His muscles tensed like hair-trigger springs ready to explode in a blast of motion.

But before he could move, Wingnut leaped at him, his clawed-hand leading the way.

Oldman was caught slightly flat-footed, and the Garou's arm slammed into his throat while the rest of him landed heavily against his chest.

They rolled backwards twice until they got caught in the doorway. Oldman could feel the claws on his throat tightening, breaking the skin and digging into the flesh below.

He raked his claws down Wingnut's chest, drawing blood, but the crazed Garou would not release his hold on him. He's strong, thought Oldman. Unnaturally so. Perhaps the Wyrm taint that had infected him was more powerful than he'd imagined.

Oldman made another attempt to break the hold Wingnut had on his throat, then saw his opportunity.

Wingnut's other hand.

The pink raw stump with two jutting fingers came to within inches of his muzzle. He reached out and snapped at it, taking away a large chunk of flesh in his teeth.

The viselike grip on his throat suddenly released as Wingnut reared back and howled in pain.

By the time Oldman got up off the floor, the Garou was out of the room and running down the hall. Oldman turned to the woman in the corner. She was cut up, and she'd be a little shaky once The Delirium wore off, but she'd be all right.

And then Oldman noticed something familiar about her. He took a closer look and realized it was Bernadine Daly, San Francisco's Master Gatherer and the sweetest old woman he'd ever met.

Rage flared within him like a rocket blasting skyward.

There could be no more mercy for this abominable Garou.

Only justice.

Only death.

He sniffed at the air to catch Wingnut's scent, then scrambled off after him, heading deeper into the building.

Holt squeezed through the opening in the back of the building and stood inside for a moment trying to figure out where would be the most likely place for a Garou like Wingnut to kill.

The answer seemed obvious to him—the basement.

Holt headed downstairs.

The trail led Oldman down a hallway, through a hole in the wall, and then twisted and turned down another narrow corridor. Oldman took a moment to stop and check his bearings and realized he was lost. It didn't really matter though because by now there was no turning back. Only forward, after his prey.

He followed the scent, stronger now, to another jagged crack in the wall. The crack was fairly wide, following the line of the bricks where they had fallen out after the last big quake. Other bricks had been pushed out to make the hole big enough to pass through, but not big enough to invite regular traffic.

Oldman squeezed through the narrow opening and realized he'd stumbled upon one of the community center's larger meeting rooms.

A small amount of light filtered in through the tiny

cracks in the wall to his left, capturing dust in its beams and just barely giving Oldman enough light to see. As his eyes adjusted to the darkness, he got a better idea of the room's layout.

What he saw made him gasp.

The normally open space was completely filled . . .

With newspapers.

Years' worth of yellowing grayish newspapers were placed in neat piles, the stacks forming little channels like the walls of a maze. Obviously, this was where Bernadine Daly had hid the newspapers she'd been collecting all these years—or at least since 1989.

Whatever the case, there were tons of old newspapers here, just ripe for recycling.

Oldman sniffed at the air and smelled the musty odor of stale wet newsprint. He tried to push the smell aside and concentrated on the scent of Wingnut.

When he was satisfied he'd isolated the Garou's scent, he followed it through the winding maze. As he moved along he felt his eyes being drawn to the headlines poking out from the piles.

PEACE TREATY SIGNED WITH JAPAN

Oldman read that one and blinked. If he remembered correctly, the Allies had signed a treaty with the Japanese in San Francisco in 1951. That meant the newspapers dated back past 1989 to who-knew-when.

Another quick scan of the piles revealed that they were made up of a wide variety of local publications. He recognized the mastheads of the *San Francisco Chronicle*, *The San Francisco Examiner*, as well as S.F. *Weekly*, *Sun Reporter*, *Nob Hill Gazette*, *Sentinel*, *Chinese Times*, *San Francisco Business Times*, and a half-dozen others he didn't recognize. There were even a few scattered editions of *The Washington Post* and *USA Today*.

Oldman realized that this wasn't just a bunch of newspapers collected by an out-of-her-mind old bag lady—it was a depository of San Francisco history. Something should be done to preserve this, he thought. Something, but what?

Just then the stack of newspapers directly in front of him toppled over, dropping down onto him with all the weight of a falling redwood.

Oldman hit the floor hard, and before he could recover, felt claws grabbing at him and fangs biting down onto the upper part of his right arm.

He struggled to get up, but Wingnut, despite his considerably smaller size, had been made strong and tenacious by The Wyrm. He felt another sting of claws in his midsection and let out a howl.

Oldman knew he couldn't go on like this for much longer. He had to get up and fight back.

Putting all his effort into the task of getting onto his feet, Oldman lurched up off the floor with Wingnut's teeth still firmly set in his arm.

Then, with all the strength he could muster, Oldman drove his right hand into the midsection of the Garou, sinking his claws and fingers knuckle-deep in flesh.

Wingnut let out a yelp and instinctively released his hold on Oldman's arm.

And then he was standing in front of Oldman, crouched over from the blow to his midsection. For a few moments the two Garou stood face-to-face, each of them catching their breath, coming to grips with the pain of their wounds.

"Why didn't you leave the city?" Oldman struggled to say.

"Where was I supposed to go . . . with this black eight ball hanging from my neck?"

Oldman didn't have an answer, nor did he feel like offering one. He bared his teeth and stepped forward. He was prepared to pounce, ready to kill. . . .

But Wingnut suddenly stepped aside, vanishing into the maze of newspapers.

He had escaped for the moment, but Oldman vowed he'd never leave the building alive. His scent was laced with blood now and easy to follow. Oldman sniffed at the air and bounded over the fallen papers.

Oldman soon found himself back in the maze, cautiously moving between the walls of newspapers, peeking around corners. Wingnut could be hiding around any of them.

He stopped dead in his tracks and listened. He could hear the Garou moving close by, perhaps just on the other side of the stack of newspapers to his right. He looked in that direction and saw a single column of newspapers wavering slightly as if they'd just been bumped.

He raised his arms to push the stack over . . .

When Wingnut dropped down on top of him.

Oldman felt fangs lock onto the back of his neck and claws rake down the length of his spine. He let out a howl of pain and twisted his body from side to side in an attempt to shake off the crazed Garou.

But to no avail.

Oldman realized then that he wasn't in a regular fight for dominance in the midst of Gaia. This was a city fight, with no rules of conduct.

He started backpedaling, gaining some speed before slamming Wingnut's back into a wall of newspapers. Wingnut grunted, but managed to keep his hold on Oldman's neck. Oldman tried the tactic again, this time choosing a less stable stack to butt up against.

On impact Wingnut grunted and released his fangs from Oldman's flesh. The force of the impact had also caused the stack of papers to fall, and bundles and loose sheets came tumbling down, several striking the two Garou where they lay on the floor.

Oldman had been expecting the deluge of paper and had put up his arms to protect himself. Wingnut hadn't been so lucky and had been hit squarely on the head by a heavy bundle of *Hokubei Mainichi*, San Francisco's Japanese daily.

He looked to be out cold.

The bowels of the community center were dark and dirty, and the air was thick with the smell of fuel oil. There were a few things that suggested that homeless people had once slept down here—food wrappers, wine bottles, old rags—but the place clearly belonged to the rats now.

No one would be dying down here tonight.

He'd have to look upstairs.

He turned to leave, and that's when he heard it—a howling yelp of pain, followed by another.

And then the building seem to shake slightly, as if a wall had been struck with tremendous force.

Holt had an idea about what was going on.

He ran up the stairs, the sound of the howling guiding his way.

Oldman stood over the prone body of the Garou, feeling the depth of the gash in his neck and the burning of the wounds down the length of his back.

He moved closer to Wingnut, claws ready to tear into his chest. He was just about to strike when Wingnut's eyes popped open and his hand shot out to rake his claws across the side of Oldman's face.

Oldman screamed a long, loud howl, and his hands came up to grab his lacerated face. Wingnut took the chance to scramble out from beneath him and climb onto Oldman's back.

Oldman could feel Wingnut clutching on his back, moving into position. He tried to shake the Garou off of him, but his face was in too much pain for him to give anything other than token resistance.

And then he felt it, a cord that had previously bundled newspapers being wrapped around his neck.

Oldman took his bloody hands away from his face and tried desperately to grab at the cord, but it was already too tightly wound around his neck, already digging deep into his flesh.

Oldman clambered to his feet and stumbled around between the piles of newspapers, his breath rasping and wheezing in great horselike gasps, trying to jar Wingnut loose.

But to no avail.

With each passing second, Wingnut was able to tighten the cord around Oldman's neck just a little more, shrinking his windpipe, making it smaller and smaller. . . . Harder for him to breath.

Oldman fell to his knees, clawing at his neck in a last-ditch effort to cut the cord with his claws, but only succeeding in shredding his own flesh in the process . . .

"Good-bye, Oldman," growled Wingnut. "It's been a slice."

"N*oooo*!"

The scream came from the corner, loud and shrill.

Wingnut turned to look in the direction the cry had come from and saw Holt charging toward him, his knife leading the way.

Holt moved fast, burying the knife hilt-deep in Wingnut's side.

Wingnut screamed in pain, releasing his hold on the cord.

Oldman fell the rest of the way to the floor, gulping for air like a drowned man who'd just broken the surface.

Holt's hands remained firmly on the knife's hilt, twisting the blade in an attempt to damage as many internal organs as possible.

Wingnut's good arm suddenly shot out, catching Holt on the side of the head, knocking him down, and sending him sprawling across the floor.

For a moment, none of the three moved.

Then Wingnut took the knife from his side, tossed it away, and headed for Holt, his clawed-hand flexing, ready to kill.

Holt moved around on the floor as if in a daze, unable to do anything as claws began to rake his skin and tear into his body.

Oldman was breathing easier now, but still felt weak. He turned around and saw Wingnut clawing at Holt and suddenly came alive with a powerful rage.

Forgetting all about his pain and the blood that was running freely from his wounds, he dove forward after Wingnut, knocking him off Holt and sending him rolling into a stack of newspapers.

Before Wingnut could right himself, Oldman was on him, grabbing one of his hind feet.

Wingnut squirmed like a small animal, kicking at Oldman's hands in an attempt to break free.

Oldman's hands quickly became bloody as Wingnut's kicking toeclaws tore at his flesh. But Oldman refused to let go. In fact he strengthened his hold, snapping several of Wingnut's tendons in the process. Finally, he pulled the Garou closer, grabbing his other leg in his hands.

Then, with a firm hold, Oldman got up onto his hind legs and lifted Wingnut off the floor, swinging him in an arc through the air and smashing his head and shoulders down flat against the floor.

Oldman finally let go of the Garou's legs, tossing them aside as if they were attached to a carcass.

Now, sure that the wind, and fighting spirit, had been knocked out of the Garou, Oldman moved over Wingnut, straddling his body. Then he fell to his knees so that he was sitting directly on top of his chest.

Oldman's rage was strong now, stronger than it had ever been in his life. It flowed through him like flame through a tinderbox, ready to explode into violent action at any moment.

He grabbed Wingnut by the neck and tore strips of flesh from both sides of it until he could hear his whining howls of pain coming out through the open wounds.

Oldman prepared for another strike, but the Garou suddenly came to life, heaving his body off the floor and sending Oldman tumbling into the nearest wall of newspapers.

Then Wingnut got up off the floor and headed back into the maze.

Oldman saw the direction he was moving in and cut him off, pushing over a stack of newspapers in front of him to block his way.

That done, Oldman waited for him to double back. When he did, Oldman was ready for him.

He charged at Wingnut with a screaming howl, his

claws out in front and his teeth bared. He clawed at the smaller Garou, his razor-sharp talons whirling in front of him as he tore chunks and strips of flesh from a dozen different parts of his body.

Wingnut tried to fight back, but that only spurred Oldman on, acting as fuel for his rage.

He clawed at the Garou's face, gouging out his eyes, tearing away his nose and jowls in a flurry of motion.

At last Wingnut fell to his knees, blood streaming through the gaps between his claws as he held his hand up to his shredded face.

Oldman did not relent. He reared back with his right arm and dug his claws deep into Wingnut's chest. After getting a hold on the flesh and bone there, he worked his fingers deeper into the cavity until he could feel the Garou's heart with the tips of his claws. It was pounding out a wildly erratic beat, like that of a frightened rabbit caught in a trap.

Then with one last push, Oldman closed his hand around the heart and slowly began to squeeze.

Wingnut's eyes opened in shocked terror as he suddenly felt a sharp pain deep inside his body.

Oldman delighted in that look and squeezed harder.

This is for the General, he thought. And this is for Sully. He looked over at Holt where he lay bleeding and tightened his fist, feeling his claws encircling the heart and digging into his own palm. And this is for Holt.

Wingnut thrashed about for a while, but his body eventually slowed along with the rhythm of his heart.

Finally, both were still.

Oldman relaxed his grip on the Garou's heart and let the body fall to the floor.

At last, the rage he'd been feeling since he'd come back from the ranch began to dissipate, replaced by a sense of calm and inner peace . . . and pain.

Without his rage, his wounds had begun to burn. The flesh on his face, neck, back, chest, and arms all felt as if it were on fire.

He stepped back from the dead Garou, knelt down, and

grabbed hold of the eight-ball fetish hanging from its neck. With a quick jerk he snapped it off and wound the cord tightly around his hand. As he looked at the ball in his palm, he was suddenly struck by a thought. Maybe there was something within the fetish that made blackballed Bone Gnawers want to kill the homeless. Or perhaps it was the Rite of the Blackball itself that was to blame . . .

Either way, it was something he'd be taking up with Bongos, and soon.

He got up onto his feet, shaky after the long bloody battle, and trudged over to where Holt lay on the floor.

Was he dead? It was hard to tell. There was too much blood—his, Oldman's, and Wingnut's—to really know how badly he was injured. He knelt down next to him and shifted into Glabro form. "Holt? Can you hear me? Are you all right?"

No answer. Holt's breath was shallow. Oldman placed a hand on his throat. His pulse was regular, but weak. He shifted back into Crinos form, lifted him up off the floor, and headed for the exit.

The gentle jostling of Oldman's first few steps seemed to awaken Holt. His eyes slowly opened and he looked curiously at Oldman. "Thanks for the lift," he said. "But I think I can make it on my own."

Oldman's lips pulled back into a smile as he gently eased Holt down onto the floor.

Holt looked a little wobbly, but managed to stay upright on his feet by putting an arm out to steady himself.

"Thank you," said Oldman, rubbing the tender part of his neck where the cord had dug into the flesh beneath his fur.

"Don't mention it," said Holt. "It was my pleasure. Besides, I owed you one, remember?"

Oldman nodded. "Consider the debt," he struggled to say, "paid in full."

After picking up Holt's knife, they left the meeting room together. On the other side of the entrance wall Oldman sent Holt on ahead while he went back to where he'd last seen Bernadine. When he got there he found the room was empty, her few belongings gone. He knew then that she'd be all right. She was a feisty old woman, a scrapper. A run-in with a werewolf wasn't going to slow her down any. Not at all. At the thought of Bernadine, Oldman's lips once again pulled back into a smile.

He hobbled down the stairs and out into the alley behind the community center where Holt stood waiting for him.

The moon hung full and bright in the night sky, shining like a beacon, helping them find their way.

Oldman was grateful for the help, but knew he didn't need it.

He could find his way back to the mission, back to his home, even in the dark.

The hospital was crowded, just like every other public building in the area. The air was filled with the smell of dried blood, sweat, antiseptic, and urine, and the sound of old men moaning on their deathbeds.

Bernadine Daly sat on a stiff examination table in a small pale beige-colored room. She wore a light blue hospital gown that left her legs bare. She let them dangle from the edge of the table, swinging them back and forth as if they belonged to a schoolgirl.

The doctor, or perhaps just an intern, stepped into the room. He was a tall, handsome young man with a thick mustache and full head of coal black hair. He moved about the room with confidence, fast without looking to be in a hurry.

When he looked at Bernadine, she smiled.

"Hello," he said. "I'm Dr. Sheldon Katz, and you are . . ."

"Bernadine," she said. "Bernadine Daly."

"Pleased to meet you, Bernadine. Now . . ." He turned to face her. "What happened to you tonight?"

"I was attacked," she said, pulling down the collar of her gown to reveal a few of the larger wounds around her neck and shoulders. She did her best not to let the pain she felt show up on her face.

The young doctor winced at the sight of the deep gouges in her flesh, but took a deep breath and quickly recovered his composure.

"What were you attacked by, Bernadine?"

"Some kind of a monster," she said without hesitation. "I think it was a werewolf."

Dr. Katz tried to hide his reaction to her words, but wound up letting out a little laugh. "R-really?"

"Yes, really. It was a big one, almost seven feet tall, covered with fur. It had sharp claws and fangs."

The doctor turned and glanced at the form attached to the clipboard, looking for any notations that said she was mentally disabled. There were none.

"C'mon, Bernadine," he said. "Everyone knows there's no such thing as a werewolf."

The suggestion seemed to cloud her memory. "No," she said, a confused look on her face. "I suppose there isn't."

The doctor turned around and pulled a curtain across the room's open doorway. *The Veil*.

"Now, before I can help you heal those wounds of yours I have to know what caused them. I'll ask you once more, Bernadine. What was it that attacked you tonight?"

There was a long pause as Bernadine tried to recall.

"I'm not sure anymore," she said. "Isn't that strange? I can't remember a thing."

23

There was a knock on the door.

Oldman was still in bed, recovering. He ignored the knock, hoping whoever it was would go away.

When he'd returned to the mission the night before, he'd spent almost two hours cleaning his wounds and applying his special salves. The creams had taken enough sting out of the wounds to allow him to sleep, and now they were just a vast network of dull throbbing pains. Every once in a while the pain sharpened, and sometimes his skin felt as if it were crawling with ants, but it wasn't anything he couldn't live with. They were all signs that his skin was busy repairing itself.

There was another knock on the door. This one more forceful than the first.

"Go away," he said, pulling the sheets over his head.

"There's someone here to see you, Father."

"Tell him to come back later."

A pause.

"It's the police, Father. They want to ask you a few questions."

"All right," he said. "Give me a minute."

Oldman rolled out of bed and checked himself in the mirror. The salves had done well to heal his skin, but he still had long red gashes on the side of his face and a big patch of red flesh on his neck. The wounds would heal eventually, leaving jagged scars, but for now he couldn't do much to hide them.

He slipped into his bathrobe, wrapped a towel around his neck, and hoped he could convince the two detectives he was feeling under the weather.

He opened the door. Detectives Garrett and Chong were standing there along with Parker. All six of their eyes widened at the sight of Oldman's face.

"I was foolish enough to try and break up a fight in the mess," he said. "We've gotten crowded, and our food supply is low. Fights are breaking out all the time these days."

The two detectives seemed marginally satisfied with the explanation and stepped into Oldman's office.

Parker remained in the doorway, looking at Oldman. "Are you all right?" he said.

"I'm fine, Parker . . . Really."

Parker nodded, then closed the door, leaving Oldman in the room with the two detectives.

"Now, what can I help you with?"

"There was another killing last night," said Detective Garrett.

"Really?" Oldman did his best to sound surprised.

"The body was found early this morning in the old Driftwood Community Center on Hyde Street."

"I know that building."

"The victim was found naked," said Detective Chong. "There were wounds all over his body. There was also a giant hole around his heart, which we figure was the fatal wound."

Oldman shook his head. "That's terrible."

Chong picked up the conversation. "The MO of the killer was slightly different than with the previous killings, but there were still enough similarities for us to consider it the work of the Homeless Killer."

"I see," said Oldman, nodding his head. "Then what brings you here?"

"The victim had a distinguishing feature," said Garrett.

"One of his hands was missing. We were hoping you might be able to provide us with a name."

"Hmm?" Oldman mused. "Which hand?"

"The right one."

Oldman toyed with the idea of telling them he knew several homeless people missing their *left* hands but none missing their right, but decided the time wasn't right for such a morbid joke. "Missing the right hand . . ." he said. "It would be pretty hard to forget someone like that." He closed his eyes and tilted his head in feigned concentration, then finally shook his head. "I don't recall anyone like that passing through here."

"Perhaps you could ask around, let us know who he is the next time we're here?"

"I don't think you'll be coming back here anytime soon."

"Why is that?" asked Garrett.

"I have a funny feeling last night's victim was the last."

"Yeah, what makes you think so?"

"Just a feeling. . . . That's all."

"Maybe he's got a direct line to the man upstairs," said Chong, smiling.

Garrett wasn't amused. "Yeah, and maybe he's just dreaming. Sorry, Father, but I need a little more than 'just a feeling' to close this case. As far as I'm concerned the case will never be closed until the killer's sorry ass is in jail, or he ends up dead." The look on Garrett's face suggested that he would prefer the latter. "C'mon, let's get out of here."

Garrett left the room. Chong hung around behind, turning to Oldman when he reached the door. "Just between you and me, Father. I hope you're right. I'd rather catch him, but I'd settle for having the killings stopped one way or another."

"Trust me," Oldman said. "It's over."

When the detectives left, Oldman returned to bed.

He lay there for an hour, unable to fall asleep. Then, when he was just about to doze off, there was a knock at the door.

"Go away," he said.

"There's a delivery here for you, Father."

"You sign for it," he said.

"I'm afraid I can't do that. It's a personal delivery to you alone."

Oldman groaned and let out a string of mumbling words under his breath, but eventually he put on his bathrobe and opened the door.

"What is it?" he said.

Parker pointed to the street outside. There was a big delivery truck parked by the curb in front of the mission.

"What's this all about?"

"Are you Wendel Oldman?" the truck driver asked.

Oldman nodded.

"Sign here." He thrust a clipboard and pen in front of Oldman, who signed a "W.O." next to the tiny X the driver had made.

"Now," he said, handing back the clipboard. "What is this all about?"

The truck driver said nothing and began walking toward the front door.

Holt came up from the downstairs dorm then, his face, neck, and arms covered with the thick white salve. "What's going on?" he asked Oldman when he saw the crowd that had gathered in the upstairs hallway.

"That's what I'd like to know," said Oldman, gesturing to Holt, Parker, and a few of the others to follow him outside.

There were more people gathered on the street, curious to see what was inside the truck.

Oldman took a moment to look up. The sky was clear and the sun shone brightly in the sky, feeling warm against his skin.

It was a good day.

The truck driver finally answered Oldman's question by hopping up onto the back of the truck and rolling up the door.

"A gift to you from a good friend of yours in Philadelphia," said the driver. "A Mr. Roland Gateway."

Oldman stood on the sidewalk in awe.

The truck was filled with pallets stacked high with bags of potatoes—hundreds and hundreds of pounds of potatoes.

"We can't possibly eat all that before they go bad," said Oldman. "We don't even have room enough to store them all."

"Ex-cuse me," said a voice from behind him.

Oldman turned around. It was L.C., pushing her way through the crowd, puffing on her cigarette like a drill sergeant.

"I'll be the judge of where we can put it and how much we can use. I've been stretching everything to make it last for so long, it'll do me good not to have to worry about where the next meal is coming from. Preston!"

"Yes ma'am," said Parker.

"You get everyone you can to help you and start bringing these sacks into the basement. I've got all kinds of nooks and crannies for you to put them in. If we run out of room, we can always put them into Father Oldman's office."

"What?" said Oldman.

L.C. smiled, giving him a wink.

Oldman had given up on trying to get some rest. He changed his clothes, went downstairs to get a strong cup of coffee, and went back up to his office to try and catch up on some of the correspondence he'd let build up over the past few days.

There were a few bills, a few envelopes that looked like donations, and a bunch of the self-addressed stamped envelopes he used whenever he wrote to corporations and companies asking for donations.

He put those aside for the moment and gathered together the bills. He was about to open one up when the phone rang.

"Hello, The Scott Mission."

"Hello, Father Oldman?"

The voice had a strong accent.

"Yes."

"This is Father Jean-Louis Trudel. . . ."

There was a pause at the other end.

"Do you remember me?"

"Oh, yes," said Oldman. How could he forget the French Canadian priest who single-handedly tried to destroy his cover? "Of course I remember you."

"I've called to apologize."

"What?"

"I know I've doubted you in the past. It was wrong for me to do so, and I'm sorry."

Oldman held the receiver in his hand and looked at it as if he expected black goop to ooze out of it at any moment. "Is this a joke?"

"No, no, Father Oldman. I assure you it's not. I've just gotten off the phone with the Cardinal."

"The Cardinal?"

"Yes, Cardinal Leger."

"Ah . . . " Oldman said.

"Cardinal Leger called me to address my concerns." The priest's voice was almost giddy. "How he heard about me I don't know, but he said you and he were great friends and that the work you do with the homeless in San Francisco is a credit to the entire priesthood."

"Well, that was very nice of him," said Oldman. "I'll have to thank him the next time I'm in . . . " His voice trailed off as if he was having trouble remembering where the Cardinal was living these days.

"Philadelphia," said Father Trudel. "The next time you're in Philadelphia."

"Yes, of course," Oldman said, suddenly understanding everything.

Oldman hung up the phone, just in time to answer the knock on his door.

"What now?" he said under his breath.

A head covered in long blond hair peeked in through the door. "Father Oldman?"

It was Caroline Keegan.

"Oh, hello, Ms. Keegan," said Oldman. "I wasn't sure I'd be seeing you again. How have you been?"

"I've been fine, just fine." She came into the room, taking a seat across from him.

"What can I do for you?"

"Well, you can appear on camera, for one."

Oldman pulled his head back and looked at her.

"I'm doing a story on how the Homeless Killer is driving the homeless into the shelters. From what Parker told me the scare has stretched your resources to the limit."

"That's right, it has," said Oldman, still wary of the reporter. She'd said she'd help the Sept, but there was still the chance that she could have some ulterior motive for doing the story. "But we seem to be managing all right."

"Okay," she said. "I just thought a spot on *Inside Affair* illustrating your situation might net you some donations from concerned viewers. I know I haven't done much yet to help the Garou, but this was supposed to be a start." She got up to leave. "Oh well, suit yourself."

Oldman was a bit surprised by her response. Obviously she was solely interested in doing some good for the Sept. "No, no, please, Ms. Keegan," said Oldman, getting up from his chair. "It sounds like a wonderful idea. Let's do it."

It took less than an hour for the *Inside Affair* crew to set up their equipment on the sidewalk outside the mission. Oldman remained in the background, making sure that Parker, L.C., and Holt were interviewed first before agreeing to be interviewed on camera himself.

"Only if you get my good side," said Oldman, referring to the still-fresh wounds on the left side of his face.

"Don't worry," said Caroline. "Your good side is the only one I'm interested in today."

The interview began, and Caroline Keegan's questions turned out to be quite well informed. And unlike in many of her previous interviews, she didn't seem to be talking down to anyone.

"Tell me, Father," she said. "What does it say about society when homeless shelters and missions like yours can be so easily filled to overflowing?"

"It tells me that the work we do here at the mission and the service we provide to the community are sorely needed."

"Do you ever think there will be a time when a place like The Scott Mission won't be needed anymore?"

"I'd love to see that happen," said Oldman, "but I don't think it ever will. No matter how much our governments do to solve the homeless problem, there will never be a shortage of people who are down on their luck and looking for a second chance at life.

"And those are the people we're here to help," he continued. "The ones who are ready to embrace a new way of looking at the world and a new way of living within it.

"For them, our door will always be open."

HarperPrism

SMALL GODS by Terry Pratchett. International bestseller Terry Pratchett brings magic to life in his latest romp through Discworld, a land where the unexpected always happens—usually to the nicest people, like Brutha, former melon farmer, now The Chosen One. His only question: Why?

0-06-109217-7 — $4.99

MAGIC: THE GATHERING™—ARENA by William R. Forstchen. Based on the wildly bestselling trading-card game, the first novel in the *MAGIC: THE GATHERING™* novel series features wizards and warriors clashing in deadly battles. The book also includes an offer for two free, unique MAGIC cards.

0-06-105424-0 — $4.99

SEAROAD:Chronicles of Klatsand by Ursula K. Le Guin. Here is the culmination of Le Guin's lifelong fascination with small island cultures. In a sense, the Klatsand of these stories is a modern day successor to her bestselling *ALWAYS COMING HOME*. A world apart from our own, but part of it as well.

0-06-105400-3 — $4.99

CALIBAN'S HOUR by Tad Williams. The bestselling author of *TO GREEN ANGEL TOWER* brings to life a rich and incandescent fantasy tale of passion, betrayal, and death. The beast Caliban has been searching for decades for Miranda, the woman he loved—the woman who was taken from him by her father Prospero. Now that Caliban has found her, he has an hour to tell his tale of unrequited love and dark vengeance. And when the hour is over, Miranda must die.... Tad Williams has reached a new level of magic and emotion with this breathtaking tapestry in which yearning and passion are entwined.

Hardcover, 0-06-105204-3 — $14.99

and Tomorrow

WRATH OF GOD by Robert Gleason. An apocalyptic novel of a future America about to fall under the rule of a murderous savage. Only a small group of survivors are left to fight — but they are joined by powerful forces from history when they learn how to open a hole in time. Three legendary heroes answer the call to the ultimate battle: George S. Patton, Amelia Earhart, and Stonewall Jackson. Add to that lineup a killer dinosaur and you have the most sweeping battle since *THE STAND*.
Trade paperback, 0-06-105311-2 — $14.99

THE X-FILES™ by Charles L. Grant. America's hottest new TV series launches as a book series with FBI agents Mulder and Scully investigating the cases no one else will touch — the cases in the file marked X. There is one thing they know: The truth is out there.
0-06-105414-3 — $4.99

THE WORLD OF DARKNESS™: VAMPIRE—DARK PRINCE by Keith Herber. The groundbreaking White Wolf role-playing game Vampire: The Masquerade is now featured in a chilling dark fantasy novel of a man trying to control the Beast within.
0-06-105422-4 — $4.99

THE UNAUTHORIZED TREKKERS' GUIDE TO *THE NEXT GENERATION* **AND** *DEEP SPACE NINE* by James Van Hise. This two-in-one guidebook contains all the information on the shows, the characters, the creators, the stories behind the episodes, and the voyages that landed on the cutting room floor.
0-06-105417-8 — $5.99

HarperPrism
An Imprint of HarperPaperbacks

PR-001